The Ground Is My Ocean

SEAN BLACK

DAVID YOUNG

SBD

About the Book

When a car wreck leaves sixteen-year-old Dylan with one leg, suddenly everyone in his life treats him differently. His girlfriend dumps him, his parents want to wrap him in cotton wool and the jocks at his new school see him as an easy target.

As he struggles to come to terms with what's happened, curiosity (and a humiliating schoolyard fight) lead him through the doors of a local MMA gym where he runs into Santana, a tough, Latina fighter with her own unique set of challenges.

With Santana as a reluctant mentor, Dylan begins training Brazilian jiujitsu, a full contact martial art that makes learning to walk again seem easy by comparison. With his body bruised and his ego dented, Dylan finds himself pushed to the edge, not just physically, but also emotionally.

Can Dylan stay the course and find the courage and determination to change not just how the world sees him, but how he sees himself?

A fresh, funny and touching story about grit, resilience and the power of friendship from the bestselling, award-winning author of the Ryan Lock thriller series, Sean Black.

CHAPTER
One

MY THERAPIST, Rich, wants me to write a list of all the good things about having one leg. That's right, the good things. As if it isn't bad enough that I only have one leg, now I'm supposed to, I dunno, look on the bright side?

Rich is a middle-aged dude from Tarzana. I see him once every few weeks to 'talk about my feelings.' Let me tell you, it's tough to tell someone how you feel about having had one of your legs cut off when they're sitting there with their two perfectly good legs crossed and this 'I feel your pain' expression on their face.

I don't mean to sound ungrateful, I really don't. I get he wants to help me. But unless he can somehow magic up some kind of operation to get me my leg back—which he can't, because when they cut off your leg it goes into an incinerator—then I don't know how talking about it changes anything. But my parents are paying for me to see him and they think it might help, so I guess I should make some kind of an effort.

I pull into the parking lot outside Rich's office with twenty minutes to go before my appointment. I dig out a notebook and pen. Let's see, good stuff. Something good about having one leg.

Wait ... I got it.

Big savings on socks. And by big, I mean an immediate, all-year-round, fifty percent discount.

I write it down. Fifty percent savings on socks. Okay, one down, but I'm going to need more than that on the good things list.

Hmm. What else? Come on Dylan, there has to be something else.

I got it!

Pedicures. It's kind of the same as socks. I've never had a pedicure, but I add it to the list anyway.

Half off pedicures.

No, wait, that doesn't work. It's not really a discount. They're only doing one foot, so you're not really saving any money.

I put a line through that one.

This is not going well. I don't have long before this therapy session, and I still have to write my good things list as well as a list of bad things and a final, maybe good, maybe bad, could go either way list.

Good things, good things. Come on, there has to be *something* else.

I look up from my notepad, glance around the parking lot, and it hits me. Duh. It's so obvious I actually feel stupid for not having thought of it before, and it's a definite perk.

Better parking.

You can park nearer the entrance at the mall. Or, in this case, your therapist's office. In fact, you can enjoy free premium parking privileges pretty much anywhere. Which is nothing to turn your nose up at, especially in the Valley.

I look down at my two-item list, relieved. Okay, two goods things may not be much, but it's something.

I startle as someone taps on the passenger side window. It's this little old lady standing with some tubby middle-aged dude in a plaid shirt, his muffin top spilling over his belt.

The old lady stares at me, her lips all puckered up like a cat's butt. She gives the window another tap.

"Young man, you shouldn't be parked here. This is a handicapped spot."

My face gets all hot. Not because I shouldn't be parked here, but because I've had this happen a couple of times and it always gets really awkward and embarrassing. Plus, I hate when people use the word handicapped.

I never paid any attention to it before my accident. Back in the good old days when I had two legs, I didn't give the word a second thought, but now I get why people get upset about certain words and other people don't understand why they're upset and call them snowflakes.

"Young man, are you going to move your car?" says cat butt lips.

I guess I could show her my parking permit. I could lower the window and explain. But why should I? It's not like she's a cop. Or a parking attendant. She's just some random Karen—no offense to any non-annoying Karens out there.

As she taps on the window for a third time, I feel myself getting angry.

I really don't need this. Not after the day I've had.

I want to raise my middle finger and give it the old slow crank, but I don't. Instead, I raise my hand and give her this pathetic little apologetic wave. I just can't get into this with her right now. If I do, I could see myself completely losing it, and what if Rich's looking out of his window and sees me yelling at some old lady? He'll probably tack on another six months of therapy.

"Okay, okay!" I tell her. "I'll move."

I throw the car into reverse and start to back out. She barely moves from where she's standing, which makes reversing out of the spot tricky. Finally, muffin top guy takes her elbow and guides her off to the side so that I don't run over her foot, although that would be poetic justice.

I clear the spot, drive around and pull into a regular one a couple of rows back. I've got like ten minutes before my appointment, and I still have to write my bad and meh lists.

I guess I can do it inside. I shove my pad and pen into my backpack, put on my sunglasses to hide my eye, open the door, and ease out of the car good leg first. Getting out of a car is a whole deal these days.

Muffin top sees me hobbling to the entrance and jabs his finger at cat butt lips. "See, I told you there was something wrong with him."

CHAPTER
Two

IN THE WAITING area there's a couch and a coffee table with magazines. On the walls are all these inspirational posters with sunsets and mountains. They say things like: *Real girls are never perfect, and perfect girls are never real.* Which is great, only I'm not a girl, being brave got me a black eye, and my only dream is to have my leg back, which isn't going to happen.

I check the time. Five minutes left. It should be enough time to do the other two lists before I get called in.

I flip to a fresh page. Next up is the meh, could be good or could be bad, depending on how you look at it list. Again, kind of dumb, but I did think about this one on the way here.

I write down leg farts.

Let me explain for you two-leg people.

Sometimes when I put my stump into the socket of my artificial leg, the air that's trapped in between them gets forced out and it makes this farting sound. It's like carrying around a fart machine, only it's one that can't be confiscated by a teacher.

At first it was kind of funny. Then today I had to adjust my leg when I was in homeroom and when I got up from my seat and put my weight on my prosthesis, there must have been some trapped air because it made that farting sound and this girl that sits next to me, Jenny Moran, who's smoking hot gave me this disgusted look.

I wanted to tell her that it was only a leg fart, not a real one, but that would have made me seem like an even bigger weirdo.

I can't think of anything else for the meh list and I only have four minutes left, so I turn to a fresh page.

Bad things about having one leg.

Okay, here goes. I could write pages—I've given this one a ton of thought. First up.

Girls don't want a boyfriend with one leg.

They might not admit it, and maybe if I looked like that guy who played the kid with one leg in "The Fault In Our Stars," they'd make an exception, but I don't look anything like Ansel Elgort, so I doubt any of them are going to want to ride this one-legged pony around the corral.

I'm pretty much going to either die a virgin, or pay someone to have sex with me, and even then she'll probably want more money because of the whole one-leg thing.

Okay, two.

People stop being normal around you. Guys will call you a spaz, or Long John Silver, or something like that. Or they'll copy the way I walk while their friends crack up.

Or they'll give you that look like they're sad for you, or somehow you're automatically brave. Girls and grown-ups are actually worse about that. Sometimes people will stop and stare at you. Or they'll just be plain weird like that old lady out in the parking lot.

Number three.

To be able to walk you have to wear a prosthesis, which is a fake leg that's attached to whatever you have left of your real leg.

It's not actually part of your regular leg so it's more like having to haul around a bag of groceries all the time. You get tired really quickly. Umberto, my prosthetist (fake leg dealer), told me that amputees burn 50 percent more calories than someone with two legs.

They make really fancy microprocessor legs that make walking less tiring, but those cost over sixty thousand dollars and for that kind of cash you could buy a Tesla, so I don't see the point.

When I was in the hospital, I asked my mom if I could have a Tesla and a regular artificial leg without a computer, but she said that wasn't how it worked because it's the insurance company that pays for it. I thought maybe I could get one and sell it on eBay or something and get the money that way, but it turns out that the depreciation on a second-hand leg is worse than on a Tesla so there went that plan. Now I'm stuck with a fake leg and a shitty old Volvo. The Volvo, aka the Dorkmobile, is because my mom wanted me in 'the safest, and slowest car possible' after the accident.

Anyway, moving on. Number four on the list of the things that suck about having one leg is phantom pain.

Where they cut off your leg are all these nerve endings that don't die so you can still feel the part of your leg they cut off, and sometimes you get these crazy painful shooting pains. It's like your body doesn't want to let you forget what happened.

I quickly flick back through the three lists and start to feel embarrassed. Everything between me and Rich is confidential, but I'm not sure I want to share all this stuff.

Just as the door opens, I tear out the pages and stuff them into my backpack.

Rich's head appears. "Dylan, come on in."

I lever myself up from the chair. Rich goes to help me up and I wave him off, but he keeps coming.

"I'm good, thanks."

"Sure, sure," he says, taking a few steps back.

He hovers there, like he's ready to jump in and grab me if I lose my balance and fall, which I might.

I've got what Umberto calls a floating knee. I started out on a safety knee, which stops you from falling because it locks in place.

The floating knee gives me more control. The downside is that it doesn't lock so if you forget to keep it straight it can give way and you fall on your ass. It's the final practice knee before I get my computerized one.

Randomly falling over for no reason is even more embarrassing than a leg fart. One minute you're standing there and the next minute it's like *woah* and you fall over. For no apparent reason. Like you're drunk or something.

I manage to make my way to the door and into Rich's office. He has books and pictures of his family on top of a bureau. He has three kids. All boys. All with two legs.

He looks at the notepad I'm holding in my hand then at my sunglasses. I think he's about to ask me why I'm wearing shades indoors, but then changes his mind.

"Are those your lists?"

"Sorry, I didn't get them done," I lie.

I flip it open to show him the blank page, hoping he won't notice where I've torn out three pages.

All I get is a nod. He's not a teacher, he's a therapist. I know he's not going to lecture me about not doing my homework.

"Okay, well, why don't you write them now. Take a few minutes. I'll wait. Just whatever pops into your head. Don't overthink it."

Ha, like that's possible. I overthink everything. It's like my brain won't switch off.

"Which one should I start with?"

"Whichever one you want, Dylan. Then maybe we can talk about your new school. This was your first week, right?"

As he says it, he stares at my sunglasses. It's like he can see through the lenses to my red, puffy eye from where I got pummeled. I quickly put my head down, pull the pen from my pocket, and click it a couple of times.

There's this horrible, awkward silence, like when the teacher picks on some kid in math class who's no good at math, and the kid's sitting there dying and the teacher won't let it go until he gives some kind of an answer. Only the kid knows that if he gives a stupid answer everyone will laugh at him, so if he's truly smart, he stays quiet.

Then it becomes this battle of wills, with all the other kids glad it's not them. Or some smart kid who does know the answer starts to say it and is maybe trying to help out the kid who doesn't know the answer, but the teacher cuts them off and repeats the question to the kid who doesn't know as if saying it again will help.

This is like that. Except there's no smart kid to help out. And 'there aren't any right or wrong answers.'

Rich clears his throat. "I have a feeling that the things you're finding challenging might be the longer list, so why don't we start with the positive things."

"I guess I save on socks. You know, like if I buy a pair, I can wear just one and save money. Or if I wear them both, and one gets sweaty I can switch them over, so I always have a fresh sock on this foot," I say, tapping my right leg.

"I'd never thought about that, Dylan." Rich beams at the first item on my positive list. He's eating this up.

"Anything else?" he asks me.

I look up at the clock on the wall behind him. Four minutes down, fifty-six to go.How come sometimes an hour zooms by and other times every minute seems to take an hour?

"That's all I can think of right now. I mean, I'm sure there's other stuff," I shrug.

Rich nods. "So what about the things that you're finding challenging?"

Challenging? That's a long list. We might need more than fifty-six minutes.

But again, I don't say any of that.

Here's the thing. I don't want to talk about any of this stuff. It's not like talking is gonna change any of it. I can't say that either because then why am I here? Plus, it's not Rich's fault. He wasn't the dumb soccer mom who was too busy texting on her phone to realize she'd drifted halfway across the median.

I don't say anything. I feel like if I get into it, I won't be able to stop. Or I might start crying or something. And forget doing that in front of a guy who wears black dress socks with purple Crocs. I'd rather cut off my other leg and never have to buy socks again than start blubbering in front of this guy.

"Okay, Dylan, shall we move on?"

Finally, he's letting this dumb list thing go. Hallelujah.

"So how's your first week at your new school going?"

"Good. You know, the usual junk. Homework. Class. I met the guys on the swim team."

"Uh huh," he says with a definite 'I don't believe you' vibe. He's staring at my eye. At first I thought I was being paranoid, but he really is.

He leans forward. "Understand that anything we discuss in this room stays between us. I won't share anything you tell me with your parents or anyone else. You can be completely honest with me. That's what makes this time valuable."

No kidding it's valuable. He charges like two hundred bucks an hour.

"Yeah, I know," I say, looking down at the floor.

"Good," he says, folding his hands in his lap. "So, shall we start with what happened this morning?"

Play dumb, Dylan. Just play dumb. He'll move on.

"This morning?" I say.

Now he's staring at me. "Yes, this morning."

There's a definite vibe going on here, like when a teacher or your mom knows what you've done, but they want you to pretend like you're George Washington and own up to it.

He sighs, which I'm pretty sure is not an approved therapist move. Then he takes out his phone, which is definitely a banned activity in here. I have to switch mine off before I come in.

I guess that's adults for you. Hypocrites.

"One of my sons forwarded this to me," he says, passing me his phone so I can take a look. "I guess it's being shared on social media."

My stomach flips over. It reminds me of the couple of seconds before my accident where I knew it was going to happen, I knew it was going to be really bad, but there wasn't anything I could do about it.

I look at the screen. It's a video. I know what it is without even having to hit play, and even if I didn't know what it was, there's a helpful title.

Kid with one leg loses ass kicking contest … ROFL.

Rich reaches over to take his phone back. "Maybe don't read any of the comments."

Too late. I already did.

CHAPTER

Three

OMG. *I was there. It was hilarious.* TheJackKim

Lol. I thought his plastic leg was going to fly off or something. RichyS-layer666

Whoever filmed this is a complete douche. AnnaBanana

If I was this kid, I'd probably kill myself. Like immediately. Ska8trBoy

Reading the comments section under your biggest humiliation is like watching a horror movie where a group of teenagers goes to see what that noise is outside their cabin in the woods. They know it's probably a bad idea. You know it's a bad idea. Literally everyone in the movie theater is screaming at them that it's a bad idea. But they do it anyway.

Why? Because they have to know.

That was me. I had to know.

Rich shoots me another 'I feel your pain' look.

"I need to use the bathroom."

"Sure," he says. "Use mine."

He must feel bad if he's letting me use his private bathroom rather than the public one down the hall.

Once I'm in the bathroom, I close the door and throw up. Postvomit, I splash some cold water over the face, rinse out my mouth, and wash my hands. As the water runs, I switch my phone on.

I have a ton of messages. A bunch of people have sent me links to the video. I really have gone viral. Guess I'm officially the kid with one leg who lost an ass-kicking contest.

I click on the YouTube link. There's a thumbnail image of me on the ground, my eyes open, looking dazed. Todd's arm is drawn back, hand clenched into a fist.

It's one of those record scratch—'I bet you're wondering how I got here'—moments in a movie. Only it's not a movie, it's my life.

How I got there was pretty simple. Todd made a joke about my leg and I threw a punch, missed, lost my balance, and fell over.

As I was thrashing around trying to get back up, Todd sat on top of me and started punching me in the face while I tried to cover up and a bunch of kids gathered around, shouting. I don't know how long this went on, I guess only a minute at most going by the length of the video. Finally the swim coach dove in (no pun intended), and hauled Todd off me. A couple of the other kids who'd been standing around helped me up and then Todd and I got marched off to the principal's office.

My throat had a knot in it, like you get before you start to cry, kind of like the one I have now. But there was no way I could let that happen. I mean, I'm sixteen. I can't start crying because I lost a fight. Not in front of people anyway. My school life would be over, if it ever really started in the first place.

When I thought about it later, after I'd been told to go to my next class and Todd was held back in the principal's office, I realized it wasn't the pain of getting punched in the face that had me almost crying. It hurt and I'd have a black eye, but that wasn't it.

What it came down to was that I felt dumb. You were supposed to stand up to bullies, right? And I had. When Todd said what he did and I took a swing at him, it felt amazing. Then a couple of seconds later not so much.

Whoever gave out that advice about standing up to bullies kind of left out an important part. If you're going to stand up to a bully by hitting them, you better know what you're doing. Even being able to put up a fight long enough for a teacher to see what was happening and break it up might have worked. But nope.

I'd been hoping that my fist would connect with his nose and bust it and he'd freak out with all the blood. We'd shake hands, and that would be that. We might not end up being best buddies, but I wouldn't get called names by him or anyone else, and I could get on with being a regular kid, which was all I wanted.

In fact, and I definitely wasn't going to tell Rich this, but I'd kind of been planning it. I knew that with my leg how it is and the way I walk, sooner or later someone at my new school was going to say something. And when they did …

BAM!

I'd hit them as hard as I could before they knew what was happening.

Like you do if you go to prison. The first guy to mess with you is a test. And if you don't stand up for yourself then you're going to have to wear a dress and lipstick and spend the night spooning someone called Bubba.

Except this wasn't prison, this was a super expensive private school in the Valley known for having an Olympic size swimming pool and one of the best swim teams in California. Plus, I hadn't thought through what would happen if my one-punch-knock-out strategy didn't work.

Like a lot of stuff you imagine, it seemed pretty good in my head.

When I come out of the bathroom Rich says, "You want to talk about it?"

I shrug and sit back down.

"How did it start?" he asks.

I tell him, leaving out my first day in prison theory.

"I can understand how someone saying that would be upsetting. But perhaps violence wasn't the answer."

Well, duh. Maybe Rich could put that on a poster next to the one about real girls, with a picture of me on the ground getting punched in the face and the words *violence isn't the answer.*

CHAPTER

Four

OVERNIGHT MY EYE went from plain old red to a deep blackish blue. With the limp and the black eye there's no need for the "Kid Who Got His Ass Kicked" T-shirt I was thinking of ordering on TeeSpring. Or maybe I could go whole hog and get myself an eye patch and a parrot, really embrace the whole pirate vibe I've got going on.

I take a shower, get dressed, and walk into the kitchen to grab some breakfast. I'm starving. Being an object of ridicule really gives you an appetite.

I stop dead when I see my dad sipping coffee. He's usually out the door and on his way to work hours before I leave. He still commutes to his office downtown and leaves super early to beat the worst of the traffic on the 101.

He puts down his coffee mug and winces. "That's some shiner you got there, kiddo."

He and mom were waiting for me when I got back from therapy. They'd already seen the video and spoken to the school. Mom was pretty upset, she wanted Todd expelled. I had to explain to her that I started it, or at least threw the first punch. Or tried to, anyway.

"I'm going to drop you off at school this morning, okay?" he tells me.

"I'm fine. I can drive."

He shoots me his 'this isn't a discussion' look. "I have to stop by the dry cleaners first. Wheels up in five, okay?"

"Sure."

He disappears, leaving me to my glass of juice. At least it's not my mom dropping me off at school. I can usually persuade my dad to let me out a block away. He gets how embarrassing it is to have your parents drop you at school like you're some first grader.

It's not even that far of a walk. Maybe a mile. I would have been able to do it easily before the accident. But then if I hadn't had the accident I would probably still be at my old school. As soon as my parents heard one of the doctors say how swimming was such great rehab for amputees and how he'd had a patient who'd gone to the Paralympics, they were all set on moving me to Meadow Grove because of its state championship swim team.

They were so worried about how I'd cope after the accident. I don't think I saw either of them smile for months. I just wanted them to go back to normal and not have to worry. And I wasn't exactly against the idea. I mean, I didn't love swimming before, it was just okay. But going to any kind of Olympics and maybe winning a medal sounded pretty cool. Before I knew it, I was in a different school.

My mom rushes into the kitchen. "Here," she says, handing me a little plastic tube. "Concealer. It'll hide that black eye."

I hand it back to her. "I'm not putting on makeup."

"It's not makeup. It's concealer."

"I don't care what it is, I'm not putting it on."

"You do not want to go to school looking like that."

"Like what? I already look like a freak. I mean, come on."

I rap my knuckle against the hard socket of my artificial leg.

"Don't say that. You are not a freak."

"Yeah, I am."

She puts her hands on her hips, a sure sign she's getting mad. "Does that make everyone like you a freak? Remember that little boy we saw when you were in the hospital, who was born missing both his legs. Is he a freak? Would you call him a freak?"

"No, I wouldn't call him a freak."

"But you think he is?" she says. She's not about to let this go. Even dad won't argue with her when she gets like this. She just digs in and won't give up.

"What? Now you're telling me what to think? Okay, maybe I'm not a freak, but I'm not normal anymore either."

"What's so great about being normal?"

Dad walks back in. He's the peacemaker in our house. He doesn't like people raising their voices or arguing.

"Hey, what's all the commotion?"

Mom slaps the concealer on the counter in front of me.

"It's not makeup," she says angrily, and walks out.

"What was that all about?" says dad.

I pick up the concealer and take off the top. It's browny pink, like skin color.

I guess the clue is in the name, but I'm still not putting on makeup.

"Mom wanted me to cover up my black eye with this stuff."

"She wants you to wear makeup to school?"

He reaches out, puts his hand under my chin and tilts my head back so he can get a better look at my eye.

"I think it looks badass. But don't tell your mom I said that."

In the car we don't say anything until we get to the end of our block. Then dad says, "Things will settle down in a few weeks. It always takes time to adjust when you start somewhere new."

I'm not sure that's true. High school's all about labels, and I already have mine. The kid with one leg. Now it's the kid with one leg who started a fight and lost.

"Right," I say.

He looks over at me. "Just hang in there, okay?"

I nod. Like I have a choice. I know from listening to him and mom talk that they've already paid the fees at Meadow Grove for the entire year. And that they wouldn't get the money back if I moved schools again.

Anyway, I'm not sure that moving back to my old school would be any better. It wasn't like my old friends went out of their way to visit me in the hospital or anything. I got this huge get well soon card, but only a couple of them came to see me, and it was super awkward, like they didn't know what to say.

Meadow Grove was supposed to be a fresh start.

"Did you ever get picked on in school?" I ask as we turn onto Ventura.

I'm guessing I already know the answer to that. My dad isn't a huge guy, but I know he was on the football team in high school and was pretty popular.

He takes a deep breath, puffs out his cheeks, and sighs.

"Not really, no," he says.

Great. Then it's just me.

"There was this one kid in my class, Mikey Collins. He had a scar on his lip. They used to call it a hair lip, although I don't think that's the medical term. Anyway, he got bullied a lot about it. I still feel bad that I didn't stand up for him more. I never went along with it, but I never tried to stop it either."

Dad looks over at me. "Sorry, I don't know why I told you that."

I don't know either. But I don't want to say that to him. I know how bad he feels about all of this.

He reaches over and jabs my arm. "But you did stand up for yourself. And I'm proud of you. Man, that was some haymaker. If you'd connected it would have been lights out for … What's his name?"

"Todd."

"Yeah, Todd."

Dad pulls over, gets out, and grabs some shirts from the back seat. He's going to drop them at the dry cleaners.

"Do me a favor, kiddo and get me a latte? Regular milk. I don't know why your mom insists on buying that soymilk stuff."

A couple of doors down there's a gym that takes up three regular-size units. It's glass fronted but the glass is tinted so you can't see inside from the street. I walk closer to get a better look.

The name of the place is painted on the glass in huge black and red letters: *Resilient MMA.* Off to either side of that in smaller letters, it says *Brazilian jiujitsu, Sambo, Mixed Martial Arts, Muay Thai.* I'm not sure about the other stuff but I know that Mixed Martial Arts is cage fighting.

I wonder if they actually have a cage inside. I go right up to the window, press my face against the glass, and cup my hands to block out the sunlight.

As I'm scoping it out, the gym door opens and three people crowd out. There's an older guy with long hair and a beard who looks like Keanu Reeves, a tough looking dude with tattoos and a shaved head, and a Latina girl who looks about my age.

The girl has long, pink hair and she's wearing cut-off indigo denim jeans, motorcycle boots, and a black hoodie with green lettering that reads *Dropkick Murphys – Signed and Sealed in Blood.* A tattoo of a rose snakes its way up from the top of her hoodie and disappears into the pink hair.

The older guy who reminds me of Keanu looks over and smiles. "Nice shiner."

Now the other two notice me.

"Damn, bro," the young guy says to me. "You should get some concealer on that."

"Concealer?" scoffs the girl. "You want him to get another black eye?"

She stares at me, unblinking, appraising. "You win?"

The question catches me off guard. From her sarcastic smile, I get the idea that it was intended to.

"Huh?"

"The fight. You win?"

Now I wish I'd waited in the coffee shop.

"How do you know it was a fight? Maybe he was playing football or something," says the younger guy.

She looks me up and down. "Football? Yeah, right."

"No, I didn't win," I say, quickly. "Sorry, I gotta go."

"Concealer," the young guy shouts after me as I limp away.

"Dude, you can't send that kid to school with makeup on," the girl says.

"It's not makeup, it's concealer."

"Duh! Which is makeup."

"What's wrong with a guy wearing makeup? I mean, you wear it," he fires back.

The girl with the pink hair flips him off.

"Hilarious, Jared," she says, punching him on the shoulder like a person who actually knows how to land a punch on target and make sure it hurt.

"Damn, girl. You been working on that jab?" he says, rubbing his shoulder before putting her in a headlock. "Let's see how your guillotine escape's coming along, chica."

As they start to roughhouse the older guy says, "Hey, hey, knock it off."

They both stop, like kids caught fighting in the back seat. She sticks her tongue out at Jared and he gives her the finger.

The older guy laughs. "I swear I'd have less trouble running a kindergarten. And I'm with Jared, what's the problem with a guy wearing makeup?"

"I'm not saying it's wrong," she says. "I'm down with it, but other people might not be."

"Hey, if it's good enough for Alice Cooper and the guy from Aerosmith," says the older guy.

"Alice who?" she says.

Jared starts singing "(Dude) Looks Like A Lady" in a falsetto voice.

The girl jams her fingers in her ears and turns to the older guy "Now look what you've started. He's singing. That's his go-to when he can't tap me any other way."

The older guy laughs.

I hear the roar of an engine and a squeal of tires as a car speeds into the parking lot. I look around to see this old vintage red Cadillac pulling up next to them. Behind the wheel is a girl with blonde hair, Wayfarer sunglasses and cheekbones as sharp as the fins on the back of the car. She looks like an Instagram model.

"That's my ride," says the girl with the pink hair. "See you tonight, Coach!" she yells to the older guy.

She runs to the car, jumps straight into the passenger seat without opening the door, and leans over to kiss the hot blonde girl. It's not a peck so much as a full-on, lips-to-lips deal, with more than a hint of tongue.

The car takes off, even faster than it drove in, thick black tire tracks the only evidence that it was ever here as it turns onto Ventura, music blasting.

I look back at the gym. The coach and Jared are watching me, kind of amused, like they enjoy seeing how people react to this force of nature with pink hair who cusses like a sailor and kisses her girlfriend right out in public.

"Hey, kid," says the coach, pointing to the Resilient MMA sign. "You ever want to learn how to block a punch, you'd be very welcome. First lesson's free."

CHAPTER
Five

WITH TODD SUSPENDED until the principal decides on his final punishment, I know I'm not about to get a warm welcome from the rest of the swim team. Todd's one of the stars of the team and they need him if they want to win another state championship.

As I stop outside the locker room and take a deep breath, I hear, "You think if Dylan goes fast enough, he'll start swimming around in circles?" Then all the guys start laughing.

I can't be sure who said it, but it sounded like Jack Kim. Jack's like this cool, yoked Korean kid. He's also kind of an asshole. As well as swimming, he spends a lot of his time in the gym lifting weights, so he's bigger than most of the other guys and he uses his size to intimidate anyone he doesn't like. If he decides to mess with me then I'm really in trouble.

I take another big breath and walk in. It goes quiet. Everyone is suddenly busy checking their goggles or stretching out.

Thankfully, Coach appears. "Practice starts in five minutes guys, so let's hustle."

I strip off my clothes, pull on my trunks, swim hat, and goggles, and join the rest of the guys at the side of the pool.

"Okay," says Coach, "let's run through our warm-ups."

Every session starts with warm-ups and stretching at the side of the pool before we get into the water. I run through the routine with the rest of the team.

As we get to the part where we jog in place, bringing our knees up as high as we can, Coach looks over at me. "Why don't you get in, Dylan. Do a couple of laps, nice and slow."

Here comes the part I always dread—taking my prosthetic leg off. I'm fine once I'm in the water because no one can see my stump. But between taking it off and getting in the pool, I can feel everyone staring at me and thinking about how gross and weird my leg looks.

I hobble over to the other side of the pool, away from the rest of the team, and sit down near the edge to take off my prosthesis. I roll the liner off and put it inside the socket. Scooting on my butt, I get to the edge of the pool and lower myself in.

The water's freezing. I get in as fast as I can so I don't look like a wuss. The best way to get warm is to swim so I push off from the side with my good leg and start out.

The rest of practice pretty much sucks. Being average at swimming is one thing. Being average when everyone else is really good is worse. And being average when you're doing things like relay, which means that the guy after you ends up starting twenty yards behind and your team loses, is a whole other level of suckage. Especially when no one is talking to you anyway because you got their buddy suspended.

I get out of the pool, dry off my stump, put my leg back on before heading into the locker room. The time it takes makes me the last one back in. Just like when I arrived, everyone stops talking and goofing around as soon as they see me.

I keep my head down and try to ignore it, but it's tough. I broke the bro code by starting a fight and letting the other guy take the rap for it and now I was paying the price.

It's almost a relief to get to class. Almost.

When I walk into English I'm five minutes late, but the teacher doesn't say anything, like they would normally. They'd all been told to cut me some slack because I couldn't run, or even walk as fast as the rest of kids. As long as I wasn't more than five minutes late it was cool, and no one would say anything.

The principal had called it a grace period. I appreciated it, I really did, but it was another thing that made me stand out. Any other student coming in late to class would at least get some kind of comment. I just get a kind smile.

And of course because I'm late, it's super quiet when I sit down. Everyone's already reading a passage from the book we're studying. So everyone hears the massive leg fart when I sit down.

Jenny Moran shoots me an even more disgusted look than last time, leans over to her only slightly less hot friend, and says, "Gross."

A couple of guys behind me snicker and I can feel people staring at me until the teacher clears his throat and stares at a couple of them with a classic 'don't test me' look that some teachers have down cold. After that everyone goes back to their reading. I can't find the chapter so I flip through the pages. Someone touches my arm. I look over to see this cute Asian girl called Anna who sits across from me leaning my way.

"Chapter six," she whispers.

"Uh, thanks."

"No problem."

I start reading but I can't focus. I hate this school. I hate swimming. Most of all I hate being me.

CHAPTER
Six

MOM'S WAITING for me after school. I'd totally forgotten that I'd been dropped off this morning, so I don't have the Dorkmobile to drive home. She hasn't picked me up from school since the third grade, but here she is, busy chatting to the principal. Not even a regular teacher, but the principal.

"Oh, there you are, sweetie," she says like I'm ten, stepping away from her conversation. "We're just down the street. You want me to bring it around so you don't have to walk?"

"No!" I say, super pissed that she's even gotten out of the car so everyone can see her collecting me like I'm a little kid.

The principal cuts in, "How was your day, Dylan?"

I look at him, feeling awkward. I don't want kids seeing me talking to the principal of the school, not out here. I guess this would be like being caught nose-to-nose with a prison warden.

"Good."

"I was just saying to your mom that we have a zero-tolerance policy for bullying at Meadow Grove and we take what happened yesterday very seriously."

Why is he telling me this?

"Okay."

"So, if anyone makes you feel uncomfortable in any way, any way at all, I want you to report it immediately."

"Sure, yeah," I say, just to get the conversation over with.

"Okay then," he says, before looking at my mom. "Zero tolerance." Then he walks away.

"I could have gotten a ride or jumped on the bus." The first part is probably a lie. I don't know anyone well enough to ask. But I guess I could take the bus.

"Well, I'm here now, so …" She smiles.

When I don't smile back, she says, "Are you okay? Did something else happen?"

Why are parents like this? Something always has to have happened. You can't just not be in the mood to smile, there has to be some deep reason.

"No," I say, raising my voice without meaning to.

"I'm sorry, I didn't think. I know you're too old for us to be collecting you from school. It's only with your…"

"You can say it. With my leg," I say.

Her smile is gone and I see a little of the same look on her face that I saw when I was in the hospital. It's a mix of scared and concerned.

"We're all trying to figure this out, Dylan."

"Look, I'm fine, okay? Nothing's going to happen to me. I can look after myself."

She doesn't say anything to that which makes me mad again.

Kids are streaming out behind me now. Oh yeah, I also get to leave five minutes early because they don't want the kid with one leg getting trampled in the halls. They all see me standing with my mom.

I see some guys from the swim team. They're laughing. One of them says, "Oh look, his mommy's here to get him."

"Can we go already?" I snap at my mom.

I walk as fast as I can toward the car. I know that the faster I walk the weirder I look, but I want to get the hell out of there. I look weird anyway, so what difference does it make if I look a little weirder?

My stump is sore and I'm hungry. I want to get home, take my prosthesis off, and lie down.

As we get into the car Mom says, "I'm sorry, Dylan. I didn't mean to embarrass you."

"Can you just drive?"

She doesn't say anything but I can tell she's upset. Before the accident we always got along. Me and my dad did too. Being an only child, we've always been pretty close, and I have lots of cousins so I never felt like I was missing out on not having brothers or sisters.

To save us having to talk anymore, I dig out my phone. I have a bunch of messages. I open the first one.

The message reads:

You're such a coward, bro. You hit Todd first and let him take the blame. I know where you live, you asshole.

I hit delete and put my phone away. Mom sees me looking at my phone but I put it away before she asks me what I'm looking at.

My phone pings again. It's a friend request with a weird username, @enjoychoke. It's probably another one of the guys from the swim team who's set up an anonymous account so he can tell me what a loser I am.

I hit delete and switch my phone to airplane mode. I wish I'd been born before the internet.

AT LUNCH the next day everyone heads outside to eat at the picnic tables outside the cafeteria.

There's a swim team table where Jack's holding court. He sees me, nudges one of the guys and they start laughing. I have a feeling they don't want me sitting with them so I scope out a free table and head that way.

Since the accident I'm not a big fan of picnic benches. I have to balance on my good leg and ease my other leg over the bench part if I want to sit in the middle. Then getting back out is a whole thing too. It's just easier to perch at the end.

A couple of girls approach to sit at the other end of the table. One of them is Anna, the cute girl that sits next to me in English. She looks over at me as they sit down, then turns back to her friend and they start giggling. I guess I can't even eat lunch without someone laughing at me. I think about moving, but what's the point?

I dig some study notes out of my backpack and read through them while I eat. I keep my head down and hope no one will notice me.

A few minutes later I look up and catch Anna looking at me again. Her friend leans over and whispers something in her ear and they start laughing again.

Something about it makes me angry. Why can't people just leave me alone? Why do they always have to stare at me like I'm some kind of freak.

If I saw someone with one arm or one leg, I'm not gonna lie—I'd probably do a double take. But I wouldn't sit and stare. And I wouldn't laugh.

I put my head down and try to concentrate on my notes, but I can't. It's like I can feel everyone looking at me. The more I think about it, the angrier I get.

Finally I grab my notes and jam them in my backpack.

"I'm going, okay? Maybe you can find someone else to laugh at," I say to Anna and her friend. It comes out way angrier and louder, than I thought it would.

They both look away and seem to be shocked that I've said anything, but they don't contradict me. As I get up, the toe of my artificial leg catches on the cement, and I almost fall over but at the last second I manage to catch myself. Falling over in front of everyone would have capped off another perfect day.

As I'm walking back inside the building someone touches my arm.

"We weren't laughing at you, I promise," Anna says.

"It doesn't matter." I still feel bad for shouting at her. "It's fine. I'd laugh at me too."

She looks at me with a really serious expression.

"You would?"

I look down at my artificial leg.

"Yeah. I would."

"Well, I wasn't laughing at you, okay?"

"Look, just forget it," I say.

As I leave her standing there my phone pings. It's another message from @enjoychoke. I delete without reading it, block them and turn off all my social media notifications. I pop in my earbuds, blast some music, and shut out the world.

As I walk to my next class, I feel another hand on my elbow. I whirl round, ready to tell whoever it is to leave me the hell alone.

It's the principal. He looks super serious and I take out my ear buds. We're not supposed to be listening to music in the corridor.

"Sorry, Dylan, I didn't mean to startle you. I just want to speak with you for a moment. In my office."

"I kind of have class."

"Don't worry, it won't take long."

"Dylan, as I said to you yesterday, bullying is something we take very seriously."

"Right."

"Anyway, I've decided to revisit Todd's suspension and while he will be returning to school in the next few days so he can continue his education, I've spoken with Coach about the swim team program, and we think it might be best if…"

My mind shoots ahead. It might be best if I leave the team?

Finally some good news. If I'm not on the swim team then half my problems go away. I don't have to take off my leg at school. I won't have to worry about people making jokes in the locker room about me swimming in circles.

I can come to school, go to class, eat lunch by myself, go home again, and wait for these next two years to be over so I can go to college where I won't be the kid with one leg who got beaten up.

The principal's still speaking but I think I misheard what he just said.

"Sorry?" I ask him.

He clears his throat. "You won't have to worry about being on the team with Todd. Not this semester anyway. We've told his parents that we'll revisit his suspension from the team next semester. And I want you to let either the coach or myself know if you have any other problems."

Wait. What? They've suspended Todd from the team, even though he's one of the fastest swimmers.

"I don't think Todd needs to be thrown off the team."

"And the fact you even say that is a credit to your character, Dylan."

He's smiling at me but I don't think he gets it. If the guys already don't like me and don't want me on their team, this won't help. It'll only make things a million times worse.

I know what I have to do. I have to tell him how I started it. That maybe Todd shouldn't have given me a black eye or made fun of me, but that I was as much to blame as he was. If I hadn't tried to punch him then none of this would have happened.

I start to speak again, but he cuts me off.

"You're already having a tough time, and the last thing I or any of the teachers want is for it to be any tougher."

I agree. That's why he shouldn't cut Todd from the team. It's like teachers don't get how any of this works.

"But it was me who …"

He looks up at the clock on the wall behind me. "Is that the time? I'm sorry, Dylan, but I'm late for a meeting."

"But …"

"You'd better get to class," he says, opening a desk drawer and starting to write out a hall pass.

The rest of the school day goes by in a haze. I float through my classes, but I can't concentrate. I can still feel everyone looking at me.

Last class of the day is AP Calculus. Jack Kim sits a couple of desks over. He doesn't say anything to me, but I can tell he must have heard about Todd being suspended from the team because he keeps staring at me like he wants to give me another black eye.

When our calc teacher reminds me I can leave early, I'm relieved. I just want today to be over. But as I gather up my work and jam it into my backpack, Jack finally decides to speak to me.

"Yo, Dylan," he whispers as I close the zipper on my bag. "Good job on ruining our chances of winning anything this year."

CHAPTER
Eight

MOM'S WAITING outside school for me again. I throw my stuff onto the back seat and get in before the rest of the kids come out.

"How was your day?" she asks.

"Fine. Can we get out of here?"

She reaches over to touch my black eye.

"Maybe we should get someone to look at that, sweetie."

I pull away. "It looks worse than it is."

That part is true. It really doesn't hurt at all. Unlike my stump, which is throbbing with phantom pain.

As the first few kids start to filter out we pull away from the curb. No one's seen me being picked up. My own private hell is over for now. Until tomorrow, when I have to face the guys from the swim team. Even the thought of it makes me feel sick.

If Jack Kim is super pissed about Todd being suspended from the team when he doesn't even like Todd, what are Todd's buddies going to be like? Hell, what's Todd going to be like when he comes back to school?

. . .

When we get home there's a guy sitting on the sidewalk outside our house. As soon as he sees our car he stands up and peers through the windshield at us, like he's not sure he has the right place.

He's wearing a hoodie with the hood pulled up and sunglasses.

My mind flashes straight to some of the messages I've been getting.

My stomach flips over, and I get pins and needles in my hands and feet. It's the same sensation I had when I was working up to throwing that punch at Todd, only worse.

I look over at mom. I can tell she's a little on edge but she's covering it.

"He's probably from the gardening service. They said they were going to send someone out today to give us a quote."

I know my dad had persuaded my mom that they should hire someone to do the yardwork because he hates doing it. But I don't see any gardening truck parked nearby. Or even a car. All our neighbors have their cars parked in their driveways. The only car on the street is a good half block down.

There's nothing else for it but to get out of the car. We can't exactly sit in the driveway staring at this dude.

As I clamber out, he pushes his hood back down and takes off his sunglasses. He has a huge, wide smile on his face.

It's the guy from the gym. The guy who reminded me of Keanu Reeves.

He walks over, super relaxed. "Hey, I'm sorry for rolling up on you guys unannounced like this." He turns to me. "It's Dylan, right?"

I nod like a dummy.

"I tried messaging you earlier, but I didn't get any reply, so I figured I'd come say hi."

My mom stares at him, and I'm not sure my dad would be too happy about the way she's doing it.

He puts out his hand.

"Martese Terra. I own Resilient MMA and BJJ."

My mom shakes his hand. "Nice to meet you, Mr. Terra."

"I ran into Dylan the other day outside my gym after we finished morning training," Martese says.

Mom looks at me, confused.

"Dad was dropping off his dry cleaning," I explain.

"Like I said, I don't mean to roll up on you unannounced, but—" he pauses, like he isn't sure what he wants to say next. "I saw the video of the trouble Dylan had at school on social media."

Great, I wonder if there's anyone who hasn't seen me get punched in the face.

"Right. Okay," says my mom, not sure where this is going.

He taps a finger in the direction of my eye.

"You know, you might want to get that looked at. Just to be on the safe side."

That's like music to my mom's ears. She taps my chest with the back of her hand. "See, what did I say?"

He turns his focus back to my mom. "Anyway, I was wondering if Dylan would like to come in and take some classes with us, no charge. I can take him through some things so he can avoid a repeat of what happened."

Before I can say anything, mom answers for me.

"Oh, Mr. Terra, that's very kind of you."

"Please. Call me, Martese," he says.

She gives him the same look that my dad wouldn't like before recovering her composure.

"We really appreciate it, but the school has already dealt with what happened, and the last thing we need is for Dylan to be getting into any more fights."

Martese Terra laughs.

"I agree, one hundred percent. Fighting is the last thing we want."

My mom looks puzzled. She isn't the only one. This dude teaches people how to fight. And not like regular boxing, or karate, or stuff like that.

I've seen some UFC fights where the whole canvas was covered in blood, and people were on the ground and the other guy was elbowing and punching them in the face until the ref pulled them off and stopped it. Like you could be knocked out cold and still get hit. That kind of fighting.

"But you do teach fighting?" my mom says. "I think I've seen your gym."

Martese is still smiling. "I know this might sound a little strange, but if you know how to fight then you don't have to fight."

He's right. It does sound strange.

"I was thinking that maybe Dylan could try one of our BJJ classes. No striking, unless that's something he wants to try of course."

"BJJ?"

"Brazilian jiujitsu. It's mostly ground based. Grappling. Like wrestling, only more fun. And perfectly safe."

Mom shoots him the same skeptical look she often gives me when I tell her I've finished my homework but in reality have been playing Fortnite in my room.

"Okay, mostly safe." He laughs again. "I'm really not selling this well, am I?" He holds up his hands. "I watched the fight you had at school. Even with as little as three months in my gym that would never have happened, and if it had you would have been able to safely deal with the situation without getting hurt or you hurting the other guy."

Now he was coming off like some kind of a kook. Okay, maybe if I practiced Brazilian Juju or whatever I could have kicked Todd's ass. But how do you do that safely? With *no one* getting hurt? Wasn't that the whole point of fighting? To mess someone up so they never bothered you again?

"The offer still stands. We have our class schedule posted on our website. Dylan, if you want to drop by, you'd be very welcome. And who knows, you might even enjoy it."

He shakes my mom's hand again and pats me on the shoulder. "Good luck whatever you decide." Then he turns and heads down the street.

I watch him walk to the end of the block and think about what he said.

If you know how to fight, you don't have to fight.

Nine

"YOU KNOW, it might not be the worst idea in the world for Dylan to learn how to defend himself."

"What if he gets hurt?"

"He almost did get hurt," says my dad, exasperated." That other kid was punching the living heck out of him before it got broken up."

Mom and Dad are in the living room talking over Martese Terra's offer. They don't know I can hear them. I feel bad about eavesdropping, but I figure if they really didn't want me hearing them they'd keep their voices down.

"And what if he injures his other leg?"

Dad doesn't have an answer to that. Something happening to my other leg and me being in a wheelchair is a big nightmare for my parents.

Just when it sounds like the discussion is over, Dad asks, "So where did you say this Martese guy was from?"

"That place on Ventura."

"I mean what country?"

"I don't know, South America somewhere."

I get up from my bed, hop to my bedroom door, then open it and peek out. My dad is tapping on his laptop.

"Okay," he says. "Here we go. Martese Terra. He's Brazilian. Hey, he has an actual Wikipedia entry. This guy's a three-time world champion. And he's coached a couple of fighters who've gone on to the UFC."

"The UFC?" Mom says, horrified. "That's like cage fighting. You want our son to be around thugs who fight in a cage?"

"I know what you're saying, but he has to be able to stand up for himself. You know what kids are like. Anyone who's different gets singled out. And Dylan's a little different now, whether we like it or not."

"Maybe we can look into self-defense classes over the summer, something that's not UFC or Brazilian whatever it's called. How about that?"

"You know, he is sixteen, it might be an idea if we let him decide."

"He may be sixteen, but he's also vulnerable."

I close the door as softly as I can and hop back to my bed, where I lie down and stare up at the ceiling.

I think I'd rather be called a total wuss than vulnerable.

I think about Martese Terra. I can't imagine anyone ever calling him vulnerable. Or any of the guys I saw walking out of the gym the other day. But if someone was dumb enough call them vulnerable, they'd kick their ass.

I didn't like being called vulnerable, but it was the truth. I am different and nothing is going to change that. It's not like I can close my eyes and click my heels together three times and go back to having two legs, because for starters, I don't have two heels to click.

CHAPTER

Ten

THE GOOD NEWS this morning is that I'm back behind the wheel. The bad news is that it's still the wheel of the Dorkmobile. I guess after they got through discussing how vulnerable I am, Dad persuaded my mom that they couldn't keep dropping me off at school every morning.

I get out of the house early, before Mom can change her mind again. Without even realizing that I'm doing it, I head for Resilient MMA. I pull into the parking lot and sit there, watching the entrance.

Last night I looked at their schedule. They have an open mat at seven every morning. I'm not exactly sure what an open mat is, but I guess it's so people can come in and train before work.

Part of me really wants to go inside, just to see what it's like. Another part of me is scared even thinking about it.

It's kind of how I felt the first day outside Meadow Grove before I went in. Only walking into an MMA gym seems even more terrifying than a new high school.

I sit there and stare at the entrance. Who am I kidding? I have one leg. How could I possibly do MMA or jiujitsu?

Swimming is something I know I can do. But MMA? It's a crazy idea.

After another five minutes of trying to work up the courage to go inside, I give up. Swim practice starts in fifteen minutes.

No one's cracking jokes about me when I walk into the locker room. In fact, no one says anything. They all act like I'm not there, like I don't exist.

This must be my punishment for Todd being kicked off the team. I already have my swim trunks on under my shorts so I strip down and head out to the pool.

I take off my leg, hop the few yards to the edge and get into the water. It's way colder than usual.

Jack Kim is next to me at the edge of the pool.

"Is the heating broken or something?" I say, trying to make conversation.

He looks straight through me, kicks off the edge and glides effortlessly underwater all the way to the other side of the pool where he starts talking to a couple of the other guys. None of them so much as look over to me.

I don't want to stay here shivering while everyone ignores me, so I kick off and start to do laps to keep warm. The lump's back in my throat. I don't know if it's the cold or the chlorine from the water leaking into one of my goggles, but I start to cry.

I have no idea where this has come from, it's just welled up in me from nowhere. I want to stop. But I can't.

I keep swimming, turning over my arms, kicking with my good leg. I can feel rage starting to build. The same rage I had before I tried to punch Todd.

Keeping my head down, I motor across the pool, turn at the end, and swim back, all these crazy thoughts crowding into my head. As I get to the far end, down by the boards, I know what I have to do. It's what I should have done before.

I swim to the steps, and struggle to haul myself up. I get my good leg on the step and somehow manage to flop my chest onto the edge and climb out.

I almost slip.

I catch someone saying, "Where's the freak going?"

"Maybe he's leaving."

"Good," says one of the other guys. "Maybe we can get Todd back."

Toweling off my stump, I roll my liner over, click my stump into the socket, and walk back into the locker room where Coach is rousting some of the latecomers. "Okay, guys, let's hustle out of here."

He stops as he sees me come in. He's looking at my eyes like he can tell I've been crying. If he asks, I'm going to blame the chlorine.

"You okay there, Dylan?" he says.

"I'm fine."

"You sure?"

"Yeah." I take a breath. "Coach, you have to put Todd back on the team."

"Are the other guys still giving you a hard time?" he asks. "You know it can take a little time for them to accept a new team member."

What's he talking about? I don't think I'll ever be accepted. Maybe if I grew flippers and set a world record for the 200 meter freestyle. But then I'd be the weird kid with flippers so probably not even then.

"No, it's not the guys," I lie. "But how's the team going to win state without him? He's one of the fastest swimmers."

"Listen, Dylan, it's admirable that you want him back on the team, but the decision's been made."

"But he didn't even start the fight. I did."

"After he said something to you."

"Yeah, but ..."

"Todd can come back to the team after he's served his suspension, but we can't be seen to condone bullying."

"But I hit him first. Well, tried to anyway."

Coach sighs and looks down at the white and blue tiles of the locker room. "It wasn't just that he assaulted a fellow student. There was more information that came to light regarding the incident. That was why we decided that his three-day school suspension wasn't a sufficient punishment."

I don't know what other information Coach is talking about. All I know is that without Todd on the team they have no chance of winning state, and they're blaming me.

"Okay, well if Todd's not swimming then I'm not either. I'll come back when he does."

Coach stares at me like he can't believe what I said.

"Dylan, I don't respond to threats. If I did, I wouldn't be able to do my job. Your parents pay a lot of money to send you to this school, and I know you're probably not the most popular kid after what happened, but you are going to turn around and get back in that pool and you're going to train. You understand me?"

A couple guys from the team have drifted in from the pool, pretending that they forgot something from their locker.

I want to put my clothes on, and walk out, and not come back. But I don't do any of that.

Instead, I pick my cap and goggles up from the bench and walk to the pool. Like the coward I am.

If I thought that maybe the guys on the swim team might give me a break because I tried to get Todd's suspension lifted, I was wrong. They ignored me all the way through practice until they absolutely had to speak to me.

No one talks to me in the locker room after practice either. I don't know how long they plan on keeping this up, but I'm starting not to care. I've done my best to make things right.

If Todd has gotten wind of me trying to get him back on team then he isn't showing it either. He looks straight through me as I walked into AP English and take a seat at the back.

As everyone comes in, a couple of the swim team guys made a big show of high-fiving him and slapping him on the back with a "Welcome back, bro!"

Maybe he hasn't heard. Maybe if he does, he'll tell the guys to lay off me. Or maybe I'll go through the next two years of high school with everyone ignoring me.

I try to concentrate on the class, but my mind starts wandering to Resilient MMA and Martese's offer. There's a Brazilian jiujitsu class at seven tonight. I could text my mom that I'm staying at school to study and go check it out.

I eat lunch on my own again. A few minutes later Anna and her friend come and sit at the other end of the bench, but only because there's no other free tables. I look over at Anna but she ignores me.

My phone pings with an Instagram message from Martese Terra.

Hey Dylan, It was good to meet you and your mom yesterday. If your family are okay with you training with us, feel free to drop by anytime. No pressure. We'd be happy to see you. Oss! Martese Terra, Resilient MMA

His message catches me off guard. Everyone at school's going out of their way to avoid me, and here's this guy who teaches people how to beat each other to a bloody pulp going out of his way to help me.

But why? It isn't like some kid with one leg is going to fight in the UFC. I looked it up and BJJ isn't in the Paralympics. The only martial art that is listed is judo, and even then they only have a category for blind people. Maybe they don't want to risk disabled people hurting themselves or something.

I don't have anything better to do so I click over to his profile and start scrolling through. There are a lot of pictures of him with fighters he's trained. And lots of pictures of him with his wife, who looks like a model.

The more I look at his awesome life, the more confused I get. Why's he trying to help me?

"Hey."

I look up to see Todd. Except I don't just look up, I flinch. The last time he was this close to me, he was punching me in the face.

He puts down his backpack and pulls out an envelope.

He practically throws it at me. "Here. It's an apology letter."

I take it from him.

"My mom made me write it," he says.

"Oh. Right."

"Anyway," he says.

"I asked Coach to put you back on the team."

"Yeah, I heard, but he's not going to do it."

"How come?"

He looks over to the swim team, then looks at me and smiles. "The video."

"You're the one who posted it?" I ask him.

"I know, totally dumb, right. But, come on, the way you fell over. That shit was funny."

He mimes me falling over. Behind him some of the swim team crack up laughing as he flails his arms and hops on one leg.

Anna scoots around on the bench and stares at Todd. "You're such a douchebag."

"And you're such a virgin," he tells her before wandering back to the swim team table where he says something and all the guys crack up laughing.

"You okay?" Anna asks me.

"Yeah, fine."

"Sure?"

"What did I just say?" I snap.

Anna and her friend get up to leave. I feel bad about getting annoyed at her, but I wish people would let me fight my own battles sometimes.

Glancing down at my phone, I look at Martese Terra standing in the middle of a cage, smiling, his hand on the shoulder of a victorious fighter. The fighter doesn't look that much older than me. He's grinning too, his face bloodied from a cut above his eye, his hand raised in the air, one finger pointing at the sky.

I look back over at Todd, laughing it up with the rest of the team. No matter how nervous the thought of it makes me, tonight I'm walking into Resilient MMA.

I'm going to learn how to fight. Not so I don't have to. No, I'm going to learn to fight so I can wipe that smug smirk right off Todd's face.

CHAPTER
Eleven

THE FIRST THING you see when you walk into Resilient MMA is the octagon. Even set up in the far corner, it's impossible to miss a steel cage with six-foot-high walls that sits on top of a platform that's almost as tall. It has eight sides, with wide corners so they're easier to get out of than a boxing ring.

I've only ever seen an MMA cage on a screen, never up close like this. It's weirdly smaller than I imagined, but also kind of scarier.

I stand there for a second, staring at it. I try to imagine what it must be like walking up those steps and through the door with someone waiting for you inside. Then the cage door is locked with both of you in there, just like gladiators, ready to fight to the death.

"Hey, Dylan, you made it!"

I turn to see Martese standing in the middle of the black mats that cover the rest of the floor space. He has a mop in one hand, He splashes the mop into a bucket of soapy water, wrings out the water, and runs the mop head across the mats.

"Welcome to my glamorous world," he laughs, lifting the bucket in salute.

I wave at him. I still have crazy butterflies in my stomach from being nervous as hell, but I'm also kind of psyched to see him and proud that I've finally made it in.

"Pretty cool, huh?" he says, with a nod to the cage. "We got it installed last month. What do you think?"

I don't know what to say. "Yeah," I say, sounding like a complete dweeb.

"Hey, Dylan, do me a favor. Take your shoes off before Santana comes in and sees you," he says, pointing to a sign by the door that says: *LEAVE YOUR SHOES AND YOUR EGO AT THE DOOR.*

"Anyone steps on the mats wearing their shoes and she completely loses it. And take it from me, she's the only person here who scares everyone."

That's the second time I've heard that name. I assume it must be his wife or someone important, but I don't want to ask. I guess if I stick around I'll figure out who everyone is.

Martese goes back to mopping and I turn to look at the wall behind me.

The sign about taking your shoes off is surrounded by a bunch of framed posters. Only these are not the fluffy, pink-cloud type posters that I see every week in Rich's office.

These posters have pictures of really scary people and they say things like: *It's not who's best, it's who's left* and *Your fears. Your insecurities. Your anxieties. Your sadness. jiujitsu will reach inside and rip them out.*

I sit down on a little bench next to a huge metal shoe rack and take off my sneakers. I'm still getting the hang of taking a sneaker off my prosthetic foot while I have my leg on. It's easier said than done.

Martese puts down the mop and wanders over.

"You see that poster?" he says.

I look over to where he's pointing. "Yeah."

A scary-looking Brazilian dude is staring out at me. He looks super intense. The words say:

One way or another, we're going to hit the ground, and we'll be in my world. The ground is my ocean, I'm the shark, and most people don't even know how to swim.

"That's Jean Jacques Machado. He's one of the greatest BJJ athletes in the world. He was born missing the fingers on his left hand. They had to build him a thumb with one of his other bones."

Martese lets this sink in.

"Adaptation, Dylan," Martese says. "Tall, short. Fat, slim. Two legs, one leg, no legs. Ten fingers or five fingers. It just doesn't matter in jiujitsu. There's a workaround for everything. It just takes time to figure it out."

"What was his workaround?" I ask, still looking at the poster.

"For missing his fingers?"

I nod.

"A crazy underhook and an even stronger overhook."

My face must look blank because Martese says, "Don't worry about it. We'll get to underhooks and overhooks."

"You want some help?" he says, with a nod to the recalcitrant sneaker.

"Thanks."

He reaches down and levers it off my foot. He holds on to my prosthetic foot for a moment and checks out the rest of my artificial leg.

"I have a buddy who lost both his legs over in Iraq. His legs are a little fancier."

"Yeah, this one's kind of basic."

"He told me that his have a microprocessor or something controlling the knee. Forty grand a pop. I told him he could get a secondhand Porsche 911 for that kind of money."

I laugh. I guess I'm not the only person who thinks like that.

"I'd be lucky to trade this one in for a Nissan."

"Guess you might as well keep it then," he laughs. "So, what do you say? You want to try some jiujitsu?"

I sneak a look at the cage. He watches me and must catch the worried look on my face because he says, "Relax, I'm not going to put you in there. We practice out here on the mats."

I shrug. "Sure. But I don't have the stuff you wear." I know that when you do jiujitsu you wear something like thick pajamas.

"I have some old gis in the back, I'll find you something. Then if you want to keep training, you can buy yourself one."

The door of the gym opens and the tough-looking guy with the shaved head, the tattoos and muscles—the one who was telling me to wear concealer—walks in.

He waves over at Martese with a smile. "Hey, Coach."

"What's up, Jared?"

Now I remember. That was his name. Jared.

"Jared's on our MMA team," Martese explains. "Hey Jared, this is Dylan. We're going to teach him how to be a stone cold killer."

"Oh yeah," says Jared. "I saw you outside the other day." He narrows his eyes. "You get some concealer for that eye?"

Jared slips off his shoes and throws them on the rack next to mine. He and Martese give each other a big hug and it seems kind of weird to me. Guys at school don't hug each other, not unless someone's scored a touchdown or a home run or came from behind to win the last leg of a relay or something.

Jared turns to me and for a moment I'm worried he's going to hug me too. If he did, he might break my ribs. Thankfully he just throws out a clenched, tattooed hand and we fist bump.

"Great to have you training with us, Dylan."

He wanders off to an area in the corner with a bunch of strange-shaped heavy bags. He pulls on light fingerless MMA gloves that are smaller than boxing gloves and starts throwing strikes and kicks at the bags.

Even though it looks like he's just warming up, not putting every-thing into his moves, the chain holding the bag rattles like crazy every time he connects.

Martese taps me on the shoulder.

"I took a fresh look at that fight you got into at school," he says, pulling out his phone. "If you want, I can go over it with you."

Man, what is it with dudes wanting to show me that fight? First Rich and now Martese. And what's there to go over? I swung. I fell down. I got punched in the face. Then it got broken up.

Without even thinking, I blurt out, "I can't think of anything I'd like to do less."

I'm worried that I've offended him. I know he's trying to help me, but he busts out laughing.

"I hear you, brother. I never much enjoying studying my losses, but in the fight game it's win or learn. And you don't learn if you don't confront your mistakes." He shrugs. "But, hey, it's totally up to you, we don't have to."

I take a breath. I really don't want to watch it again. I've only seen it once, when I first saw that someone posted it. I clicked it off before it was even halfway through, it was so embarrassing.

But win or learn? I hadn't won. That was for definite. So maybe I could learn.

"Okay," I say.

Martese already has the clip ready to go on his phone. He angles the screen so we can both watch it.

My stomach turns over as Todd tackles me to the ground, gets on top of me and pins me down. When he starts to punch me I cover up as best as I can and wait for someone to stop it.

"This kid, what's his name?"

"Todd."

"Okay, so Todd clearly isn't trained, but he does a couple of things right. First, he slips your punch and takes you down to the ground. Then he establishes a dominant position by moving straight to mount. Apart from taking your back, mount is probably the strongest position there is."

Take the back? *Mount*? Martese is speaking a totally different language.

He picks up on my blank expression. "Don't worry about the terminology, we'll get to that. Here, let me show you. Lie down on the mat," he says slapping the edge of one of the squares.

Wait. I thought we were watching it, not doing some kind of a crime scene reenactment.

"Actually hang on, you need to see it. Jared, I need to borrow you for a moment so I can show Dylan a couple of things."

Jared jogs over and lies down with his back on the mat.

"I'm going to take a high mount," Martese says, sitting on Jared's chest.

"Bro, you ended up on bottom?" Jared asks me, like he can't believe anyone would be that dumb.

I didn't know that's what it was called, but I guess I did.

"Yeah," I say, feeling totally lame. I still don't see how any of this is helpful. I already know I messed up and that I'm worse in a fight than I am at swimming. I have the black eye to prove it.

"Oh, man," says Jared, with this big grin. "That sucks, dude."

He looks up at Martese.

"Hey Coach, remember that fight I had against Velasquez where I spent about a minute of the second in bottom mount while he ground and pound the living sh—" he stops and corrects himself. "The living heck out of me."

Jared laughs at the memory of being punched in the face. When I first met him he reminded me of a pit bull, but now as he laughs about getting his face smashed in he seems more like a golden retriever— happy with whatever's going on.

"Hey," Martese says to Jared, with a nod up at me. He's serious, indicating that story time is over and that he wants to show me something.

"Sorry, Coach."

"So, Dylan," says Martese. "Mount means that someone has passed your legs and they're sitting on top of you. A high mount means that they've scooted up your chest. It's very difficult to escape from a high mount and it means they can land strikes with the benefit of gravity."

He mimes throwing punches and elbows at Jared's face. Jared mimes blocking them.

"In your fight, Todd established mount and then goes for a classic ground and pound. You actually did pretty good by covering up. If you could have broken his posture down and pulled him more into you, got control of his arms that would have been better, but your instincts were good."

I wasn't sure if that made me feel better or not. It still looked humiliating.

Martese gets up and pulls Jared back to his feet. "Don't look so bummed out. Even fighters who know what they're doing lose. You can't avoid taking the odd L."

I think about the learn part he'd mentioned. "What should I have done?"

"How did it start? It looks like he just went for you, but that's not usually how fights start."

I took a deep breath. It's going to sound lame, but I may as well tell the truth.

"He called me a name, and I took a swing at him."

I was expecting Martese to ask me what name Todd had called me. That was the first thing every other adult had asked, from my parents to the principal. But he doesn't.

He stands in front of me and says, "Okay, I'm Todd. I call you a name, and you do what?"

Jared is watching us. A couple of other people have begun to drift into the gym. I don't want to show anyone how weak my punch is, never mind an audience made up of people who actually know how to throw one.

"Show me how you were standing first. Like where were your feet?"

I try to remember how you should stand and move so I'm side-on to Martese. I feel like I'm getting ready to punch a brick wall.

"Okay, good. Not great, but not terrible."

"Now, throw the punch you threw. It was an overhand right, correct?" he says miming throwing a punch.

I have to think about it. Right hand. Yeah, I guess that was it. I clench my fist.

"Okay, I get the picture," Martese says, stepping back and saving me further embarrassment.

"So, what should I have done?"

"He called you a name?" he asks.

I nod.

"Then ask him not to call you that."

That's it? This is the amazing MMA coach's advice. Did this guy ever go to high school? You ask someone not to call you a name and they'll just laugh in your face.

I'm starting to feel like this whole thing is a waste of time. What kind of advice am I getting here?

"You don't believe me?" says Martese. "Dylan, you ever hear the expression 'give someone enough rope to hang themselves?'"

"Yeah."

"What do you think it means?"

"If someone's messing up then let them keep doing it?" I venture.

"Exactly. So, if you ask him to stop and he does, that's awesome, you've de-escalated the situation."

"And if he doesn't?"

"Hey Jared, square up to me, show me some street thug."

Jared's expression changes. I know he's acting, but it's still scary. His eyes blaze with anger and his chest puffs out, fists clenched. "What you looking at, homie?"

Martese stands in front of him, one arm across his chest, his hand on his chin. "Nothing, man. I'm minding my own business."

Jared puffs himself up even further. "Oh, I'm nothing to you? That what you're telling me?"

He's getting closer and closer to Martese. Even though I know this isn't real I feel my heartbeat speed up.

Finally, Jared chest bumps Martese. I'm not exactly sure what happens next, because it's so fast. One second Jared's in Martese's face and the next Martese has spun him around and is standing behind him with the blade of his forearm across Jared's throat. Martese reaches over and behind and grabs the bicep of his other arm, which is tucked behind Jared's ear. He starts to squeeze.

Jared reaches back and taps Martese's arm. Martese lets go.

I'm impressed, but confused.

"But you said I should de-escalate the situation." I'm pretty sure strangling someone doesn't count as de-escalation.

"Yes, and I tried to. More than once. But as soon as he touched me, I defended myself." Martese puts his hand on my shoulder. "Dylan, someone calls you a name and you pop them one, that's one thing. You just increased your chances of getting in trouble, maybe even getting sued or arrested, or ending up in court. But if you try to de-escalate the situation first, then someone puts their hands on you and you protect yourself from being assaulted, that's something else. You're within your rights."

I guess he has a point, although I'm still not sure a teacher would see it like that. It looked kind of brutal.

"Jared, are you hurt?" Martese asks. "Broken bones? Black eye? Cuts? A bruise?"

Jared smiles and shakes his head. "Nope."

Martese turns to me. "There you go, Dylan. The only thing that might get injured is the other guy's ego, and that's no bad thing."

He claps his hands together. "Okay, you ready to try this out?"

IN THE GUY'S locker room, Jared shows me how to tie my gi pants. There's a thick cord and you have to thread it through some loops at the front before you tie it. I put on the jacket, which is a little too big for me. He fixes my belt, cinches it tight, and stands back.

"There you go. You're now officially the most dangerous man in the gym."

"Dangerous?" I ask him.

"Brand-new white belts are always the most dangerous. They got no chill. You take 'em down and they start spazzing out." He gives me a friendly pat on the shoulder which almost knocks me over.

Martese walks in.

"Come on guys, let's go. Class is about to start."

He looks down at my prosthesis. "You're probably going to want to take that off."

Now I'm totally confused. "My leg?"

"The knee's metal, right?" he says.

"Yeah. Titanium."

"You catch someone in the head with that thing and you'll open them up."

I can see the logic, and I was already worried about getting my foot stuck and messing up my hip if someone threw me or something. At the same time, I'm not sure I feel comfortable taking off my leg in front of a room full of strangers.

It's bad enough in the swimming pool, even though it's mostly underwater. But this would be different. No water. Nowhere to hide what I look like.

Martese smiles. "Look, Dylan, everyone's going to be too busy doing their own thing to be looking at you. And if they do look, so what?"

"But it's weird," I say, looking down at my stump, safely hidden away in the socket of my prosthesis. "I look like a freak."

"A freak?" he says.

"Well, I'm not normal, am I?"

Martese puts his hands on my shoulders and looks me straight in the eyes. For a second I think he's going to give me the same 'you're not a freak, you're just different' speech I get from my mom.

"You think the people who come in here every day are normal? You think I'm normal? You think Jared's normal? Normal people don't last long around here." His brown eyes bore into me. "Who wants to be normal anyway? Freaks are the people who change the world."

As I hop out of the locker room to the mat, I can see that a bunch more people have arrived for class. One guy does a full-on doubletake and nudges the guy next to him.

This is a bad idea. I want to go back into the locker room. To take off the gi, put my prosthetic leg and my regular clothes on, and get the hell out of here.

But it's just one class, I tell myself. One hour. I can get through it.

"Okay, guys. End of the mat," says Martese. "Two lines, and let's start the warm-up with forward rolls."

Wait. Forward rolls? I thought we were learning to fight.

This looks like gymnastics class in pajamas. Everyone forms two lines and forward roll their way down the mats to the other end.

Martese waves me over to the side of the mat and shows me how to do it properly. "Roll over on your shoulder, not your neck."

I try it. It's a little bit like a racing turn in the pool. I kind of get it on the third or fourth try. Then we were on to the next exercise which is, drumroll, backward rolls.

Again the secret here is to roll over on your shoulder, not your neck. Martese shows me that one too. I watch the other people in the class as they tumble their way back up the mat. The guy who'd nudged his buddy when I'd walked in shoots me a thumbs up as he back rolls past me.

Martese stands back up. "Now, shrimps!"

What?

Did he just say shrimps?

He comes back to the side of the mat next to me. "Shrimping is probably the most important movement you'll learn in jiujitsu."

He demonstrates the move. Shrimping involves lying down, placing the sole of your foot on the mat, and using it to push off and move your hips so that you scoot your butt backward. It looks about as goofy as it sounds.

"It's all about the hips," Martese told me.

I'm still not convinced. Forget the hips—how could pretending to be a shrimp help you kick someone's ass? The world was full of scary animals: lions, bears, cheetahs, snakes. I don't think the shrimp had ever made that list, but if Martese says it's all about pretending to be a shrimp then I'll go along with it.

The last part of the warm-up makes more sense. We do neck exercises, then sit-ups and back raises, and finish off with leg raises where you have be on all fours and move one leg at a time. I stake out a spot near the edge of the mat where I can't tell if anyone is staring at me while I do my leg raises with only one leg.

When everyone is finished with the warm-up, Martese waves Jared back over. The two of them sit in the middle of the mats and everyone else gathers around to watch.

"This week we're covering back escapes. Grab yourself a partner."

I watch as everyone pairs off. I get that sinking feeling you get when teams are getting picked and you know you're going to be last. Not only am I brand new but there's the whole leg thing.

Someone jostles my elbow and I turn to see this smaller Asian guy.

He's a few years older than me and looks kind of geeky. He's wearing a blue belt instead of a white one, which I know from reading stuff online is kind of a big deal. It's not like a lot of martial arts where you get promoted just for showing up. In BJJ it usually takes a couple of years of solid training to get a blue belt.

"Kyle," he says, introducing himself.

"Dylan."

He bumps my fist with his, and then slaps my hand, which seems like it was what people do here instead of shaking hands.

We all watch as Martese lies on the mat and Jared scoots underneath him, both of them face up, like Martese is giving Jared a piggy back ride, only with them both lying down.

"Okay," says Martese, "so I messed up and Jared here has taken my back, which is pretty much the worst position I can be in during a fight. And he has his hooks in."

When he says that, Jared, who already has his legs snaked around Martese's legs, places his heels against Martese's hips.

"And he's setting up what?" Martese asks.

"Rear naked choke," someone calls out.

"Exactly. Which means if I don't defend and escape, it's either tap or take a nap and if this is out on the street, then they're not going to stop just because I tap. So my first job is to hand fight against the choke. Two on one."

He grabs one of Jared's hands. "One hand on his hand, right here up against the thumb. Second hand slightly lower, more toward his wrist, so I can begin to pry his arm away. Once I have control of his arm, or at least once I've stopped the immediate danger, I can start thinking about my escape."

He shows us the escape, which involves what looks like someone wriggling hard to get their shoulder onto the mat.

He finishes showing us the rest of the move. "Okay, try that with your partner. On three. One, two, three."

At the end of the three count everyone claps and breaks off into their pairs.

I scoot on my butt over to one side and Kyle 'takes my back.' He put his heels against my hips and wraps his arms around me, one arm snaking up around my neck.

I've already forgotten what Martese just said about using your hands to hand fight and where my hands were supposed to go. I'm so confused that Kyle has to literally move my hands into position.

"One there and one there."

Slowly, with every piece of strength I have, I manage to move the blade of his forearm from under my chin. I know he's letting me do it, and he could totally choke me out if he wanted to, but he doesn't.

Once he's let me do a pretty horrible version of the super-smooth escape Martese showed us, it's my turn to take his back and let him practice the escape.

I have a problem. I only have one heel, and you use your heels to control your opponent's hips to stop them from sneaking out. There's nothing to stop Kyle escaping on that side.

He takes his time and works his escape slowly, but he could have done it straight away if he'd wanted to.

I'm not going to lie. When I watched Martese demonstrate this move, my mind flashed to my fight with Todd. I could see myself taking his back, sliding in a hook and then choking him out.

If I'd been able to do that, things would have been totally different. Not only would I have been a legit badass that no one messed with or so much as teased, it would have been even cooler because when he'd tapped, I could have let him go. Just like one of those Roman emperors who gave a thumbs up in the Coliseum when he wanted to spare a gladiator.

Beating someone up isn't nearly as badass as submitting someone. I get that now.

But how can I get that far when I can't hold them in place? I feel like I'm back to square one, and all because of having only one dumb leg.

"How we doing here, guys?"

I look to see Martese standing over us.

"I don't really have a hook on this side," I explain.

Martese takes a step back. "Try pressing the end of your stump into his hip. It should do the same job."

I wince at the thought. The end of my stump is still sensitive. There's only so hard I can press it into Kyle's hip before I get a sharp needle of pain that shoots up into the rest of my body.

"Sorry, it's kind of sore."

"Okay, let me see," says Martese, lying down and taking my place.

He puts his left leg way out to the side like it's missing.

"Hmm," he says, like he's trying to figure out a math problem, which I guess he is.

Moving his right leg straight across the line of Kyle's hips, he reaches down with his left arm and grabs his right ankle. "Okay, Kyle, try to get out."

Kyle wriggles and struggles and tries to get his shoulder to the mat, but he can't manage it. Suddenly Martese lets go of his ankle. As Kyle starts to wriggle free, Martese's right arm shoots up, lighting fast, and goes across Kyle's throat. He reaches over, grabs the ball of Kyle's shoulder joint, and squeezes.

Next thing, Kyle makes this choking sound at the back of his throat, reaches up and taps Martese's arm.

"Okay, try that," says Martese, scooting out from under Kyle and letting me move back into position. "Let go of your ankle and let him think he's out. Then move your other arm in for the choke."

I do it. My movement isn't smooth, but I get the blade of my forearm across his throat.

"Good, now reach up and grab his shoulder. Perfect."

He taps. He actually taps. He definitely lifted his chin to let me get my arm in under there and I'm pretty sure he could have grabbed for my choking arm, but it still worked. Kind of.

"See!" Martese says. "It's all about adapting. Don't worry about what you don't have, use what you do."

After class ends, I sit on the edge of the mat and watch everyone else roll. Rolling is live sparring. It looks like barely controlled chaos with people wrestling on the ground, trying to choke or joint lock each other, but everyone seems to be enjoying it.

It's the weirdest thing. All these people are trying to choke out their partner or break their arm, but no one gets mad, and they all seem to be having fun.

Two people pair off for a round and each round lasts five minutes. There's a big digital display timer mounted on the wall that beeps at the start and end of each round.

Just before the timer beeps to signal the start of a round, the opponents fist bump, slap their fingers together, and go at it until one person taps. Then they reset and do it again, continuing until the five minutes is up.

At the end they bump fists again or hug, or one of them will show the other person the move they just used or how to escape it. Then they pick a different partner to roll with and it starts all over again.

I get so caught up in watching it that it's only when I look up at the other clock on the wall that I realize I have to get home. Like Cinderella if she'd been a dude with one leg, I hustle to find my prosthesis and put it on before the clock strikes midnight.

On the way out, Martese hands me some papers.

"If you want to keep training, you need to have one of your parents sign this, and here's the payment information. If money's a problem I offer a reduced rate for students who help clean up and keep the place tidy."

I hesitate. "My parents don't know I'm here."

He gives me the same disappointed look he did when I told him about how my fight with Todd started.

"I don't think my mom was in love with the idea," I explain.

"Then ask your dad, but I need that waiver signed if you want to come back."

Just then the gym door bursts open. The girl with the pink hair and tattoos, barrels through it. She's wearing MMA gear—shorts and a rash guard. She takes off her shoes, throws them near the door, and runs straight across the mats to the cage with her training bag.

Jared opens the cage door for her with a flourish, like he's a doorman at a fancy apartment building. They both step inside. She digs a gum shield out of her bag and pops it into her mouth. Next she takes out a single MMA glove and throws it down onto the cage floor.

"You forget your other glove again, Santana?" says Jared.

Santana smiles and flips him off. She lifts her right arm, grabs her left arm just below the elbow, and yanks off a prosthetic arm which she tosses into her training bag.

I stand there, mouth open, shocked. I hadn't even noticed the one arm thing before. Like, at all. It was as if someone unscrewed their head from their neck or something. Surreal.

I must still be staring, because she whips around and gives me a death stare.

"What are you looking at?"

"Sorry, nothing," I mumble.

Martese comes to the rescue. He claps a hand on my shoulder.

"Santana's on our fight team," says Martese. "She's fighting ammy at the moment."

Ammy? The look on my face must be as blank as my mind.

"Amateur," he explains. "You can't fight pro until you're eighteen, so she has to stay fighting ammy for another year."

Santana is seventeen? I know girls can look a lot older, especially with makeup, but she comes off a lot older than the sophomore, and even senior girls, at Meadow Grove. She's just way more confident.

I wonder if that's maybe why I didn't notice her arm before now. There's so much else going on with the pink hair and the tattoos. Maybe it's not even that though. It's just the way she is, her presence.

Back inside the cage, Jared has picked up a huge kick pad. He straps it around his chest.

"What you want to work on?" he asks her.

"That flying knee."

"Gamebred style. I like it," grins Jared.

"Yeah, I'm going to Masvidal that ho," she says, pushing her chest out and placing both arms behind her back as she settles into the cage mesh.

Her head whips around again. Her top lip peels back over her gum shield. Instead of bright white teeth there's now a row of tiny illus-trated skulls.

I shake myself out of it.

"I gotta go," I say to Martese.

As I walk off the mat, Santana runs full speed across the cage, leaps into the air, and slams her knee high into the pad that's strapped around Jared. He stumbles back from the force of it.

"Beautiful!" he shouts. "That's a recovery room KO, baby."

Santana prowls back to her starting position, hand on her hip like a total badass.

CHAPTER
Thirteen

"HOW WAS STUDY HALL?" Mom asks as we sit down to a dinner of chicken fajitas and salad.

I raided the refrigerator as soon as I got home, but I'm still starving. Between swim practice and my first BJJ class I must have burned through a crazy amount of calories today.

I knew Mom was going to ask about study hall. She always does. I'm not going to lie, but I wait until she has a big forkful of fajita in her mouth before I answer.

"I didn't go."

She looks across the table at Dad. It's weird how parents have those looks. This one was somewhere between their 'uh-oh' look and their 'do you want to take this one or should I?' look.

"Something happen at school?" asks Dad.

"No, school was fine." Of course it wasn't entirely fine, but I don't want to get into the whole being a social outcast thing because it won't change anything and Mom will only get upset.

"So where did you go?" she asks.

I brace myself. "You remember that Brazilian guy who came around the other day? I went to his gym and he showed me what I did wrong in that fight with Todd. Then I stayed and took a class. But it's okay, it was jiujitsu."

I want to add *and see, I'm perfectly fine. I didn't break anything, or crumble into dust,* but I think that might be pushing my luck.

"I just wanted to see what it was like. I'll finish up my schoolwork after dinner."

Mom's fork clanks down onto the plate. "You went where?"

What is it with parents? You tell them something and they immediately want you to repeat it, even though you know they heard what you said. But if you repeat what you just said then they think you're being a smart-ass.

I already knew Mom would flip out, but I have an ace up my sleeve, and I decide that now was as good a time as any to play it.

"There's a girl who trains there who has one arm."

"What?" says my Dad .

"Yeah, it only goes to here," I say, showing him with my arm.

"She have an accident?" asks Dad.

"I don't know."

"And she trains this Brazilian jiujitsu stuff?"

"Yeah, but she's an MMA fighter. She's amateur right now, but she wants to go fight in the UFC."

"With one arm?"

"Yeah."

"How does she fight people when she has one arm?"

Dad is super into this unexpected turn in the conversation, but Mom isn't so easily distracted.

"Dylan, you are not training at some cage fighting gym," she says, super firm, like that's the final decision.

"I won't be cage fighting. It's jiujitsu, there's no striking. It's pretty safe."

"I don't care what it is, you're not doing it."

"Why not?"

"Because it's dangerous," she splutters.

"Mom, it's not. If you think you're going to get hurt, you tap and the other person has to stop."

I look over at Dad, hoping for some back up but he seems distracted.

"This girl with the one arm," he says.

"Santana."

"Her parents must be okay with her going there."

I have no idea if they are or they're not, but I'm not going to say that.

"Yeah, totally," I lie.

"Well," says Mom, turning to the next page of the big book of mom clichés, "we're not her parents, we're your parents. Even if it is safe, which I don't see how it can be, but even if it is, you have swim practice and school. You're taking your SATs next year, you really need to focus on your academics."

"Swim practice is mostly in the mornings, and this is after school. Plus, they have weekend classes for teens. I was thinking maybe I could do those. That way it wouldn't get in the way of school or swimming."

Mom isn't about to give up, no matter what I say. "Dylan, you'll have swim meets on the weekends."

"I'm not going to be on the team for meets. I'm way slower than the next slowest guy they have. There's no way Coach is going to be putting me in to compete at a meet."

"Well not with that attitude he won't," she says.

As usual, Dad tries to play peacemaker.

"Why don't we do this," he says. "Dylan can go do these classes until he makes the team and as long as his schoolwork doesn't suffer. Sound fair?" he asks me.

"Sure," I say.

"And what if he gets hurt?"

Not this again. I am so sick of hearing about how I might get hurt. So tired of people treating me like I'm a weakling because of my leg.

"Duh! I'm already hurt," I say, tapping my knuckles against my artificial leg. "Or haven't you noticed?"

As soon as the words are out of my mouth, I feel horrible. It's a complete asshole thing to say. Mom doesn't know but when I got out of the hospital after the accident, I used to hear her crying some nights.

She would wait until I went to sleep and then lie in bed next to my dad and cry while he tried to comfort her.

She gets up from the table and rushes back into the kitchen. I look at my dad. "I'm sorry. I didn't mean it."

He shakes his head. "She worries about you, Dylan. We both do."

I start to get up but he waves for me to sit back down. "Give her a minute."

I sit back down. My appetite's gone.

I think I just blew whatever chance I had that my parents would sign the waiver so I could train at Resilient MMA. Even if I could get the money to pay for the classes, there's no way Martese is going to let me train without that piece of paper.

Fourteen

AFTER I FINISH my homework I take my laptop into my room and find a video of the very first UFC tournament. Martese had recommended I watch it so that I understood a little bit more about the history of BJJ and why it's become so popular.

The UFC, which stands for Ultimate Fighting Championship, was the first big organized Mixed Martial Arts tournament in North America. The idea was to let fighters who used all kinds of different fighting styles battle it out in a cage to see which one worked the best. Boxers against wrestlers against judo players against karate black belts.

Spoiler alert. The winner was BJJ.

BJJ was developed by this guy called Helio Gracie in the 1930s. He was this little guy who'd been sick a lot as a kid and I guess got picked on because of it. Anyway, he took regular jiujitsu from Japan and switched it up. His idea was to create a fighting style that used leverage to allow a smaller, weaker person to beat a bigger, stronger person.

He taught this new style of grappling to his eight sons and pretty soon they had this bad-ass fighting dynasty. Then they moved to California to spread the word of how effective it was and started teaching it to people like Chuck Norris.

It was still this kind of underground secret, but the Gracie family were so sure that BJJ worked that they had an open challenge where anyone could come in and fight one of them. If they got beaten, they'd give the person ten times the amount of money the other person put up. Quite a few people tried but no one managed to collect the money.

Then they helped set up the UFC. There were no weight divisions, and you could fight any style you wanted. The only things that weren't allowed were biting and eye gouging. To prove their point, the Gracie family picked the smallest of the eight Gracie brothers, Royce Gracie, to represent them in the cage.

I'm right in the middle of watching this crazy Dutch fighter named Gerard Gordeau beat up this massive sumo wrestler called Teila Tuli when there's a knock on my door and my dad walks in.

"Where's this piece of paper I have to sign?" he says.

"Really?"

"You can try it out, but do me a favor, would you, kiddo?"

"Sure."

"Maybe don't talk about it around your mom. And no more black eyes."

"Oh sure, no more black eyes," I say, as on my laptop screen two of poor Teila Tuli's teeth fly out of his mouth from a vicious head kick.

"Hey, so what are you watching?" Dad asks.

"Oh, nothing."

If I tell him it's the first ever UFC tournament, then he'll want to take a look and maybe change his mind about letting me train at Resilient.

"Well, don't let your mom catch you watching *nothing*," he says, putting up air quotes when he says *nothing*. "You know what she thinks about that kind of stuff and how it degrades women."

He thinks I'm watching porn.

"Oh, no, it's not …"

Wait. It might be safer to let him think it's porn. I close my laptop.

"Little bit of advice for you," he says.

Oh God, he's not going to talk to me about sex, or watching porn, is he?

"Don't go confusing some of the things you see on the internet with, you know, real girls. I mean, obviously they're real, but you know, they're acting."

"Right."

I can tell that now he wishes he hadn't said anything almost as much as I do.

He puts his hand on the door frame. "So, any girls you have your eye on at school? There must be some cuties."

Yeah, Dad, I feel like saying, *there are lots of cute girls. Dozens of them.* But I don't think they want to have anything to do with a guy who does leg farts and walks with a limp and got someone kicked off the swim team.

"I guess."

"And what about this girl at the gym? The one you were telling us about, you know, with the one arm. What's her name?"

"Santana."

"That's the one."

I think back to Santana kissing her girlfriend full on the lips.

"Yeah, somehow I don't think I'm her type."

"You might be surprised," says dad.

I really don't think I will be.

Fifteen

CRAZY IRISH PUNK music pumps through the gym speakers as I line up against the wall for the start of my first teens BJJ class. It takes me a second to tune into the lyrics which are all about a sailor with one leg who's Shipping Up To Boston, whatever that means.

Santana stands in the middle of the mat, hands cocked on her hips. When I arrived and gave Martese my signed waiver and my payment details, he told me that Santana teaches the teen class. I don't know what's up with her music choice, but no one else seems to have registered it.

"Okay," she yells, grabbing a remote and inching down the volume on the song about the guy with one of his legs missing.

"Two lines. Forward rolls."

I hop to the end of the mat with everyone else and jump in behind a girl who looks like she's thirteen. When I first walked in, I wondered if I had the time wrong and it was the kid's class, because apart from a couple of people, everyone seems younger than me.

"Shrimp down and back," Santana shouts over the music.

This is the one move I've been practicing every night since my first time at Resilient. Shrimping looks about as goofy as it sounds, but it seems like it's super important. It's all about moving your hips and creating space when you're on the ground so that you can get your guard back. Guard is using your legs, or in my case, leg and stump, to stop your opponent.

All the other kids shrimp down the mat and I do my best to keep up. I'm already breathing hard and we're only halfway through the warm-up. By the time we finish my gi is damp with sweat.

Santana calls one of the older kids, a tall, skinny girl with cornrows, out into the middle of the floor. She has a white belt on but there are four black pieces of tape around the end of it. Stripes are like progress markers before you move up to the next color belt.

"So today we're working single leg takedowns," she says.

Next, she demonstrates what she means. Crouching down, she grabs the tall girl's leg and scoops it up with her arms. Then she circles around so that the girl loses her balance and falls onto her back.

She does it twice more, talking through each of the steps from head position to making sure you keep the person's leg between yours, and then the rotation.

"Okay, six single legs each, then switch. Then we'll look at a quick counter using a guillotine choke."

By the time I start to look around for someone to partner with, it seems like everyone has already paired up with someone. First the song about a peg leg and now I'm standing (on one leg) on my own while everyone finds partners. I look over to Santana but she's busy talking to the girl with the cornrows and another really tall girl.

Someone taps my shoulder. I turn round and for a second I don't see anyone. Then I look down and there's a kid who looks like he must have snuck in from the kids' class that runs before this one. He's a foot shorter than me and super skinny, with huge brown eyes that make him look like he's from a cartoon.

"Come on," he says. "Single leg me."

"Okay, I'll try."

We bump and slap hands, and I reach down to lift up his leg. It's really hard to keep my balance but I manage to lift his leg up and hop to one side fast enough that he falls over. The only problem is that I fall with him.

He gets to his feet and puts out his hand. I grab it and he hauls me up. He's way stronger than he looks.

"Do it again," he says.

I crouch down, like we've been shown, promptly lose my balance, and fall onto my side without even getting hold of his leg. He helps me back to my feet and I try again. The calf muscles in my right leg are on fire from all the standing and hopping around.

I make a couple more attempts, then we switch. Of course the first time he grabs my leg and raises it off the ground I fall straight over. I'm not even a good practice dummy, but he doesn't seem to mind.

Santana claps her hands together. "Now we're going to look at a counter to the takedown."

"Latisha, go for a single leg, and I'm going to counter with a guillotine."

Latisha steps in, drops down for the level change, and picks Santana's leg up. As she does, Santana slips her half-arm under Latisha's neck, reaches her other hand under to grab her arm-stump, and falls back. Latisha immediately lets go of Santana's leg, I guess to stop being choked, but Santana falling backward brings Latisha down to the mat.

Santana throws a leg over Latisha's back and yanks her arm-stump up, all the pressure going into Latisha's throat.

Latisha taps her hand on Santana's side and Santana lets go. Latisha makes this half groan, half coughing sound and a bunch of the kids laugh.

Latisha smiles and rubs at her throat.

"One more time," says Santana.

They repeat the same move. Latisha grabs Santana's leg and Santana immediately puts her in the weird front headlock, falls back, and uses her good arm to yank her half-arm up into Latisha's throat.

"Now you guys try it. Six reps each then switch."

I go first but as soon as Konrad grabs my leg, I fall over before I can get one arm to his neck, never mind grab it with my other hand so I can guillotine him.

"I can't get this," I say, after he pulls me back up for the second time.

Santana comes across the floor.

"Having trouble?" she asks.

I don't know if she's making fun of me again or what. I mean, duh, it's kind of obvious that I'm having trouble and that partnering up with me is a big waste of Konrad's time.

"I can't keep my balance long enough to get it," I tell her.

"Maybe try a standing guillotine," she says.

She motions for Konrad to stand in front of her.

"So let's see how we work t his," she says, suddenly thoughtful, like it's a math problem.

She lifts her left foot off the mat so that she's hopping on one leg like me.

"Okay, Dylan, place your right foot back so it's harder for him to single leg you."

I do it. I see what she means—if my leg is out of the way, it's harder to grab. Anyway, in a regular fight I'd have my prosthesis on so it wouldn't be an issue.

"Okay, go to grab me," she says, hopping back.

I try it. As I move in, she grabs the back of my neck, pushes my head down and guillotines me. It's so fast that I don't even feel her arms, just this crazy pressure on my throat and neck. I panic tap.

"Right, try it on Konrad."

Santana steps to the side and Konrad closes in. I try the choke, putting one arm under, grabbing my other hand, yanking up and then falling back.

I make a total mess of it. I'm so bad that Santana shows me again and literally has to move my hands for me. Then she lets me try on my own and I kind of get it.

Next, it's Konrad's turn. He's slick. He yanks on the choke and even though I tap fast I can feel my head start to swim. Coughing, I hold my hand up.

"You okay, dude?"

"Yeah, yeah, I'm fine," I say, sounding like a cat coughing up a hairball.

We do a few more repetitions and then I ask Konrad if he's ever tried to guillotine someone in a fight. Konrad looks at me. "A fight?"

"Yeah, like at school."

"Why would I get in a fight at school? My mom would go nuts."

Santana slaps her hand on the wall, signaling that we're moving on to the next section of the class.

"Okay, this week we're working on our escapes from mount bottom. Dylan, you might want to focus on this one," she says and this time there's a definite smirk on her face.

Santana lies on her back in the middle of the mats. Latisha sits on top of her, her heels pinched in against Santana's hips, all her weight on her. It's the exact same position I was in. I feel a shudder of recognition as I think about Todd's face looming over me, his fists pummeling my face since I couldn't move.

"So, first thing, what do we say if you find yourself in mount bottom?" Santana asks.

She looks at everyone clustered around watching the demonstration.

A tiny blonde girl who also looks like she should be in the kids' class shouts out, "You messed up a long time ago."

"Okay, all together now," says Santana. "If you're here …"

"… You messed up a long time ago," the whole class says in unison.

I feel my cheeks flush. I look around to see if everyone is looking at me. They're not. Everyone is focused on Santana.

"But" says Santana, "it happens. You get caught with a takedown, or your guard gets passed, or your opponent transitions from knee on belly, and you find yourself here. What do you need to do next?"

"Escape," someone shouts.

"Exactly," says Santana. "You don't want to hang around on bottom getting your ass kicked, and you don't want to let them improve their position and make things even worse for you."

I'm not sure how being flat on your back with someone on top of you could get worse, but apparently I'm about to find out.

"So," says Santana. "Elbows in! Legs flat! No bending your knees or bringing your feet up to your butt until you're pulling the trigger on the escape, because?"

She looks around.

"You don't want to be grapevined!"

"Exactly," says Santana, bringing her feet up to her butt so that her knees are bent.

Latisha hooks her heels under the back of Santana's knees.

"So now she's grapevined me, I can't straighten my legs, which means I can't generate the momentum I need to bridge."

I'm totally lost, but I try to stay focused. It's like learning a completely different language.

"The other thing your opponent might try to do is move to a high mount position."

Latisha pushes Santana's elbows and scoots up so that she's sitting on her chest.

"If you let that happen, look—you can't bridge," says Santana, thrusting her hips up from the mat. "So today we're going to work on a really basic escape from mount."

Once Santana shows us the basics of the escape, we have to practice it with our partner. Konrad lies on his back and I take a low mount.

Looking down at him I don't see how he's possibly going to move me. I'm way heavier than him, and I know exactly what's coming. He's going to try the escape that we just watched.

We bump and tap hands. As I'm thinking *good luck, kid*, he grabs my right arm, pinning it down to his chest at the elbow so it's trapped. Next, he moves his left foot so that it's trapping my right foot and bridges hard.

Next thing I know I'm lying with my back on the mat and Konrad is looking down at me. It was like being inside a washing machine as it gets switched on. One second I'm looking at the floor, the next I'm looking up at the ceiling.

We reset with me on top again. He does it a second time—grabs my arm, traps my foot, bridges his hips, and *oopa*, I'm right back to looking at the ceiling.

He does it twice more. I try to crush my weight down onto him, but it doesn't make any difference. In fact, it seems to make it easier. Never mind breaking a sweat, he's not even out of breath.

"Your turn," he says.

We switch so that I'm lying with my back on the floor. It's not a flashback or anything, I don't see Todd's face, but I remember the sensation of him being on top of me as he pulls back his arm to punch me in the face. My stomach does a flip.

I push the memory to one side and focus. Okay, step one, grab the arm. Santana said that if the person's arms are out of reach, you can still bridge their hips. That will bring them forward and most times they'll reach their hands down to the floor to stay balanced.

I grab Konrad's arm at the elbow and secure his hand so that he can't move it. I move my right foot up and trap his left foot, then push my hips up into a bridge. He doesn't really resist. It's almost like he half falls off me, but I'm able to get off my back.

"Do it again," he says.

We reset and run through it a few more times. I still feel like he could stay in mount if he wanted to, but I manage to get him off me.

"Just keep practicing, bro," he says. "You'll get it."

Santana claps her hands together and after a few seconds everyone settles down again.

"Okay," yells Santana. "Shark tank!"

A tiny girl with pigtails punches the air with her fist as everyone runs to the wall. Konrad helps me up.

"Everyone line up," says Santana. "I'll give you a number."

I hop over and join the line. I don't know what shark tank is, but I don't like the sound of it.

CHAPTER
Sixteen

SANTANA WALKS down the line giving everyone a number from one to three.

"Okay, number ones out on the mats. You're going to take mount bottom."

I watch as the number ones spread out across the mats and lie down.

Santana looks back to the number two and three kids standing against the wall. "You guys come off the wall, take mount top. Your job is to retain mount for fifteen. On bottom, number ones, your job is to escape before the fifteen is up. Got it?"

Everyone nods.

"Number ones stay out until I call time. Everyone else, when you're done, you go back and join the end of the line. And remember, no submissions! We're only practicing the escape. That means no arm bars, no kimuras, no chokes. You hear me?"

More nods.

"Okay, let's go."

I'm near the top of the line, and I've drawn pigtail girl. Maybe I couldn't keep Konrad pinned down, but I must be at least twice her size, maybe more. All I need to do is flop on top of her and there's no way she'll be able to get me off of her.

I hop out onto the mat and take up position. When I look down, she's closed her eyes. Before I can ask if she's okay there's a loud bell and Santana yells, "Go!" and I'm immediately upside down.

I can still hear the letter "—o!" as pigtail girl stands up. She looks past me to the line, raises her hand, and yells, "Next!"

I crawl out of the way and hop over to the end of the line as someone from the front takes my place. When I look over at Santana, she's smiling.

Even with all the swimming I've been doing, which I figured had made me super fit, I'm out of breath, not to mention soaked in sweat.

I think I might be in shock. How could a girl half my size move me off her that easily?

I guess I hadn't really sunk down on her. I wasn't ready. It must have been something like that.

The line moves fast as people jump into the shark tank. I watch some of the battles in the middle of the mats as people on top struggle to hold their mount position and the ones on bottom work their escapes.

Before I know it, it's my turn again. This time it's a kid about my age and size. I hop out, take up mount position, we bump-tap, and he bridges me off in less than a second.

Okay, it must just be easier than it looks. Although if that's true, how come I couldn't move Konrad?

Back to the end of the line I go. It keeps moving then I'm up again.

It's pigtail girl again. This time, I'm going to focus. I won't let her trap my arm and I'll sink all of my weight down onto her.

She looks up at me.

"Ready?"

"Yeah—"

And I'm looking up at the ceiling. That was even faster than the first time.

She's already standing up and waving her hand at the next person on the conveyor belt of opponents.

• • •

Eight minutes later it's my turn to be out in the middle. I lie with my back flat on the mat and wait for someone to run off the line.

It's pigtail girl. Okay, here we go. Time to give this pocket-sized ninja a taste of her own medicine.

She clambers into mount. She has her game face on, all business.

We tap-bump, and she immediately sinks down, putting her arms out over my head and onto the mat. I bridge my hips to get her off, but she moves her weight. I do it again. She shuffles her kneecaps up so that they're digging into my armpits.

Now I really can't move. I bridge my hips up into thin air.

I can feel myself getting angry, although I'm not sure who I'm angry at. Her for making me feel like an idiot, or me for not being able to get her off.

No wonder Todd beat the crap out of me. I suck!

The longest fifteen seconds of my life is over and someone else runs off the line.

I can't escape from them either. The fifteen seconds runs down.

Then there's someone else. I flail and bridge and grab arms, but none of it is any use. I can hardly catch my breath.

It doesn't seem to make any difference what size they are, I can't move them. I'm pinned and I stay there.

It feels like someone's taken my brain and thrown it into a clothes dryer.

A kid not much bigger than pigtail girl takes up mount position. "You okay?" he asks.

"Yeah," I lie.

I am very far from okay. It's not exactly being cut out of a car wreck bad, but it's a lot closer to that than I ever could have imagined, which seems as crazy as it sounds.

We bump-tap and I do my best to focus. Okay, all I need to do is grab the kid's arm, pin it, and bridge my hips.

Grab. I get hold of his arm. I even manage to trap it the way we were shown.

I put my head back at an angle and make sure I'm looking behind me.

Here we go. I bridge as hard as I can and he moves. This is it … I've got it …

Nope.

He yanks his arm free, sits back down on top of me, and I'm back where I started.

The buzzer goes off and I lie there, staring up at the ceiling, spent.

I haven't been punched in the face. But that's only because strikes aren't allowed. Pretty much any of these kids could have whaled on me and given me a matching black eye.

Even pigtail girl. Hell, particularly her.

The only thing I've actually learned coming to teens' class is that I could easily be beaten up by a thirteen-year-old girl.

Oh, and I got to listen to a song about a sailor with one leg, and generally got made to feel like crap. If someone had been organizing a prank that was designed to deliver maximum humiliation, they couldn't have done a better job.

"Okay, guys," Santana says. "Good class."

I don't see anything that was good about it. But unlike swim team, I don't have to come back here. Mom will be relieved if I don't. Dad probably will be too.

I hop over to the edge of the floor to grab my leg, roll my sleeve over my stump, and click it into my socket. A bunch of parents are standing near the entrance waiting to collect their kids. Some of them have younger children with them.

A little kid, maybe five or six, is staring at me. I know kids can't help but stare at me sometimes, but it pisses me off even more than usual. Not that I'm going to say anything. He's still wearing his gi from class, which means he could probably beat me up too.

I pick up my bag and make for the door. I guess I should say something to Santana, like thanks, but not after she played that song at the start of class and some of her other little digs at me. I get that she doesn't want me training here, and that's totally cool with me.

"What happened to your leg?" asks the kid.

"A shark bit it off," says Santana.

"Woah!" he says. "Was it the same one that bit off your arm?"

I stare at her. Why is she doing this?

She shrugs at the kid. "Could have been. Human flesh can be pretty delicious."

"That's it," announces the kid. "I'm never going swimming again."

"Thanks, Santana," the kid's mom says with a hint of sarcasm, shepherding her son away.

Santana smiles. "You're welcome."

She looks at me. "What?"

I'm done. The shark thing is the last straw. I get enough of people making fun of my leg at school. I don't need it here too.

"If you don't want me here, just say so," I tell her.

"What do you mean?"

Anger and frustration boils up inside me.

"Come on. I'm a sailor peg and I've lost my leg. Single leg take-downs. 'Dylan knows all about mount bottom.'"

I sound even angrier than I feel, but I'm sick of always being the punchline. A couple of the parents look over at us, but I don't care. I'm not coming back.

Santana stares at me. "I honestly have no idea what you're talking about. *Sailor peg?*"

"The song."

"Dude, that's the first song on the playlist. It was my walkout music from a couple of fights back. It's always the first song on the playlist. If you don't believe me, ask anyone."

The bad thing is I do believe her. Now I can add embarrassed to angry and frustrated.

"We always practice at least one takedown at the start of every class, and this week it happened to be single leg. You want me to not show it to everyone else because you might get your panties in a bunch?"

Now I want the ground to open and swallow me up. She's right.

"What I said about you and mount bottom, I'll give you that one. Maybe I shouldn't have said that. But it's true. And what did I show you? How to get out of that position, right?"

I don't know what to say. I still want to get out of here.

Santana's expression softens a little bit.

"Look, Dylan, what we do here? It's for anyone, but it's not for everyone. Most people don't even have the cojones to step inside, so you got that going for you. But if you want to do this, you're going to need to get yourself some TTFU cream."

"TTFU cream?"

She locks eyes with me. "Toughen. The. Frick. Up."

CHAPTER
Seventeen

I CAN'T MOVE. Every muscle in my body aches. I can't even lift my arm to grab my phone and switch off the alarm. I try, but it's so sore that I give up.

Instead, I lie in bed staring up at the ceiling and listen to it beeping.

I feel like I've been beaten up. Then I remember that, oh yeah, I have.

My mind slowly starts to whir to life. Yesterday's class comes back to me in fragments. The Dropkick Murphys song about a sailor with one leg. Getting humiliated by the tiny girl with pigtails. Santana telling me to get some TTFU cream.

I don't know about cream, but I could really use some of the morphine they gave me in the hospital after the accident.

I close my eyes again. I need to get up and into the shower, but I'm not sure how I'm going to do it.

But before any of that I have to switch off my phone alarm. I talk myself through it, step by step.

First I need to roll over on to my side so I can reach my phone. My arm is so heavy I can barely move it.

Toughen up, I hear Santana say.

I count down from three and manage to shift my hips so that I'm on my side. I scoot a few inches, reach out, and grab my phone. I've basically done that shrimping movement they taught me to be able to reach it.

Maybe that's why you learn that move? It's not to help you escape, or create space, or whatever Martese said, it's so you can get out of bed after training.

So now the alarm is off. Next I have to figure out how to get to the bathroom.

It's only maybe ten steps—or hops—away. But it seems like a mile. This will not be fun.

Toughen up, Dylan, I say to myself.

Somehow, with what seems like a crazy amount of effort, I manage to swing my leg out and over the edge of the bed. I grab the top of my prosthetic socket, pull out the sleeve, and roll it over the stump.

Weirdly, my stump isn't that sore. I just have kind of a pins and needles sensation near the end. Compared to how all my other muscles feel, it's almost pleasant.

Walking into the bathroom definitely isn't pleasant, and there's worse to come as I stand in front of the sink and look in the mirror. My chest and arms, even the top of my shoulders, are covered in bruises.

Down near my wrists and up near my biceps there are finger-size bruises where someone clamped down during training. Then there are a couple of huge black and blue patches on my chest.

Shifting around so I'm side-on, I see another big mark that runs from my armpit to the bottom of my rib cage. I have no idea how I got that one.

One thing's for sure, I'm going to have to wear a long-sleeved shirt today and stay covered up until they start to fade. If my mom sees them she'll freak out.

After I shower, I towel off, and lifting my arms so that I can dry my back takes about three times as long as it usually does.

Getting a shirt on is even worse. It's like all the muscles in my back and shoulders have seized up. Even after a warm shower I can still barely lift my arms. I try to shimmy my way into my shirt.

My mom calls from the hallway. "Dylan, hurry up! You're going to be late for swim practice."

I don't know how I'm going to drive to school, let alone get through an hour of swim practice.

In the kitchen, Mom sips coffee and goes through some work emails on her tablet. She looks up at me as I walk in.

I'm starving hungry, but eating before swimming is out. Unless I want to risk cramping up, I'll have to wait until after practice.

Mom looks up from her emails. "Are you okay, sweetie?"

She asks it like she already knows that I'm not, but she wants to see if I'll tell the truth. I know I'm shuffling across the floor like some kind of Egyptian mummy, so I can't really deny it.

"Yeah, I'm good," I say. "Just a little bit sore after jits class."

"How did it go? You didn't say much when you got home. We were worried that you didn't enjoy it. I know Mr. Terra went out of his way to invite you, but you know you're not obligated to do it."

"It was fine. Hey, is there any coffee left?" I say. I really want to get off this particular subject.

The truth is, when I got home from class, I sat in my room and typed out a message to Martese, thanking him for letting me train at the gym, then making some lame excuse about how I didn't really have the time.

In a way, it wasn't an excuse. Mom had been right when she said I already had enough to do between school and swim team and therapy.

But I realized something else too. If you want to do something, you find the time.

The problem with Santana after the class was that I really wasn't sure I wanted to train at Resilient. It wasn't only that I was exhausted, bruised, and sore. It was that I felt stupid, and as much as Martese had talked about adapting and finding strengths in the areas where I was weak, I didn't know if that was true.

Thanks for letting me train, but I'm so busy with school right now ...

I'd looked down at the message, been about to hit send, but I hadn't. I kept thinking about what Santana had said to me about needing to toughen up. If someone else had said it to me, it might have been different. But it felt different coming from her.

"TTFU," I say under my breath.

Mom looks up. "What's that, sweetie?"

"Oh, nothing. Just something Santana said."

CHAPTER
Eighteen

"SO, DYLAN, HOW ARE YOU?" Rich asks, leaning forward with his elbows planted on his knees. "I mean, how are you really?"

Oh, here we go. I tug my sleeve down over my wrist. Most of the bruises from my first class with Santana have faded. But I've picked up a bunch of fresh ones, including a couple of new fingerprint ones above my right wrist where Santana demonstrated a "Dagestani hand-cuff" on me.

This is the first time I've seen Rich in a couple of weeks. He was at a conference and then on vacation and then I rescheduled this appointment so I could jump into a no-gi class at Resilient.

"I'm good," I say, and I kind of mean it.

"That's great," he says. "What's changed? Last time I saw you, you were struggling with things at school."

"Oh, yeah. That."

I really don't want to get back into talking about the whole getting my ass kicked thing, although I think that's where Rich's steering this.

"So how are the other kids treating you?" he asks.

I don't know what to say to that. The swim team still isn't speaking to me. I talk to some kids in class about homework and stuff. Anna and her friend hang with me at lunch and we talk about all kinds of things. She's pretty cool.

"The same, I guess," I tell him.

"I'm sorry to hear that."

"Okay."

The truth is I don't even think about it. Apart from the guys on the swim team and a couple of the girls, most of the kids at school are basically background. They're there, but that's about it.

We're back into one of our awkward silences.

"Have there been any more incidences of bullying?"

I'm not sure what to say to that. I haven't been beaten up, apart from at Resilient MMA during training, and then all I have to do is tap out. Plus I go there voluntarily, so that hardly counts.

I still get comments at school, mostly from the swim team guys like Todd and Jack. But most of that isn't to my face. They're too scared that the coach will hear them. It's more like they ignore me and make it clear that they don't want me on the team.

"Not really," I say.

"It's just that when you sat down I couldn't help but notice you had a pretty big bruise on your arm there."

Damn. I really need to work on my sleeve game. I guess it must have ridden up when I sat down.

"Oh that, that's nothing."

Rich looks skeptical but he doesn't say anything.

"I've been training at an MMA gym. I'm mostly doing Brazilian jiujitsu, but I'm going to do some MMA classes soon too."

"And that's where you got that bruise?"

"Yeah, I have tons more than that one," I tell him, rolling up my other sleeve.

Rich looks slightly horrified. It reminds me of something Santana said to me after class last week when she was telling me about how some people freak out when she tells them she's an MMA fighter.

"Dude, we're not like other people."

At first I thought she was talking about how we're both down one limb. Then as she looked around the gym at everyone training or sparring, I realized that she was talking about Resilient.

"You're never going to be able to explain why we do what we do to a civilian," she said.

Civilians is what Santana calls people who don't train. She kind of looks down on them. I'm still sort of a civilian in her eyes because so far I only train BJJ, and don't do striking or MMA.

When she said it, I didn't quite get it. I don't think she's that different. But now with Rich's horrified look as he scans my bruises, I see what she means.

"They're not really sore or anything," I say, trying to reassure him.

"And you got these …?"

He's starting to sound more like my mom than a therapist. He's usually pretty good at keeping a poker face.

"Doing Brazilian jiujitsu. It's kind of like wrestling, only you're trying to choke the other person unconscious, or break their arm or their shoulder, or their leg."

I stop. I'm really not selling this to him, am I?

"But if you think you're going to black out or your arm might snap, you tap and the other person stops. So it's totally safe."

Rich doesn't say anything to that. He just stares at me, blinking like an owl.

"If anyone asks me why I have so many bruises I just tell them I'm really into bondage," Santana says, smirking.

We're sitting inside the cage at Resilient, taking a break. I dropped by after therapy and somehow got roped into holding pads for Santana.

"Somehow I don't think announcing that I'm into bondage would be a good explanation to give my mom or my swim coach."

She laughs. "So, you have a therapist, huh?"

"It's to help me 'come to terms with losing my leg.'"

She takes a sip of water from the big jug she carries everywhere and offers it to me. I wave it off.

"Has it?"

"Not really. Usually I hate it, but today wasn't so bad."

"Let me guess, you spent most of the hour telling him how to set up a kimura trap?"

"Rear naked choke."

Santana says you can tell someone trains jiujitsu the same way you can tell if someone's vegan. *Because they won't shut up about it.*

"Must be nice to have some money for therapy."

"It's insurance money from the accident," I say, a little defensively. "We're not rich or anything."

"Dude, you go to private school, your parents own their house, they ain't renting. You have a car. Believe me, you're rich."

"Well, I don't feel rich."

She gets up and grabs her gloves from the cage floor. As she opens the cage door, she stops and looks back at me.

"Yeah, that's kinda your problem."

"What, I should be grateful that I'm like this?" I say, looking down at my leg.

"Yeah, you should. You're alive, aren't you? You have a family who loves you. You go to a great school with good teachers and live in a nice house. You have a car. You have a fancy prosthesis so you can get around."

She reaches down and grabs her fake arm with her good arm and waves it at me.

"You know how I got this?"

I shake my head.

"Martese organized a charity rollathon for me when I joined. You know how embarrassing it is to rely on people's charity? You don't even have to think about where you'll get the money for your next leg."

I don't say anything. She's right. Compared to Santana and a bunch of other people, I am lucky. It's just I don't feel lucky. I feel overwhelmed.

Her face softens. "Look Dylan, I get it. This stuff is still new and you're dealing with a bunch of preppy assholes who want to make your life a misery. It's raw. But you'll get through it."

"How?"

"This place," she says, taking in the cage and the mats. "This right here, it's like the best therapy in the world."

I'm not convinced. Sure I enjoy being here, and the people are cool. I get treated the same as everyone else. I think Santana being here has made it easier for me. But I don't see how rolling around on the ground is all that life changing.

"You know what you should do?"

I don't.

"You should start rolling."

Rolling is BJJ code for sparring. It's not something that Martese allows beginners to do—you have train for at least three months first. And even after three months some people never roll. They just come to class and drill the moves and go home.

"You think I'm ready?" I ask.

She laughs. "No. Not even close."

"But you just said …"

"You'll never do anything if you wait until you're ready. Just trust me, okay?" She grins. "It'll be fun."

CHAPTER
Nineteen

ROLLING with Santana feels like being drowned. It's as if she's dragged me down to the bottom of a pool and is holding me there, only she has an oxygen tank and I don't.

I can't breathe—the pressure on my chest is unbearable. My heart is pounding and my mouth is completely dry.

I've had glimpses of this kind of sparring during shark tank. But rolling is shark tank with the volume cranked up. We have three minutes of a five-minute round left, but it may as well be an hour.

I'm on bottom, pinned down and lying on my back, completely unable to move even an inch. Meanwhile Santana wedges the side of her shoulder into my neck. It's a technique called the shoulder of justice, but I'm not sure where the justice part comes in. It's not really a submission, because it's not designed to cut off your carotid artery so that you pass out. It's just supposed to be really uncomfortable, and it is.

Santana adjusts her position and the pressure against my neck eases, but the relief doesn't last. Now her shoulder is jammed into my face, covering my mouth and nose. Now I really can't breathe.

The panic I'm feeling shifts up a notch. Sweat is pouring out of me and I can't seem to get any air into my lungs. I try to remember what I'm supposed to do.

I know I've drilled an escape from this position, but I can't think of the first step, never mind how the rest of the thing goes. And even if I could I'm not sure it would work against Santana, who prides herself on her 'pressure game.'

There's only one thing for it. I'm going to have to tap. If I tap it's over.

I reach my hand up and tap my fingers three times against her side. She slides off me and sits cross-legged on the mat.

The pressure eases and I can finally breathe. It's pure relief.

She scowls. "Why did you tap?"

"I couldn't breathe."

"You're such a wuss! Come on, let's restart."

"Hang on, let me fix my belt."

As I retie my belt she looks even more disgusted. I'm buying time, running down the clock, and we both know it.

"Ready?" she says.

We've barely fist bumped and I'm right back where I was. Lying flat, shoulders pinned to the mat with Santana's good arm under my neck and her shoulder jammed hard into the side of my neck.

Just when I think my situation can't possibly get any worse, it does. She pops up and jams her knee into my stomach, at the V where my ribcage ends. It's called knee on belly position, and we've been drilling how to get out of it all week.

Santana has one foot balanced on the mat as she grinds her knee into my stomach. I feel like it's going to go right through me, through the mat, right into the floor.

I try to push through, deal with the pressure. Try to handle how uncomfortable it feels to have this unrelenting pressure on my chest. And that's the thing—it's not pain, not like I've experienced. It's discomfort. But it stays there, feeling like it will never end. And it won't. Santana could stay here all day if she wants, slowly grinding the air from my lungs until I tap.

Without even really deciding, my hand comes up to tap on the knee that's causing so much misery.

Santana's kneecap does another little circle. I tap my hand harder, anticipating the relief when she gets off me.

"Hey, I'm tapping," I manage to say, although I can barely breathe, let alone speak.

The pressure on my solar plexus eases a little. But Santana doesn't get off me.

"Come on, you can't tap to knee on belly."

"Yeah I can," I wheeze. "I just did."

"You know the escape. Work it."

"What?"

She digs her knee back in. "Work. Your. Escape."

I can't believe this. You can't not stop when someone taps. That's the first commandment of BJJ. If someone taps, you stop.

She eases up again.

A switch flips in my mind. I have to focus.

Think, Dylan. The escape.

Keeping my elbows close, I put my knee into Santana's butt, bring my outside hand under the knee that's digging into me so she can't move it, and turn into her, flattening my leg and stump out behind me. I come up on top.

I'm out and I feel a surge of euphoria. A few seconds ago, I'd given up. Now there's not just relief that I would have gotten from the tap, but there's something else.

Santana shoots me a rare smile, and even rarer compliment. "See, I knew you could do it," she says with a more common Santana-type sting to it. "All you had to do was stop being such a wuss."

I know she eased up on purpose. I know she let me work the escape. If she'd decided to keep me there, I wouldn't have been able to do anything about it.

But that's not why I'm happy. I'm happy because I didn't give up. Sure, I wasn't given much of a choice. But I got through it.

"Why have you stopped?" says Santana.

"I got out."

"Big deal. The round's not over," she says, getting back on top of me. She grabs my arm, swiveling her legs around my head and chest and pushing her hips up so that my arm is about to snap.

I try to put my thumb up to work the hitchhiker escape, but it's too late. I can feel all the tendons in my arm strain.

"Tap, you idiot," says Santana.

She lets go as a second later the bell rings for the end of the round.

"You told me not to tap."

"You tap when someone's about to break your arm, dummy," she says, standing up.

She puts her hand out and hauls me up.

"Any other advice?" I say, pissed off.

"Yeah, your breathing sucks."

How can my breathing suck? You breathe in, you breathe out. What else is there to it?

She starts making these exaggerated breathing noises like someone having an asthma attack.

"It's like you're hyperventilating or something. It's not really your fault, pretty much everyone's breathing sucks when they start. And your balance is terrible. You need to work on that too."

"Of course my balance sucks, I have one leg," I protest.

"Really? I hadn't noticed. Oh, and one more thing."

"I know. Toughen up."

"Well, yeah, that too, but I was going to say be here tomorrow morning at six for extra training."

CHAPTER

Twenty

IT'S STILL DARK when I pull the Dorkmobile into a spot outside Resilient and park next to the red vintage Cadillac that Santana's girlfriend, Mia, drives. I guess they must have gotten back together because the last time I saw them together, Santana was out here in the parking lot screaming at Mia in Spanish while half of the MMA team crowded at the window watching. When Santana came back in, no one said anything because it turns out that I'm not the only person who's scared of her.

Santana has this aura around her. She's confident, but not in the same way Martese is. His confidence is super chill. With Santana there's more of an edge, like she's confident that she can kill you with her bare hands.

Inside the gym three pink yoga mats are laid out in the middle of the mat area. The Dropkick Murphys and Black Flag have been replaced with the sound of waves lapping on a beach.

"We're doing yoga?" I say, trying to keep the surprise out of my voice as I drop my bag onto the floor and sit down to take my prosthesis off.

I guess I could keep my leg on, but by now I'm so used to not wearing it on the mats that it would feel weird. I still catch myself feeling self-conscious, especially when a little kid is staring at me, but it doesn't bother me as much as it used to.

"First we're doing some breathing exercises," says Santana, sitting cross-legged on her mat. "Then Mia's going to take us through some yoga poses. Dylan breathes like an asthmatic with a sack over his head," she says to Mia.

You can't exactly cross your legs when you only have the one, so I tuck my good leg over my stump and try to keep my spine straight and my shoulders back as Santana tells us to close our eyes.

We start by taking thirty deep breaths, breathing in through our nose and exhaling through our mouth. Santana tells us not to pause between breaths. By the end I'm starting to feel a little lightheaded.

When we reach thirty, we exhale and hold our breath. With all the swimming I've done I thought I knew how to hold my breath, but by the time the sixty seconds is almost over, I really want to inhale.

Santana counts down the last five seconds and it's all I can do not to breathe early. I have pins and needles in my fingers and all ten toes, even the five I don't really have. My chest feels tight like someone's tightening a belt around it, or a big guy is sitting on me in a high mount.

"Now take a deep breath in and hold it for fifteen."

Relief floods through me as I take a deep breath in.

We go through the same exercise twice more; thirty deep, fast breaths, then holding our breath before inhaling again and holding it for fifteen seconds.

We hold our breath a little longer each time. The pins and needles get more intense, so does the tight feeling around my chest. On the third and final round I get a head rush like I'm about to pass out and I can feel myself starting to panic but I manage to get through it.

I lie back on the mat, my head still spinning.

When I open my eyes, Santana is staring at me.

"Cool, right?" she says.

She claps her hands together. "Now yoga."

After thirty minutes of downward dog and child pose and me

falling over a half dozen times as I stand on one leg, we're done and I have to admit I feel pretty good.

"Wanna roll?" Santana says.

"Sure."

We stay in what we're wearing, and Mia starts the timer for a five-minute round and for those five minutes I'm back in the tumble dryer.

People joke that BJJ is like folding clothes while the person's still wearing them. I'm definitely the fold-ee rather than the fold-er.

As we roll I can tell Santana is going a little harder than usual. She takes top, and I feel like my ribs are going to shatter into hundreds of tiny pieces.

"Okay," she says. "Slow your breathing. Stay calm. Think the position through."

I do my best to follow her instructions and grab her arm, pinning it to my chest to bridge and roll. I can't move her, but for once I'm not flailing around like a fish on the bottom of a boat.

At the end of the five minutes, I've been submitted a half-dozen times and I'm soaked in sweat and gasping for breath. Santana's totally relaxed and the only sweat on her clothes has come from me.

"Can I ask you something?" I say.

"Sure."

"Why are you helping me?"

It's a question that's been bugging me for a while. Santana helps me out and shows me things, but she's not exactly encouraging. In fact, a lot of the time she behaves as if she doesn't like me.

"You really want to know?" she says.

"I asked you, didn't I?"

"You see that?" she adds, pointing to the Resilient MMA & BJJ rash guard I'm wearing.

"Yeah."

"You're walking around with the name of my gym on your chest, and you got whaled on by someone named Todd. It's freaking embarrassing."

I don't know what I was expecting her to say. I knew it wasn't going to be some warm, fuzzy Hallmark moment. It is Santana, after all. But really, that's why she's helping me? Because I'm an embarrassment?

She gets up with a shrug. "If you think you might not like the answer, then don't ask the question."

CHAPTER
Twenty-One

I'M STILL THINKING about what Santana said as I open my swim locker and grab my trunks, cap, and goggles.

"BJJ," says Jack, reading my rash guard. "What's that stand for? Blowjob jockey?"

A couple of the guys laugh.

I stare at him but don't say anything. He's not as easily thrown by me staring as Todd is.

"What, you wanna throw down or something, bro?"

He walks over to me and squares up.

"Well?"

I'm not going to fight him. But I'm not going to back down either. I stand there looking at him.

"Yeah, that's what I thought," he says, turning around and walking back to his locker as the others laugh.

It would be so easy to jump on his back, throw on a rear naked choke and squeeze until he passes out. For a second I think about it.

I can hear Santana's voice in my head, telling me to do it. Especially as he was making fun of my shirt with the Resilient logo on the front. Then Martese's voice floats into my head, and he's reminding me they're only words.

Martese wins out. I've been training at Resilient. But Jack is way bigger than Todd. I don't even know if I could beat him in a fight, and even if I did, I can't keep getting into fights at school. And either way it's not going to help the other guys on the team accept me.

I take off the rash guard and stuff it in my locker.

"Guys, listen up. Here's the team lineup for next month's meet in La Cañada," says Coach. "I wanted everyone to know ahead of time so you can really focus. Especially for the guys taking part in the two relays."

I kind of tune out as he starts reading off names. It's going to be a big meet, with five other high schools competing and the school that's hosting it has been our school's big rivals over the years.

"Okay, so finally, the 200 relay. Not in any order yet but it's going to be Jack, Toby, Alex, and Dylan."

I look up. Did I hear my name being called for the relay?

All the other guys are looking at each other. A couple of them mutter to each other.

Coach stares at us. "Is there a problem?"

"Coach, come on," says Jack. "Dylan? We want to win this, right?" he says, looking around at the others.

Even with what happened before practice between me and Jack, I agree with him. Me swimming the relay is like starting the race three seconds down. Even if all the other guys swim personal bests we still won't win.

"This is a team," says Coach. "That means we look out for each other. You want to win? Then help your teammates improve. Okay guys, that's it."

Someone else starts to say something, but Coach cuts them off.

"Hey," he says. "You don't want to be part of this? Go play softball."

Oh man, this is the worst. If the guys on the team didn't hate me before, they're really going to now. They want to win, but they won't do it with me swimming relay.

The meeting breaks up and everyone drifts back into the locker room. I keep my head down. All I want to do is get changed and get to class.

Maybe but I could quit, or say I'm injured. But if I fake being injured so that I can't swim then my parents won't let me train at Resilient either. And I can't quit without seeming ungrateful—Mom and Dad are paying a lot of money to send me here because of the swim program as much as the academics.

I don't see any way out of this. I can try to improve my time but there's no way I'm going to be fast enough by next month to help them win the relay.

One of the guys comes out of the showers and heads over to the locker next to mine.

"Okay, very funny," he says, looking around and singling out Jack who's checking his phone. "Where did you put my clothes?"

"Why are you asking me, dude?" says Jack.

Hiding someone's clothes is a regular prank. I'm amazed they haven't played it on me yet, but they haven't. I think Jack and the others are afraid of what would happen if Coach or the principal found out. No one wants to get suspended from the team like Todd was.

The guy is running around opening lockers, looking for his clothes. He's getting more and more frantic. The more annoyed he gets, the funnier some of the others find it.

"I'm gonna be late for class," he pleads, but that only makes it worse.

I remember that I have a spare pair of pants and a T-shirt in my bag. I finish getting dressed and pull them out.

"Here," I say, passing them over.

We're roughly the same size. The pants might be a little short, but not so much that anyone will notice.

"Oh, man," says Jack. "That's super gay."

He grabs the T-shirt from the guy and holds it up.

"Does this one say blow job jockey too?"

I look at him. "You seem kind of obsessed with guys giving blow jobs, dude. You got something you want to get off your chest?"

The other guys start to laugh. But this time they're not laughing at me, they're laughing at him. It feels good, but I get the feeling that I'm going to pay for it.

TODAY IS GRADING AT RESILIENT. Grading is when people are promoted to the next level of belt. White to blue, blue to purple, purple to brown, and finally, brown to black. Martese told me that it usually takes ten years of consistent training to get a black belt.

Not everyone's going to get a new belt color so they also give out stripes to show people's progress. Santana thinks stripes are 'mostly bullshit, like the kind of crap you see in McDojos' but I'm pretty psyched to see if I get one.

The atmosphere when I walk into the gym is a mix of excitement, anticipation, giddiness, and nerves. There's a lot of people here. Maybe eighty or ninety, four times as many people as I've ever seen at even the busiest classes. It's a mix of the gym's MMA team and those who only train jits, but everyone's in their gi with their belts tied neatly around their waists.

Martese stands in the middle of the mats, rocking his black belt. Jared and a couple of the higher belts who also coach, including Santana, stand on either side of him.

"Okay, if everyone could line up against the wall in belt order— higher belts this end, white belts at that end," announces Martese.

Everyone shuffles into place against the wall, checking out the belt and the number of stripes of the person next to them and then doing another shuffle, until the whole gym is standing along the wall in ranked order.

I stand at the very end, a no-stripe white belt, the lowest person in the pecking order. But I don't mind. It is what it is.

Martese calls out the names of people who have four stripes on their belt and are ready to move up a level to go out to the middle of the mat. A couple of people with four stripes aren't called and look a little dejected. The people who are called space themselves out. They look kind of nervous.

"If you thought you were going to be graded for a promotion but you haven't been called, I don't think you're quite ready yet. Keep training and you'll get your shot next time," says Martese, looking at the four-stripe people who are still standing against the wall. "Likewise if you're being graded tonight—there's no guarantee that you'll be promoted. Even if you get through the Iron Man."

Everything I've heard about Iron Man makes me happy that I'm not rocking any stripes. It sounds brutal.

Martese looks back at the people who've been called out. "If you tap, that's fine. You'll probably tap a lot tonight. But if you walk off the mat, even to visit the bathroom or get water, then you can't be promoted. You stay out here fighting until I say so. Everyone clear?"

The people in the center of the floor nod. One guy crosses himself and looks up at the ceiling.

Martese matches the people in the middle with people from the line. If someone is looking to move up to a blue belt, they get matched with a similar-size blue belt opponent. If they're moving to purple, they have to roll with a purple belt.

"Time on," he says, and a half-dozen sparring sessions start on the mats. Bodies fly everywhere as people vie for position, fight to take grips, pass guard, pull guard, and try to smash their fellow club member into the mat, choke them out, or break one of their limbs.

It's full. On. Intense.

The people being graded try to show they deserve to be promoted. The people they've been matched against go full throttle, probing for any weaknesses or chinks in their game that can be exposed.

Within minutes the people on the mats are soaked in sweat and the air is thick with humidity. Everyone on the wall stands and watches as people start to get caught in a submission, tap, and go straight back at it with their opponent.

About ten minutes later, Martese calls time and the sparring stops. A couple of people flop down onto the mats gasping for air.

The people being graded barely manage a few sips of water before Martese orders them back into the middle.

"Okay guys, it's free rolling, like a shark tank," he says. "These guys stay out here and you guys come off the top off the line. If you submit or get submitted, you go to the end of the line. Everyone got it?"

He signals for the other coaches and some of the higher belts to match up against someone who's being graded. The timer sounds and the organized mayhem resumes, only this time everyone gets a chance to roll with the people being graded.

I watch as Martese rolls with a purple belt looking to move up to brown, the final belt before you receive your black belt. The purple belt is a big guy with a beard I've seen in the advanced classes. He's good, but no match for Martese, who quickly takes his back and chokes him. The purple belt taps and Martese gets up and signals for the person at the top of the line to come off the line to be the big guy's next opponent.

The line moves up. It's like a checkout line at the market, but instead of groceries, the goods rolling down the belt are chokes and joint locks.

Watching the higher belts roll like this is strange. While I huff and puff and strain, they seem to expend almost no energy, unless they're up against someone of the same size and ability. Then it's like a couple of stags smashing their antlers into each other.

Now I'm at the top of the line and ready to jump, or hop, into the chaos. You can't choose who you get. It's the luck of the draw and I have to roll with whoever's next.

I scan the bodies on the mats. Someone gets up, defeated by a purple belt guy who's grading to move to brown, so near the top of the food chain.

I head over to the purple belt and we slap and bump. He's sitting down so I grab for the bottom of his gi pants, looking for a Toreando pass. He shakes off my grips with a flick of his legs. I fall forward. He sits up, hooking his forearm under my neck, and guillotine chokes me. I panic tap and that's it, I'm done.

The roll lasted maybe ten seconds. I hop back down to the end of the line. I've been training long enough not to feel bad about being submitted so fast.

I go back to watching the action. I can see the people in the middle starting to run out of gas. The pace is relentless. As soon as they finish rolling with one person, the next person is right there.

Martese is off to one side now, watching everything. He has a piece of paper and he's busy taking notes.

The gym gets hotter. Someone yelps as Santana catches them with an arm bar and they tap. She gets up while they sit there, rubbing their elbow. Then they signal for the person at the top of the line.

There's no quitting at grading. If you're injured, you find a way to battle through.

A few more minutes pass and I'm back at the top of the line. A younger guy who's grading for blue is open. He's gasping for air, exhausted.

I manage to pass his guard and take side control. I start fishing for his collar, trying to get grips so I can choke him. He hand-fights, fending me off, and I manage to scoot my stump over and move into a top mount.

I experience a brief moment of elation. This guy is way more experienced and bigger, but I have the dominant position. Not only that, I got there because of my stump, not in spite of it. You can't grab for a leg that isn't there.

I flop down, trying to stay loose and relaxed, which makes for better pressure. I manage to slide my arm in under his neck, establishing a cross face, and cementing my position.

Suddenly, as I start to relax, he lifts his hips and bridges onto his side, scooting his knee up as he moves back to guard. I slip my stump back between his legs and now I'm in a half-guard.

There's nothing in my head apart from him and me and what I do next. I slide one hand under his collar, palm up. My other hand comes in under the first. I fall off to the side, my forehead resting on the mat as I bring my elbows together.

He taps. I did it. I subbed him.

I've only ever gotten submissions on other noobs before now. The guy's exhausted, which probably explains why he didn't defend like he would have if he was fresh. But all the same, I got it.

Would I have beaten him if he was fresh? No way. But at the stage I'm at, I'll take my wins where I can. It's a rare victory in a sea of defeats.

Fifty minutes later, over an hour after the Iron Man began, Martese calls time. It's over.

The people grading lie on their backs, limbs stretched out like starfish. They barely move. They're completely spent, in a state that's beyond exhaustion.

Martese stands at the side and applauds.

"Well done, guys."

Santana and the other coaches join him as they call people forward one by one and give them their new belt. Everyone claps and cheers as Martese ties each person's shiny new-colored belt around their waist.

Martese and the other coaches hug them, then they walk down the line of the people who just tortured them for an hour, shaking hands, fist bumping, and hugging. Everyone is happy. We all saw what they had to endure. We were all part of it.

It feels like watching an award ceremony you see on TV, but the smiles and congratulations aren't fake or forced. We're all happy for everyone getting their promotion.

I watch as someone receives their blue belt. I'm not jealous because I know how hard they've had to train to get it, and what they just had to go through. But I feel a twinge of something else.

It's a hard thing to get. It has to be earned. You don't get one for showing up every week. It takes literal blood, sweat, and tears. Hours of rolling, being submitted probably a thousand times, maybe more. Dozens of bruises.

In other words, it takes resilience. You can't weather just one storm, you have to endure dozens. Some rounds are easy, but even the easy ones challenge you somehow. And most rounds are tough.

And then, right at the end, on a night like this, you have to survive a freaking hurricane.

Once all the colored belts are handed out, Martese calls for silence. Santana stands next to him, cutting strips from a roll of white tape.

One by one Martese calls people out from the line. Santana wraps a piece of tape around the end of their belt, marking their new stripe. Martese shakes their hand or high fives them, and everyone claps or cheers.

Some people already have a stripe or two. For those who have three, the fourth stripe means that next time they'll be out in the middle doing the Iron Man.

Just like when trying to move up a belt, there's no guarantee you'll receive a stripe either. I wait, nervous. I've been training hard since I started. I go to as many classes as I possibly can and I've started rolling. I usually get five rounds in.

All of that should count, but it's down to Martese.

The white belts start to be called forward to get their stripes. Martese calls my name.

There's a huge cheer as I hold up the tip of my belt and Santana wraps the tape around it.

"Great work, Dylan. You've earned this," says Martese.

Martese shakes my hand.

Santana gives me a hug. "Good job, gimpy," she says.

As I make my way back to the wall, I feel a surge of emotion. It's like a mix of happiness, pride, and relief. People slap my back or reach out for a fist bump as I walk down the line.

"Good job, man."

"On your way to being a killer, bro."

"Oss!"

I melt back against the wall, but I can't help looking down at the white stripe against the black band of my belt. To someone outside the gym it doesn't mean anything, it's just a piece of tape wrapped around some cloth. But to me it means more than I can put into words.

"One more thing before everyone leaves," says Martese. "Next week is the charity rollathon to raise money for the summer camp. Sponsorship details are on the website, and I'd like a big turnout."

Santana told me once that every summer the gym helps with a kids' camp and the rollathon helps cover the cost of running it.

The rest of the night passes fast. A lot of pictures get taken as people stand with their friends and teammates. After the grind of the Iron Man, everyone's happy and smiling.

Finally, people drift off to get showered and changed. It's close to eleven by the time I walk outside to my car. I text my dad to let him know that I'm heading home.

Pulling into the driveway, the lights are still on. I grab my training bag and my backpack and head inside.

Mom's reading and Dad's watching the news. He looks up as I come in and drop my bags on the floor.

"You should get to bed," says Mom, not looking up from her book. "It's late."

I'm hoping this isn't going to turn into another conversation about how I spend too much time at Resilient.

I open my training bag and pull out my belt.

I hold it up for my dad to see. "I got my first stripe."

"That's terrific, Dylan."

He says it in the 'I'm happy that you're happy' tone that parents give you, but I don't mind.

Mom looks up from her book. "Good job. *And* you're on the team for the swim meet. You're really not letting anything hold you back."

By *anything* she means my leg.

"We're both really proud of you, kiddo." says Dad.

"Thanks."

What's weird is that I don't see the two things as being equal. Not even close. I earned the stripe but I didn't earn my place on the team. One's an achievement, and one's really not.

For a second I think about telling them more about the Iron Man and how long it went on and how grueling it was. But I know the more I tell them, the more Mom will worry, so I don't say anything.

In a way, I don't mind that I can't share much about it. Sometimes it's enough that you yourself know.

Climbing into bed, sore and exhausted, I smile into the darkness. Today was a good day.

CHAPTER
Twenty~Three

WE TAKE a bus from school to the swim meet in La Cañada. There's some seats for supporters and Todd has come along. He's sitting in the back with Jack and a couple of the other guys.

I'm sitting by myself a couple of rows in front of them. I've worked my ass off in the pool the past few weeks. My personal best is way better than it was when I started, but I'm still miles off from the kind of time I need if we're going to stand any chance of winning the relay.

Behind me I can hear Jack telling Todd how it's complete BS that he's off the team while I'm on it, and how it means they have zero chance of winning anything this year.

The funny part is I agree with them. It doesn't make any sense. But there's nothing I can do about it. I tried to explain things and get Todd reinstated.

The past week I thought hard about faking an injury. Nothing serious, just something like a pulled muscle that I could recover from quickly without it seeming suspicious. But Mom has really been on my dad about me doing too much. By too much she means training at Resilient.

If I suddenly get injured and miss a swim meet, I know which activity she'll make me stop and it won't be swimming. I need

Resilient right now. It's my sanctuary. They talk about kids having a safe space. Well, my safe space just happens to be an MMA gym.

I decide I'll have to get through the swim meet as best I can. It's not as if the rest of the swim team can get that much worse.

Everyone still pretty much ignores me. And when they're not, it's only so they can make jokes about BJJ standing for blow job jockey and how gay the whole thing is. Oh, and they still make jokes about my leg.

So, yeah, what else can they say that they haven't already?

I'm hoping that when we get smoked by the other schools in the relay that Coach comes to his senses and drops me for the next meet. Or maybe when we get there, he'll drop me and reinstate Todd.

We pull into the parking lot and everyone gets off the bus. The team heads for the locker room that we have to share with a couple of the other teams.

I'm suddenly nervous. I know I'm going to be too slow but what if I really mess up? Miss the transition, or go too early and get us disqualified so that we don't get any points for the relay.

All these thoughts of disaster come crowding in from nowhere. And now they've arrived, I can 't seem to banish them. They're like unwelcome visitors that have taken over the inside of my head.

What if this?

What if that?

As they flit around, bouncing off the inside of my skull, I feel myself starting to panic. I should have stayed home. Missed the bus. Called in sick. Anything so I wouldn't have to be here now.

I need to get a grip and calm down or I'm going to be completely burned out by the time I have to swim. Suddenly I remember Santana's breathing exercises. I dump my bag in one of the lockers and go looking for somewhere quiet, away from everyone.

Outside there's a football field next to the school's parking lot. I sit down at the fifty-yard line, close my eyes, and start to breathe. Thirty steady breaths, sucking all the air I can into my lungs, then exhaling and not letting any time pass between breaths.

When I hit thirty I stop. When I feel like I can't hold my breath for a second longer, I breathe in, hold it, and count down from fifteen.

I take a few seconds and do it twice more, thinking about how Santana told me she does this before every fight.

By the time I've completed three rounds, I'm still nervous but I don't feel like I'm about to jump out of my skin anymore. Something in me has settled down.

As I walk back to the pool, something else hits me and my stomach turns over so hard that for a second I worry I might throw up.

I'm going to have to take my prosthesis off in front of all these kids from other schools, and people in the stands. And I won't be able to slip quickly into the water because I'll have to stand there waiting for my teammate to touch the side before I can dive in and hide my gross stump.

I've been so worried about costing us the relay I hadn't even thought about any of this until now.

I do it at Resilient and in front of the swim team, but that's different. Apart from maybe a new kid, no one at Resilient stares. There I'm just Dylan, the one-stripe white belt who's hard to foot lock.

Jack and a couple of the other guys on my team won't let me forget what I look like, but I'm used to that. It's like getting choked or arm barred when you're rolling. It's never as shocking as the first time. It's unpleasant and you try to avoid it, but that's about it.

The calmness from the breathing ebbs away. Fear stacks upon fear, and my heart is racing again. I walk back to the edge of the football field, sit down, and start again with the breathing. But this time I can't focus.

Part of me wants to start running and just keep going. But I can't do that either.

Twenty~Four

THE RACE IS ALREADY UNDERWAY, and we're in the lead by the time I click the button on the side of my leg to release the catch and slip my stump out of the socket. I peel off the liner and stand next to the diving block of our lane.

One of our team is already standing on the block. I'm next.

I glance over to the stands. Most people are watching the race, but I catch a couple of people looking over at me.

Our first swimmer comes home first. As soon as he touches the wall, my teammate launches himself off the starting block.

It's a smooth transition. He keeps the lead and even gains a few yards. I scoot my butt up onto the white starting block, roll my shoulders, and try to stay loose.

A couple of the guys I'm swimming against are already standing on their blocks. I wait until the swimmers in the water are headed back down the pool. My good leg is a lot stronger than it was and my balance is better from yoga and jits, but standing on one leg is still tiring and I get wobbly from time to time.

Our team now has a convincing lead and Jack, our strongest swimmer, will be closing out the race for us. Maybe if I can hold onto the lead, or at least not give up too much of it, we'll still have a chance.

I need to focus, get the handover right, and dig in. Finally I stand up on the board.

Now I can feel more people looking at me. I push out the thought, take a couple of deep breaths, and focus. As soon as my teammate touches the wall, I push off with my good leg and dive in.

I settle into my stroke, pulling myself through the water with my arms, shifting my body to minimize drag. I find a rhythm, but I can already see a shape coming up in the next lane as I tilt my head to the side to take a breath.

Upping my rate, I plow on down the pool, putting everything into it as we come up on the wall. As I make the turn, I see someone two lanes down move ahead of me.

I keep going. It's all I can do. I might have lost the lead, but I need to stay close and give our team a chance on the last leg.

Halfway back down the pool, I glimpse more swimmers slip past me. I dig in. My lungs are bursting. I'm exhausted, but I push on, doing my best not to get demoralized.

Come on, come on, I tell myself. Push. Push harder.

As I touch the wall, Jack Kim launches over me and into the pool.

I tread water as I catch my breath. I gave it everything but turning around and looking down the pool, I see that we're second from last. He's making up ground as he powers down the lane, but it's an impossible task.

I swim to the side, grab the ladder rails, and haul myself out. I'm so spent that I don't care who's staring at me as I grab a towel, dry off the stump, and put my leg back on.

The rest of the team stand together, shouting for Jack. He's on his way back down and he's moving up. Fifth place. Then fourth.

If he had another lap, he'd cruise it. But he doesn't.

All around us teams are screaming and cheering. In the stands, parents and school friends are on their feet, urging the swimmers on.

Right at the death, Jack finds another burst of energy. He touches the wall. The third swimmer home.

He grabs the side, whips off his googles and slaps the water in frustration. He's angry, and I don't blame him.

I look across to see Todd glaring at me.

Coach comes over to me and shows me my time.

"Good job, Dylan. You dug in. That's a new PB for you."

It's cold comfort. I did my best but we still lost, and I'm going to take the blame.

I tell him thanks and head for the locker room. I plan on taking a shower, getting dressed, and waiting on the bus so I can stay out of everyone's way.

I'm finishing up my shower, rinsing off the soap. When I turn around, my leg is nowhere to be seen. I'd leaned it against the wall, under the hook where I hung my towel.

My towel's gone too.

I can see someone snatching up my towel by mistake, but not my prosthesis. Maybe someone was worried about it getting wet so they moved it into the locker room.

There's a couple of guys from other teams around but I feel weird asking them if they've seen my leg. I hop across to where it was. I look closer, but it's definitely gone.

Now I'm wet, buck naked, and stuck with only one leg. All I can do is hop back into the locker room like this.

It's busy. A couple of guys look at me then turn away. I don't see any of the guys from my team.

Thankfully, there's a stack of towels sitting on one of the benches. I don't think I've ever been happier to see a towel before in my life, especially when I open the locker I was using and see that my bag's there, but my clothes are gone.

Now I know what's happening. This is payback. Only it's doubly embarrassing because it's at a different school with more people around.

Rage starts building up inside me. I don't want to hop out to the pool with just a towel so I sit down on the bench and decide to wait it out.

A few minutes later Jack wanders back into the locker room. He's with Todd.

"Very funny. Where'd you hide it?" I say to Jack.

He looks at Todd with a smirk and then gives me an exaggerated innocent look. "Put what?"

"My leg."

He looks down at me and points at my good leg. "Dude, your leg's right there."

Todd laughs.

"Where is it?"

I didn't see him do it, but it's the only thing that makes sense. Even if he didn't take it himself, he knows who did.

"I don't know what you're talking about, dude," he says, a hint of menace dropping into his voice.

It doesn't work. I spend hours at Resilient getting my ass kicked by professionals. Jack or Todd or any of the other guys don't intimidate me.

I look at Todd. "Just give it back, and we'll forget about it, okay?"

He laughs. "What are you going to do? Kick my ass?"

He turns and walks back out with Jack, both of them laughing.

One of the guys from the home team has been watching us. "What's up, bro?" he says to me.

I explain how my teammates sometimes prank each other, and how they probably took my clothes and my leg. I don't get into any of the other stuff.

The guy turns to some other swimmers. "Anyone seen this kid's leg?"

No one laughs at the question. Probably because they're not complete assholes.

"I'll go take a look around," he says to me.

I sit in a thick stew of anger and impotence. I can't even go outside to the pool area, not with one leg and only a towel around me.

Screw those guys, I repeat over and over in my head.

I check my bag. I still have my phone. I could call my folks, but that would mean even more drama.

I hate everyone right now. My parents for making me attend this dumb school. The coach for making me swim in the relay when he knew I wasn't good enough and it would mean the team would lose.

Most of all, I hate Jack and Todd more than I've ever hated anyone in my life.

The guy who went looking comes back. "Sorry, bro, I didn't see it. I can probably scrounge up some shorts and a T-shirt for you if that helps."

I don't like accepting his help, but I don't have a lot of options. If I have clothes, I can at least go out there and look for myself.

The locker room door opens, and our coach comes in. He's with a couple of guys from our team.

"Come on," he's saying to them. "The bus leaves in ten."

He sees me. "You okay there?" he asks.

There's no way I'm telling him what's going on.

"I'm good, Coach, thanks."

"Okay then, don't just sit there, get dressed and get on the bus."

He walks back out. A couple guys from my team are trading looks. They know that if I'm not on the bus Coach will come looking for me and he'll figure out what's going on. Then all hell will break loose.

One of them leaves and a minute later Todd walks back in with him. He has my prosthesis and my clothes. Only the clothes are soaking wet.

"What do you know? They were out by the pool. You should be more careful where you put stuff, and maybe don't go accusing people. You know, my dad's an attorney and I'm pretty sure he's sued people for making false accusations."

CHAPTER
Twenty-Five

"NOW, ladies and gentlemen, are you ready for our next contest of the evening?"

Jared nudges me with his elbow. We're sitting cage-side to watch Santana fight, and I'm glad that I'm here with some of the crew from Resilient because the crowd is super drunk and noisy.

In the middle of the cage the announcer, who's wearing a suit covered in blue sequins, continues. "A featherweight women's contest over three rounds. Fighting out of Alliance MMA here in sunny San Diego, weighing in at one hundred twenty-five pounds, standing five feet, six inches tall, and holding a record of three wins and one loss—in the red corner, please welcome Gabriella Rich."

Music starts up, and the spotlight whirs from the cage over to a set of double doors where Santana's opponent appears flanked by her two cornermen. She holds up gloved hands, acknowledging the crowd as she takes the short walk toward the cage, the music cranked up super loud.

She reaches the cage, and the referee checks her over. Her coach pops in her mouthpiece and she runs up the steps and into the octagon. She jogs around as the spotlight shifts back to Mr. Blue Sequins and the music abruptly cuts out.

Jared nudges me.

"Here we go, baby."

I'm suddenly nervous. Gabriella looks older than Santana by a few years and she's shredded. She stands off to one side, shadow boxing and throwing spinning back kicks as she psyches herself up.

"And her opponent," says the announcer. "Fighting out of Resilient MMA in Los Angeles, weighing in at one hundred and twenty-four pounds and standing at five feet, eight inches tall, with an amateur record of five wins and no losses—in the blue corner please welcome Santana Dominguez."

I'm not gonna lie, as he says *Resilient MMA*, I get chills. I'm not a fighter like Jared or Santana but that's my gym. I'm part of it in a way that I've never felt part of anything before, even before my accident. It's like we're a gang or a tribe and there's a bond between us that comes from sweating, and sometimes bleeding, together on the mats

Santana's music starts, another song by The Dropkick Murphys called "Rose Tattoo." The doors open and she appears, flanked by Martese and another guy from the gym. She doesn't raise her arms or showboat. She walks slowly toward the octagon, her face emotionless.

I get up along with the guys from Resilient MMA and cheer as the referee checks her over. Then she puts in her mouth guard and walks up the steps and into the cage.

Santana jogs slowly around the octagon as the announcer leaves and the referee joins the two fighters in the middle of the cage.

Behind us someone in the crowd says, "Check out that chick's arm."

"Holy crap," says his buddy. "How is that allowed?"

"I don't even think women should be in there."

Jared turns round and stares at them until they go quiet. They're drunk but not drunk enough to mess with Jared.

In the cage, Santana stares at Gabriella as the referee gives them instructions. They touch gloves and retreat. Santana leans with her back against the cage.

The bell rings and the referee drops his hand, moving back as Santana sprints full-tilt into the middle of the octagon. She's been drilling a flying knee, hoping that her opponent ducks for a takedown so Santana can catch her full-force in the head with her knee.

Gabriella doesn't duck or level change though. Instead she stays standing and throws a chopping low kick, which Santana checks before throwing back one of her own that catches the back of Gabriella's calf muscle.

Santana circles to the outside. They dance around each other, feinting and faking kicks and punches as they try to find an opening without getting caught themselves. At least that's how Santana explained it to me one day after training.

She said that people who don't fight wonder why there can sometimes be all this dancing around. It's because each fighter is feeling out their opponent. Trying to get a sense of their timing.

There's another reason too. One wrong move and you can get caught with a head kick or a spinning elbow or a punch and the fight's over.

In boxing, if someone gets knocked down or even if they stumble and fall, their opponent backs off while the ref counts. In MMA, their opponent doesn't have to stop. They chase them down to the ground with punches, and if it's a professional bout, with elbows. It's called ground and pound, and even with one good arm and a stump, Santana is an expert at it.

Gabriella gets more aggressive. She circles around and throws a one-two punch. Santana rolls her shoulders, deflecting the jab but getting caught flush in the face with an overhand right.

She rocks back for a second, blood dripping from her nose. Gabriella hesitates. Santana backs off, raises her gloved hand, and waves Gabriella on, like 'come get me.'

Accepting the invitation, Gabriella rushes back in. Santana drops down to change levels and shoots in for a takedown.

It's timed perfectly. Gabriella falls back and Santana goes with her.

The two of them scramble for position. Gabriella wraps her legs around Santana's waist, bringing her into a close guard. It's weird seeing stuff we do in class happening up close in a cage fight.

Santana launches a fist at Gabriella's face that opens a cut above Gabriella's eye.

Gabriella goes to grab under Santana's armpits and pull her in, but Santana rears up and throws another sharp elbow at Gabriella's face. Gabriella gives up on what she was trying and covers up.

Santana pushes down on one of Gabriella's knees with the end of her stump and Gabriella's legs, moving into half guard. Now one of Santana's legs is trapped between Gabriella's thighs, but her upper body is on top of Gabriella.

It's a stronger position. Not as good as mount, but better than before. Gabriella fires back a couple of short elbows to the top of Santana's head, but Santana shrugs them off and goes to work with her own ground and pound, showering Gabriella with a tornado of blows.

Gabriella does her best to fire back and pull Santana back down onto her, but lying on her back it's tough to generate any force.

After a few more exchanges Gabriella tries to escape, pushing off against Santana and shrimping back, hoping to recover her guard.

As Gabriella tries to retreat again, Santana gets onto her back. Jared raises his arms and screams: "Hooks in, Santana! Hooks in!"

But Santana is ahead of him. She's draped over her opponent's back. She slips first one foot and then the other just below Gabriella's waist so that the backs of her heels are pressing into Gabriella's pelvic bone.

"Yes!" Jared screams and all of us from Resilient are on our feet now because we know that unless Gabriella acts fast, Santana has taken her back, which is the last thing you want to happen.

Just like in BJJ, giving up your back is all kinds of bad news. You can't attack your opponent with strikes, and you're open to a bunch of attacks.

I look up at the clock. There's still three minutes left in the round.

Santana stays busy. She slides her stump under Gabriella's chin and with her good arm, she punches Gabriella in the side of the face. The blows are slow and methodical.

Gabriella flails, trying to shake Santana off her. But with her hooks in, Santana controls her hips. Santana closes her hand and changes the angle, launching hammer fists into Gabriella's face, careful not to hit the back of her head, which isn't legal.

Trying to do something to stop the barrage of blows, Gabriella rolls onto her side. As she moves, her chin comes up and Santana slips her good hand underneath it. She tucks her head in next to Gabriella's so they're ear-to-ear, and her good hand grabs her elbow.

Santana begins to squeeze the choke. Gabriella reaches up with both her hands again, trying to grab Santana's choking hand, but all she finds is the smooth, bony end of Santana's stump.

Like a boa constrictor, Santana squeezes. Everyone is on their feet and screaming, even the civilians behind us who a few minutes ago were saying how women shouldn't be allowed to fight MMA.

I look up from the cage to the big screen on the far wall in time to see Gabriella raise a yellow glove and reach back to tap Santana.

The ref throws himself down to the canvas and grabs Santana, pulling her away. She lets go of the rear naked choke, rolls onto her back, and punches a single triumphant fist into the air.

Jared is jumping up and down. He turns and grabs me, dragging me into a bear hug.

A win. In the first round. By her trademark one-hand rear naked choke submission.

Santana gets to her feet. She leaps up onto the edge of cage, swings a leg over and sits on top of it, punching her fist into the air.

As the spotlight catches her blood-speckled face, I think back to something she said to me about the moment she'd realized that only having one hand could be an advantage.

"You can't grab a hand that's not there."

Twenty-Six

SANTANA JUMPS down from the top of the cage and walks over to Gabriella, who's finished being checked over by the doctor. Santana sits down next to her and gives her a hug.

I can't hear what she's saying but she pulls Gabriella onto her feet and gives her another hug. Then she races to the other side of the cage and hugs Martese, who wraps her up in a huge bear hug, lifting her off her feet to twirl her around.

The referee calls the two fighters back into the middle of the octagon and Mr. Blue Sequins announces Santana as the winner in the first round by submission. There's a moment when the ref gets confused because he's taken hold of her half arm, but then recovers and holds it up anyway.

Santana gives Gabriella another hug, and Martese shakes hands and hugs Gabriella's corner team. Then they all make their way out of the cage and back toward the changing area.

Jared jostles me. "Come on, let's go congratulate the winner," he says.

I follow him down our row, out into the aisle, and over to the door. There are a couple of big bouncers guarding the doors.

"Are we allowed in there?" I ask Jared.

"Sure," he says, greeting the biggest bouncer by name, and pushing the door open for us.

We walk through into what's just a big room with some dividers so people can get changed in privacy. The wallpaper and carpet are a reminder that this is just the conference and meeting area of a big hotel.

A couple of fighters are doing some light sparring to stay loose. Others pace back and forth with their game faces on, like method actors trying to stay in character before they go on set.

I spot Martese standing with the other corner guy from Resilient. Then I hear shouting. It's Mia and she's screaming at Santana in Spanish.

Santana screams back at her. They alternate between Spanish and English. Mia seems super angry.

"I saw her message on your phone!" Mia's shouting at Santana.

"Why were you looking at my phone?" Santana screams back. "Estas loca!"

"Me estas engañando!"

"Estsas loca!" Santana repeats.

Mia grabs for the phone that Santana's now holding and Martese jumps in between the two of them.

"You spoil everything," Santana shouts.

"Me? I'm not the one messaging other girls."

Jared looks at me and shrugs. "Santana drama," he says, as if that explains everything. Which it pretty much does.

"We're through," says Mia. "I'm done with your sorry ass."

Mia stalks out, pushing one of the bouncers out of the way as she goes.

If Santana's upset, she doesn't show it. "That girl is crazy," she says to everyone and no one.

She walks over to Jared and me and throws her good arm and stump up, mimicking closing a rear naked choke. She grins, the argument with Mia seemingly forgotten.

"You see that?" she says to Jared.

"Slick!" says Jared.

"I know, right?"

She dances around on the balls of her feet, shadow boxing.

"All the way to the UFC, baby."

CHAPTER
Twenty~Seven

SANTANA SITS in the passenger seat of the Dorkmobile, looking distinctly unimpressed. She reaches over and taps her knuckles on the speedometer, like she's wondering if the needle is stuck.

"I know, it's super slow," I say.

"Kind of suits you."

As I merge onto the freeway, she leans back against the door and narrows her eyes, studying me.

"So what's going on with you?" she asks.

"What do you mean?"

"You've been real quiet since you came back from that swim meet."

I wonder if somehow she knows what happened, but I don't see how she could. I haven't told anyone at Resilient. Or anyone else for that matter.

I shrug off the question. "I'm quiet sometimes."

She tosses her hair back. "Bullshit. I can tell when something's up. What is it? Is it school? Your parents? You get yourself a girlfriend?"

"No," I say too quickly.

"A boyfriend then?" she laughs. "Nah, it can't be that. You're about as straight as I'm gay."

I don't know if I should tell her about what happened at the swim meet.

The only person I've told is Rich, and I only told him because he's paid to listen and it gave me something to fill the hour. I'm also pretty sure a therapist can't tell anyone what I tell them unless it's about me killing someone.

Telling him didn't help. It didn't make me feel any better. It was kind of humiliating, and he didn't offer me any advice that I could actually use. He suggested that I speak to someone at the school, which would make me a snitch, or talk to Todd, which would be even worse. Adults either have no idea what high school is like, or they've completely forgotten.

I tell Santana what happened. I'm kind of surprised because as I tell her, she doesn't interrupt, not once. She stops staring at me and stares through the windshield.

I finish up and she still doesn't say anything.

I'm waiting for her to ask where Todd lives so she can kick his ass, or something along those lines.

She's still silent.

"So?" I say, finally. "What do you think I should do?"

"You don't know?"

I tell her what Rich suggested. That draws a laugh.

"Your parents pay this therapist money? That's the worse advice I ever heard. No one likes a snitch."

"I'm not going to snitch," I protest.

"Then what are you going to do?" she says.

"I don't know."

She grabs the dash with her one hand, pulls herself forward, and stares over at me. "You really don't know! You've been training with us for months, learning how to choke someone out, and now when someone messes with you, you don't know what to do."

"I couldn't fight him. Not at the meet. I'd get suspended."

"Oh no, not *suspended*," she says, super sarcastic.

"My parents pay a ton of money to send me there. They'd go crazy."

She sighs and I think she's about to shout at me again, but she doesn't.

"Okay, so maybe fighting at school isn't a good idea. But you can't just let it go."

"I kinda already have."

"Hey, Dylan, listen to me. He punked you, and he's going to keep punking you until you stand up for yourself. That's why you train, right?"

I don't have the heart to tell her that I mostly train because I enjoy it. I train because it's like a never-ending puzzle. And because it's hard. Also because after I finish, I feel completely calm and at peace, even if I'm sore and bruised, and I don't get that feeling from doing anything else. Kicking someone's ass is way down my list of why I keep showing up.

"What about Martese telling us that we should learn to fight so we don't have to fight?"

She throws her head back and lets out this big belly laugh like one of the three musketeers. "Yeah, Martese says a lot of stuff."

"What about the other week when that guy stole his parking space and he didn't do anything?"

"Yeah, that's Martese now. That's not what Martese was like back in the day. You never heard of gym invasions or the Gracie challenge?"

"Martese did those?"

"Hell yeah. He'd fight anyone who came in looking for a fight. No rules. Everything was allowed, apart from weapons."

"That's what I should do? Challenge Todd to a fight?"

Santana looks over at me. "Hey, you wanted my advice."

Twenty~Eight

I WALK over to the swim team lunch table and sit down. Jack, Todd and a couple of the other guys look at me.

"No one said you can sit here," says Jack.

I ignore him. I'm here for Todd.

"Yeah," says Todd. "Shouldn't you be with the special needs kids?"

"I know it was you who hid my stuff at the meet and dumped my clothes in the pool," I say to Todd.

"So what if it was? You going to tell on me?" He says the last part in a whiny, little kid's voice.

"You know where Resilient MMA on Ventura is?"

"The gay wrestling place," says Todd.

The others laugh.

"Meet me there at midnight on Saturday."

"Like a date?" he smirks, and now Jack and the others are laughing so hard that people at other tables are looking at us.

"Yeah, exactly like a date. You and me in the octagon."

"I already told you I'm not into that gay wrestling, blow job jockey stuff."

"That's cool. Punches, kicks, knees, elbows … You can throw whatever you want."

He looks at the others for confirmation then back to me.

"You want to get your ass kicked again?" he says.

I think about what Santana told me about the stare down before a fight. How she never breaks eye contact. How she searches her opponent's eyes and waits for them to blink first or look away.

"You scared?" I ask.

"Of you? Yeah, right."

"Good. Bring Jack. He can corner you."

Jack rocks back and forth, chuckling. "Oh man, this is too funny." He turns to the other guys. "Hey, how hilarious would it be if Todd loses?"

Sometimes I forget that Jack and Todd aren't really friends. Before I joined the team apparently Jack would rag on Todd all the time, and Todd would play pranks and make fun of people to worm his way in with him.

As soon as the words are out of Jack's mouth, I see Todd react. It wouldn't be like losing a regular fight. It would be worse than that. Way worse. If he loses Jack and other guys won't let him forget about it.

The stakes just got raised. And Todd knows it.

"See you Saturday," I say, getting up and slinging my backpack over my shoulder. "Oh, and don't forget a mouth guard. You'll need one."

Twenty-Nine

"SO WHAT'S THE PLAN?" Santana asks me as we sit together on the mat.

"I thought you were going to tell me."

She taps a finger against her chin. "It's in the cage so you're gonna be wearing your leg, right?"

"Yeah," I say, a little uncertain.

"Problem?"

"Well, what happens if I catch him with my knee?" I say, reaching down to tap the titanium knee joint.

Santana looks at me, confused. "What do you mean?"

"Well, I could really hurt him."

She reaches over and play slaps me across the face. "That's kind of the idea, Dylan. It's a fight. In a cage."

"I know that, but there's still rules."

"I never read any rule about whether a dude with one leg could wear his fake leg or not." She leans forward, suddenly serious. "Listen, he's going to try to hurt you, so you need to try to hurt him. That's kind of the entire deal. If you don't think you can do that then maybe you need to call it off."

"There's no way I can back down. Not now."

It's true. Ever since I challenged Todd it's been the talk of the school. Social media has gone wild. There are even teams. Team Todd and Team Dylan. It's mostly Team Todd, but I have a few supporters, mostly the geekier kids who've been bullied, and even better than that a whole lot of girls.

There's also been a ton of smack talk online. A few weeks back I posted a video clip from one the jits classes at Resilient and Todd, Jack, and a bunch of their buddies jumped into the comments.

SO GAY!

Is Dylan playing touch butt?

I can't believe he wants Todd to kick his ass again.

Yeah, but how funny would it be if he kicks Todd's ass. OMFG that would be hilarious.

Todd posted beneath that comment:

Yeah, right. I'm going to beat him like a redheaded stepchild.

Then the others weighed in:

Could you beat him hard enough that he's off the swim team? I'd like to win some relays this year. Lol.

I've even had people ask if they can buy tickets or come along to watch. The whole thing has taken on a crazy life of its own and it's out of control.

The only hope I have of it not happening is if somehow one of the teachers or a parent finds out about it and calls Martese, but the kids at school are way too excited to go squealing about it.

They want to see me fight Todd. And, not gonna lie, I want to fight him. I just haven't given that much thought to my plan. I know that if it goes to the ground, even with the small amount of training I've had, I'll win. We've had enough noobs start since I've been training and I can handle them on the mat, even some of the smaller adults.

It's the stand-up part that worries me. Santana's been working with me on my punches and elbows, and I'm not dumb enough to throw another big overhand right out of the gate like I did last time I got pummeled by Todd. But I don't have any real boxing, kickboxing, or Muay Thai or any other stand-up skills to speak of. Not even Tae Kwan Do.

"It's simple," says Santana. "Don't get caught on the way in. Close the distance, take him down. Ground and pound and use your BJJ. If you do get caught and end up on your ass, stay down there, and let him come down to you. Sweep him, take top and beat the crap out of him until he gives you his back, then choke him."

"So," I say to summarize, so I can get it clear in my own head. "Close the distance, take him down, ground and pound, and choke him out."

Santana nods. "Or G and P the crap out of him until he cries."

She jumps to her feet and hauls me up. "Throw your leg on and we'll go into the cage. You need to have a feel for it. We don't have time to do a ton of cage work, but it's at least got to be familiar."

Cage work is what coaches and fighters call the things you have to know and the techniques you need when you find yourself pressed up against one of the cage's eight sides. Because you can't fall through the ropes like you could in a boxing ring, fighters can spend a lot of time up against the cage sides or padded pillars.

You can use the cage walls to get back to your feet. Or you can press your opponent into it and use the mesh walls to grind them down and exhaust them. Santana says it's the third discipline of MMA after ground game and stand up.

We walk into the cage and she bolts the door closed. The floor feels strange under my foot, firmer and springier than the mats we grapple on.

I stand in the middle and turn around. It feels smaller than it looks from the outside, more claustrophobic.

Santana looks like she belongs in here. I most definitely don't.

"You'll both start standing, so let's work on that first. Forget kicks or throwing big shots. We need you to get within range for a takedown without getting caught on the way in."

CHAPTER
Thirty

FOR THE FIRST time since I started, I enjoy coming to school. Rather than sitting in my car, dreading what's coming and waiting until the last possible moment to go in, now I park and walk straight inside.

I'm being looked at and talked about, and not only because of my leg, although who am I kidding, that's still part of it. I might still be a weirdo, but me challenging Todd has revealed one thing. A lot of kids don't like him, or Jack, as well as some of the other guys on the swim team.

I guess it's what happens when you have a sports team that's really successful. At most schools it would be the football team, but our football team sucks so they don't have a lot of swagger. But the swim team has won so much over the years that they're this school's equivalent.

It turns out that a couple of juniors are big into MMA, and they know all about Resilient. Some of them even know about Santana and a couple of the other MMA fighters and are asking me if I know her. She's gotten a lot of media attention because of the arm thing, and because she keeps winning.

When they ask if I know her, I say sure and play it off as no big deal, but it's kind of cool. Her one-armed choke in the last fight went viral, and a lot of people think it's ironic that her trademark submission is a choke that involves both arms when she only has one and a half.

Santana told me that visualizing things can be as good as actually practicing them. I thought it was BS, but I looked it up and it turns out it's a thing.

So that's what I find myself doing when I walk into swim practice and see that Todd is officially back on the team and standing in the locker room. I put down my bag and stare at him.

In my mind's eye, the fight is here, now. I close the distance on him with my hands up and my elbows in tight. I throw a couple of quick jabs and as he counters with an overhand right, I level change and double leg him, taking him to the ground and passing his guard before he realizes what's happened.

Just as I'm starting with the ground and pound, I hear Jack say: "Yo Todd, you think Dylan has like a crush on you, bro? And that's why he wants to do this?"

A couple of the guys start laughing. Todd's not one of them.

I stop staring, grab my bag, and go through my swim gear. I guess if you're going to stare at someone, a locker room filled with a bunch of guys in Speedos might not be the best place to do it.

The team filters out to the pool. A few seconds later Todd walks back in and goes to his locker to retrieve his goggles.

"You sure you want to do this?" he asks, trying to come off tough, like he's doing me a favor by giving me an escape route.

I look at him. "Yeah, I'm sure. Why?"

"Well, like, I beat you pretty good last time. What if you get hurt?"

"Oh, you mean like what if I lose a leg or something?"

I smile. I'm enjoying this. I don't know if Todd is scared, but he's definitely uncertain. He knows as well as I do that neither of us is going to back down.

Like Santana always says, you can talk all the smack you want to on social media, but when that cage door closes behind you, it's all just noise.

I stare at him. My anger is still real, but it's not wild and emotional. It's cold. Ice cold.

I don't just want to win the fight. Once I have him on the ground and pass his guard he's going to be in my world. His two legs won't count for anything.

"Dude." He says it like we're buddies, and now I really know he's the one who doesn't want this. "What happened at the meet was a joke. Everyone gets pranks played on them."

"You don't. Neither does Jack."

That's the truth, and he knows it as well as I do. The pranks, the teasing, the bullying—it's all one-way. There are the bullies and then there are the targets, except now Todd's my target, and all of a sudden he wants to be pals. Well, too bad.

As he sees I'm not backing out, his mood switches.

"Fine. But don't go crying to anyone when I beat you up again."

"Tell you what," I say to him. "You apologize, and we'll forget it."

"Like I said, it was a joke, dude."

I look at him.

"Okay, I'm sorry." He puts out his hand. "We good?"

"Not here. Do it at lunch, in front of everyone. Admit you're a bully and I'll let it go."

I know he's not going to go for it. There's no way he can. He looks angry, but I know what's really behind it. It's fear. Fear of being embarrassed. I recognize it because I've been there.

"There's no way a gimp like you is going to beat me. I'm just trying to save you from getting your ass kicked again!"

I roll my shoulders, relaxed, smiling. That was another Santana tip. "Smile, it confuses the hell out of people."

"Guess we'll find out," I tell Todd.

At lunch I stake out my usual table. As I eat, I pull up a video on my phone. It's about controlling your opponent's wrist when you have them on the ground. Trapping the wrist means you can control their position while you hit them with your free hand.

Anna comes over and sits down. For once her friend isn't with her. I'm thinking something's up. Man, I can see why people get addicted to this whole celebrity thing. I guess she's heard about me calling out

Todd. Santana told me that fighters get a lot of attention, although being Santana, she phrased it as, "Fighters pretty much drown in pussy. Even the ugly ones, which is good news for you."

"Are you really going to fight Todd?" Anna says.

I look up, a fork speared with a piece of chicken halfway to my mouth.

"Yup," I say, trying to play it cool.

"Why?"

It's weird—more kids have spoken to me outside class in the past few days than in all the months I've been here, but not one of them has asked me that.

"He won't stop messing with me," I say.

I don't want to get into all the details. Even now I don't like talking about it. Discussing it with Rich was bad enough.

"That doesn't sound like a good reason to fight someone. Can't you sort out some other way? I mean, say you beat him up, what does that prove? The whole thing sounds totally dumb."

Her friend appears and sits down with us. "I think it's kind of cool. I'm totally Team Dylan," she says. "You've been training at that gym on Ventura, right?"

"Yeah."

"So you should win, right?"

"Yeah, I'm gonna win," I say.

I believe it too. Not because I'm arrogant or because I've spent hours practicing in front of a mirror, or have been throwing shapes in thin air like that Karate Kid bullshido.

I know I'm going to win because I've rolled and sparred dozens of rounds. My body is different than it was. It doesn't bruise as easily. I'm conditioned for being in all kinds of situations that happen in a fight.

I've been strangled. Santana's taught me how to check a leg kick so it doesn't hurt me, and roll with a punch so that I absorb the impact.

But more than any of that, I'm comfortable with being uncomfortable. I know how to stay calm in the middle of the storm. I know how to breathe and think my way out of a bad position. I'm happy on the ground. It's not like when I 'fought' Todd before. If that got replayed now, I'd reverse him as soon as we were on the floor, pass his legs, and be able to keep him pinned.

I've been submitted dozens, probably hundreds of times, and slowly, especially over the last month, I've started submitting other people. I've failed over and over and over and it's for that reason more than any other that I'm confident.

Anna's still looking at me. A strand of hair falls over her eyes. She reaches up and tucks it back behind her ear.

"I still think it's dumb."

Her attitude is starting to annoy me. She hasn't had to deal with all the stuff I have. Maybe if she had then she'd understand.

I shrug and fork another piece of chicken. "Yeah, well."

"Oh, come on," says her friend. "Todd's a total douche." She smiles at me. "I hope you win."

"I hope you both lose," says Anna, and it's the first time I actually feel like maybe I shouldn't be doing this.

IT'S CLOSE TO MIDNIGHT. Resilient MMA is dark. I pull into a spot, turn off the engine and wait for Santana to show up with the keys.

She's roped Jared into acting as referee for the fight so that she can corner me. I'm so nervous that part of me is hoping he's told Martese and the whole thing is about to get called off.

I've been nervous before, but this is different. I'm so anxious that I feel like I might puke. The feeling's been with me from the moment I woke up and remembered that today was the day.

I even thought about sneaking one of my mom's valiums—she got some from her doctor after my accident—but I have to stay sharp.

What's weird is that this whole week I didn't feel any nerves. The opposite of now. I've been so busy training and visualizing, and yes, I admit, enjoying all the attention, that I've felt hyped.

Now all that energy has turned against me, and I'd do almost anything, make any kind of promise, as long as I didn't have to go through with this. It's like having to take a test you haven't studied for times a thousand. Or bungee jumping when you're scared of heights.

Right now, I hate the old Dylan way more than I hate Todd. Todd wasn't the one who made this happen. That was old Dylan.

Old Dylan has totally screwed me because the new Dylan doesn't want to do this. I just want to go home and go to sleep. But I have to go through with it.

My hands are trembling. They're shaking so much I don't know how I'm going to put on my gloves, never mind step into the cage.

Santana warned me this would happen, but like a bunch of stuff she's told me, I didn't really believe her.

"My first ammy bout," she said to me after our last training session this week, "I was so terrified beforehand that I puked everywhere! And I do mean everywhere. Martese had to get me a new rash guard."

Headlights sweep across the front of the gym as a car pulls up. Jared gets out with Santana. If I was going to run away, my chance is gone.

I get out of the Dorkmobile, grab my gear, and walk over to them. At first I thought about telling my parents that I was going to a party, but that would have meant sneaking out with my training bag, and getting a lecture about not drinking or taking drugs if I was driving. Instead, I told them that I was helping Santana prepare for a fight and that she likes to train late at night, which is true.

As Jared unlocks the door, Santana looks at me. "How you feeling?"

"Sick to my stomach."

She laughs. "Told you."

Jared holds the door open and I follow Santana inside.

"If anyone asks, I wasn't here," says Jared.

"I don't think anyone is planning on telling Martese," says Santana.

We all know that Martese would never agree to this.

"Go get changed and we'll warm up," Santana says.

I grab my bag and head to the locker room, relieved to have something to do that doesn't involve sitting around thinking about all the things that could go wrong and how my life will be basically unlivable if I don't win.

I change and take my water bottle, mouth guard and gloves out into the gym. Santana's already grabbed pads. We've rehearsed the start of the fight over and over.

Defend. Close the distance. Takedown. Pass the legs. Go to work, and do not under any circumstances let him get back on his feet.

Santana climbs into the cage. I follow her inside. She holds the pads as I throw a couple of jabs, level change, and shoot for a double leg. I pass her guard. We rest and do it again. This time she steps back and I wait for her to come back into the pocket before I shoot.

We do it a half-dozen more times and I can tell some of the tension and nerves are leaving me as my muscles warm up.

"Hey, maybe your swim buddy isn't going to show," says Jared as Santana lifts the water bottle to my lips so I can take a sip.

"He probably won't," says Santana.

I hope she's right. Todd chickening out would be perfect.

I check the time. Maybe they're right.

If he doesn't turn up, then I'm not going to need proof. I can probably livestream it so that people can see I'm here, ready to go, and he's not.

I take off my gloves and as I'm getting out of the cage to find my phone, I see Jack's BMW pull into the parking lot.

CHAPTER
Thirty-Two

MY STOMACH DOES backflips as Todd and Jack get out of the BMW. Jared goes to open the door for them and shows Todd where he can get changed.

"You got beat up by that dude?" Santana says, staring at Todd's back.

"I wasn't training then."

Santana stands with arms folded, watching them.

"Look at him, he looks like he's going to piss his pants."

Todd did look nervous when he walked in. What's more surprising is that so did Jack. Then I remember the first time I ran into Jared and the first time I walked in here. It's intimidating.

Now Jared's just Jared, but back then he was scary. So was this place and everyone in it. Now it's just a gym.

It hits me how much I've changed, and I feel a little better.

Santana slaps a hand against my chest. "Come on, put your gloves back on. You need to stay loose."

Jack walks back in with Jared. He pulls out his phone and holds it up, filming the place. Jared puts his hand over the phone.

"No phones, man. No recording. Nothing on social media. This is off the books."

"What? Like Fight Club?" Jack says, putting his phone away.

Jared doesn't smile. "Yeah, like Fight Club—if Fight Club was real and not a movie."

With Santana and Jared here, I haven't heard any mentions of gay wrestling from Jack. In here he seems like what he is, your standard Valley-bro bully.

Todd walks back out of the locker room and Santana starts laughing, but catches herself. He's wearing board shorts, wrestling shoes, a Tap Out T-shirt, and boxing gloves.

She leans into me. "Has this guy ever seen an MMA fight?"

"Lose the shoes and the T-shirt," Jared tells Todd. "I'll find you some proper gloves, okay?"

Jared disappears into the back as Todd takes off his shoes and T-shirt. Jared comes back with the fingerless gloves that MMA fighters wear and helps Todd put them on.

He waves me over.

"Okay, I want you both to be clear on the rules here. It's standard MMA rules like you've seen on TV. There's no biting and no gouging or poking the eyes, so keep your hands closed when you're throwing a punch. No groin strikes or kicks, and no kicks to the head of a grounded opponent. You got all that?" he asks, looking at Todd.

Todd nods. I can see he's nervous, and that gives me a bit of relief.

"There's no rounds, we keep going until someone taps or I stop the fight. Obey my instructions and defend yourself at all times."

He looks from Todd to me and then back to Todd. "You both ready to do this?"

I nod. So does Todd.

"Okay," says Jared. "Let's get in the cage."

He stops.

"You have a mouth guard, right?" he says to Todd.

Jack reaches into the pocket of his hoodie, like a best man giving the groom the wedding ring. I think they might have forgotten to put it in if Jared hadn't asked.

"You?" Jared asks me.

Santana hands me my mouth guard. It's custom fitted. I put it in, making sure it's snug.

"Right, gentlemen," says Jared.

"Wait!" shouts Santana.

She rushes over to the side of the cage and taps her phone. Music starts up. "Shipping up to Boston." What else?

"You're probably never going to do this again, so I thought I'd give you some walk-on music," Santana tells me.

Todd walks into the cage and I follow him. Jared shows Jack where he should stand. Santana takes up her place outside the cage, elbows propped on the apron.

I jog as best I can around the inside of the cage. The butterflies are back, except they're more like flying monkeys. My mouth is dry.

The music cuts out. The sudden silence is strange and suddenly it's all very real.

Jared secures the cage door and calls us into the middle.

"You're both clear on the rules?"

We nod. I stare at Todd. Todd stares back.

"Okay, go to your corners and wait for the bell," says Jared.

We don't have a bell, so Santana uses an app on her phone that plays through the gym's sound system. I back up against the cage wall, Santana behind me. "You got this, Dylan. Keep your hands up, close the distance, and do what you've done a hundred times."

I look across the cage, past Jared to Todd. Jack's shouting encouragement at him but it sounds muffled to me. My vision is suddenly narrow, super sharp where I'm looking and blurred outside that. I can hear the blood pounding in my head and my mouth is completely dry.

At the sound of the bell, Jared claps his hands together and steps back. Now there's nothing and no one between me and Todd, only the floor underneath us and the cage fence surrounding us on eight sides.

Todd rushes out into the middle. I go to meet him.

CHAPTER
Thirty-Three

TODD IS two-thirds of the way across the cage. I keep my hands up, elbows in tight, and chin tucked as he throws a wild punch and catches the side of my head.

My glove absorbs most of the impact, but I stagger back, rocked more by the shock of the blow than its force, and I almost fall. After months on the mats and sparring with Santana, my balance is way better than it used to be. But it's still not as good as someone with both their legs.

Encouraged, Todd pushes forward, throwing wild punches as he barrels toward me. A boxer, or someone skilled in stand up would have picked him off by now, but I'm no boxer. He backs me up against the cage and digs a short, sharp jab into my stomach.

I'm in a panic. My mouth feels like it's filled with sand. It's one thing knowing what will happen before a fight, the reality is something different. Everything is chaotic. Things move so fast in front of my eyes that they blur into each other.

"Underhooks! Underhooks!" Santana screams.

I must have heard her shout that instruction a thousand times by now. I don't even have to think. My body just reacts.

As he closes in, I slip my hands under Todd's arms, wrapping him up so that we're chest to chest. Moving my prosthetic leg back, I brace the heel of it against the cage so that the metal knee joint locks.

"Beautiful, Dylan," Santana shouts. "Now, head position and link your hands."

Again, I don't have to think. I bend my good knee and shove the top of my forehead in under Todd's chin. I grab for my right glove with my left and join my hands together, wrapping Todd up in kind of a bear hug.

His right hand jabs me in the side but we're so close there's nothing in his punches. The initial shock from his rush across the cage and then catching me by surprise is gone. The shock was just that—shock. Like the rush you get when you first dive into cold water.

My heart still hammers in my chest, but my mind has started to clear. I can hear Jack shouting, "Push him off you, dude. Get free."

But I have underhooks and my hands are linked so the only way Todd can get free is if I let him go or he catches me in a transition.

Santana talks me through everything step by step. It's the same, calm methodical set of instructions I've heard Martese call out to her during a fight, like someone telling you what buttons to push on a video game controller.

Across the cage, Jack's instructions are like someone jabbing their finger randomly at the buttons. "Punch him, dude. Push him off. Mess him up, bro."

"Okay, Dylan, step and reverse," says Santana.

This wasn't the plan. I was going to shoot for a takedown in the center of the cage. But training has taught me that sometimes you have to work from where you are, not where you wish you were.

I wait until I feel Todd tense and press hard, trying to move me. I step my right leg out, adjust my body, and allow his momentum to carry him around. Now his back is to the fence, and I'm pushing him against it, using my head under his chin and the underhooks to hold him there.

The more he tries to push me away, the harder he breathes. That's the idea—grind your opponent into the cage and drain them of their energy.

"Beautiful!" Santana shouts.

Jack shouts at Jared, "Break 'em up. Don't you have to break 'em up?"

"This ain't boxing, dude," says Jared.

As he says that, I level change, lowering my hips. I sink down and shoot for an ankle pick takedown, grabbing Todd's right ankle, pulling it forward. His foot lifts off the floor, and caught by surprise, he falls.

Santana screams and applauds.

"Yeah, baby! Takedown!"

Todd sits with his butt on the floor and his back against the cage, like a toddler who's being dumped into a playpen, and he's just about as clueless as a baby as to how to get out.

I move past his legs and into a side control position, and drive my shoulder into the side of his neck while I secure his wrist. He throws a few weak jabs into my side with his free hand as I consolidate my position.

He's gasping for air now, his mouth open as he sucks in his breaths. He gives up on the short jabs and tries to bench me off. I recognize his anger and frustration. It's the frustration everyone encounters when they're new to the experience of being pinned.

I sink down into him. The more I relax, the heavier I am. The heavier I am, the harder it is to move me. After a few seconds of pushing, he gives up, out of ideas.

The squall at the start of the fight has subsided. I weathered it, and now it's my turn to bring the storm. It's an almost-perfect feeling, made all the more delicious by the fact that he has no idea what's about to happen.

"Strikes, strikes!" barks Santana. "Let's work."

Scooting my butt up, I adjust my body and throw two short sharp elbows into his face. He tries to block them with his gloves, but the second one slides through, catching him above his left eye, opening up a gash.

Blood starts to ooze from the cut. It trickles down the side of his face.

Todd makes another attempt to push me off but it's pointless. He needs to cover up and wait for me to move. Maybe try to time his escape, try to re-establish his guard by shrimping to the side, and getting his legs between us. Instead, he grabs for my arms and tries to muscle me off him.

"Deep water! Deep water!" shouts Santana.

Todd and Jack may not know what she means, but I do. Deep water is the middle of the cage, away from the fence that a fighter can use to leverage themselves back to their feet.

I let him wriggle off the fence. He puts a hand down on the mat as he tries to get up. I reach one hand down and grab behind his knee, pulling him farther away from the cage wall.

As he starts to get back up I shift position, controlling his hips and dragging him even farther away from the fence.

Moving up his body, I re-establish side control, reaching one arm around his neck to get the cross face.

Now I have the position for what I want to do next. I throw another short elbow with my free arm, giving him something to think about.

Fighting with my prosthesis on worked when we were both standing. But now I don't need it. If anything, it makes things harder. On the ground I never wear it, and in this position it makes moving into a mount a lot harder.

It's time to switch things up. Time for the kid with one leg to kick some ass.

Throwing one more elbow, I reach my free hand down and click the button on the side of my socket, which releases the pin mechanism. I slide the socket off my stump, kicking my prosthetic leg across the cage with my good foot.

If Todd somehow manages to get back to his feet now, I'll be screwed. But he's not going to. He's in my world, away from the fence, out in the deep water.

I'm going to drag him to the very bottom, and then I'm going to drown him.

Thirty-Four

"STAND THEM UP. STAND THEM UP!" Jack screams at Jared.

It's pretty much what you hear from casual fans who don't understand that MMA is as much about ground work as striking. As long as the attacking fighter is active then the fight doesn't get stood up.

Jared ignores the pleas from Todd's corner as I transition to mount.

Usually to move into a top mount the fighter on top has to swing their leg up and over their opponent's leg. That risks their opponent blocking the movement, or worse, using their move to mount to escape or reverse the position.

But I don't have a leg to block. I simply move my stump over and go straight to mount. Quickly, before Todd can bridge his hips to get me off, I scoot up his torso into high mount.

Now I'm where he was in the locker room. In the most dominant striking position of all. And I plan on taking my time.

I slam a punch into his face, aiming for where he's already cut. His arm drops and he covers his bloodied face.

My mind fills with a cold, clear rage. Looking down I don't see him bloodied and scared, I see the arrogant smirk he had when he was on top of me. Laid over the smirk is a looping scroll of all the social media comments. All the insults, all the barbs, all the 'jokes.'

"You wanna know if I swim in circles?" I ask him, slamming my forearm into his throat.

He rasps and his hands move down to his throat. I punch him hard in the eye with my other hand.

I stop for a second, rearing over him. I want him to look at me.

I crack three short elbows into the side of his head. There's blood all over me. All over the canvas.

Pausing, I look over at Jack. All his bravado has evaporated.

I keep looking at him as I flick another sharp left elbow and open up a fresh cut on Todd's face.

It's not even Todd I'm hitting anymore. Not really. Not in my mind.

It's all of it. Everything. Everyone. The lady who wasn't paying attention while driving. My shitty luck for being on that street at that second.

I'm hating and hitting and punishing all of it. Every thrust of phantom pain. Every look of pity I get. Every moment I wake up and remember that this is my new reality.

I can hear Jared now. He's speaking to Todd. "Todd, you have to start moving or I'll have to stop the fight. You hear me?"

Todd throws a hand up, catching me in the stomach with all the force of a kitten pawing at a ball of wool.

Something about Jared's voice brings me back from wherever I was. I hit him again, but the venom isn't there anymore. It's time to finish him, but not like this. I don't want to do any more damage, but I still want the tap and I know exactly how to get it without messing up his face any more than I already have.

I shift my weight over to my left side, easing the pressure on him. Instinctively Todd starts to roll onto his side, covering up so that he won't be hit in the face anymore.

As he rolls, I move my right leg over his hip, the back of my heel finding his pelvic bone. Before he knows what's happening, I slip my right arm under his neck. He tries to push it away, but it's half-hearted.

I press the end of my stump into his opposite hip bone, taking his back. My right hand reaches across to his shoulder and then up. I open up the glove and clasp the hand around my left bicep.

I start to squeeze, bringing my elbows together to finish the rear naked choke. As I tighten the choke, cutting off the blood to his brain, he reaches up and taps hard three times.

I let go and Jared jumps in, reaching under my arms and hauling me off to the side just to be sure.

Kneeling on the cage floor, I look over at Todd, lying there spent and bloodied.

I did it. I won. He tapped out.

I crawl across the cage, grab my prosthesis, slip it back on and stand. Santana bounds into the cage and hugs me.

"Great sub! Beautiful."

I look across to Todd's corner. Jack isn't there. I look around, expecting to see him in the cage, checking on Todd.

He's not inside the cage either. Then I catch sight of him, heading for the exit. Shaking his head, he pushes through the door of the gym and out into the parking lot.

Todd is sitting up and Jared is kneeling down next to him. He spits out his mouth guard as Jared pats his back.

"It's okay, take your time," Jared says to him.

I've thought about this moment ever since the challenge. Thought about all the things I'd say to Todd. All the smack talk I could unleash.

Now the moment is here, saying any of the things I'd planned on saying seems stupid. He tapped. I won. He lost. It's over.

I'm happy that I beat him. But more than anything, I'm relieved. I squeeze Santana then let go and walk over to Todd. I want to make sure he's okay.

Thirty-Five

I HAND TODD my water bottle. He looks at it, then he looks at me, like maybe I'm playing a trick on him. Finally, he accepts it and takes a big gulp of water as he wipes off some of the blood covering his face.

He looks over to his corner.

"He left," I say.

"Figures."

"You almost had me at the start," I tell him.

He doesn't say anything.

I reach down, grab his hand, and pull him back onto his feet. "Good fight. You hung in there a lot longer than most people would have."

For a second I think about how weird this all is. A minute ago I was on the verge of choking him unconscious. If he hadn't tapped, I would have.

Now I'm giving him water and making sure he's okay. I've never thought about fighters hugging it out after a fight before. It happens at the end of most fights, the victor consoling the vanquished, but I never understood it.

Now I know that it's about respect. You both went through something together. One person had to win and one had to lose, but you both had the courage to step inside the cage. Courage demands respect.

Jared comes back into the cage with a fresh towel.

"Come on, I'll help you get cleaned up," he says to Todd, handing him the towel as he ushers him out.

Santana dances around me. "Oh man, when you took your leg off? That's some of the funniest shit I've ever seen."

She stops and looks at me.

"What is it?" she asks. "Aren't you happy?"

"Yeah, sure."

"Dude, you won. He tapped out."

She stares at me.

"I know."

"Hey, think about all the shitty-ass stuff him and his buddies have done. Calling you names, stealing your prosthesis, doing their best to humiliate you. He had that beat-down coming."

I know she's right. He did do all those things. But when I was throwing those elbows it wasn't about any of that. Not if I'm being honest. It was about everything. All the rage, all the anger, all the negative things I have inside, I took it all out on him. While I was hitting him with elbows and fists it felt great, way better than telling Rich how I feel. But now, when it's done …?

If I'd taken him down, controlled him and then submitted him that would have been different. But I didn't. I didn't just want to win. I wanted to hurt him. Punish him for things he'd done, yes, but also for things that have nothing to do with him.

I think about explaining this to Santana, but something stops me.

"Dylan, it's a fight, dude. You think for one second that he wouldn't have done the exact same thing to you?"

I know she's right, but it doesn't help. I'm not Todd.

"I'm gonna go see if he's okay," I say.

Santana rolls her eyes.

As I'm walking out of the cage, Jared comes back out of the locker room.

"He's fine. Bit banged up, couple of nasty cuts, but he's not concussed. You really got him good with those elbows."

Jared's also fought MMA. He has the same attitude as Santana. It was a fight. The end.

Maybe they're right. Maybe I'm overthinking it and making more of this than it is. How bad would Todd have felt if he'd done to me what I did to him?

Perhaps I should enjoy it. I won. I beat him. And it wasn't a fluke—I didn't get lucky, I won because I trained hard, had a plan, and executed it.

Unlike the last fight I had with Todd, I knew what I was doing. Even when he caught me with that one punch, I didn't panic. I stayed calm, or as calm as anyone can be.

I weathered the storm. I can go home to bed, take it easy tomorrow, and know that on Monday when I go back to school my life will be better. No one's going to be making fun of me like they have been. Not when they see Todd's face.

I'm the kid with one leg who won the ass-kicking contest.

Thirty-Six

THE BLOOD and sweat have been mopped from the floor of the octagon. Santana and Jared wiped down the gloves and threw the bloodied towels into a laundry bag. Usually, stuff from the gym that needs to be cleaned goes to the laundry place a few doors down, but they might mention it to Martese, so Jared throws the bag into the trunk of his car to wash it at home.

Todd and I have changed back into regular clothes. He has a cap that he pulls down low to hide his eyes, concealing the big gash over his left eye and the smaller cut over his right.

My eye is starting to swell and there's a yellow tinge to the skin. It must be my third or fourth black eye since I started training. I don't even think about them or the rest of the bruises anymore. The only time I worry is when one of my ears starts to fill with fluid and I have to get Martese or Jared to drain it with a needle. Even though Santana tells me chicks dig it, I figure I'm a little too young for cauliflower ears.

Jared locks up, and he and Santana get into his car and take off down Ventura.

I'm about to get into the Dorkmobile when I notice Todd standing there. Jack was his ride.

"Need a ride home?"

He looks at me for a second. I can tell he's wondering why I'm being so nice to him.

The truth is all the hatred I had for him is gone. I see him for what he is, just a dumb kid who's been a bully.

I open the trunk. "You can throw your bag in here."

He walks over. "Thanks."

I get in the car with him and back out of the spot.

"Wanna tell me where you live?" I ask him as we turn onto Ventura.

"Oh, yeah, sorry," he says. "Take a left, then go down six blocks and hang a right."

I've never been to Todd's. I haven't been to the home of anyone from Meadow Grove. I don't get invited over to study with people and I don't get invited to parties. Maybe the other kids at school think I'm a loner.

A lot of my social life revolves around Resilient. School's just a place I have to be, like a job. The gym is somewhere I want to be.

"You get nervous driving?" Todd asks me.

I shrug. "Nah, not really. My mom does though."

"Right," he says, going back to staring out the window.

"Get some ice on your face before you go to bed. It'll keep some of the swelling down."

"Yeah."

We stop at a light.

"It wasn't my idea," says Todd. "Stealing your fake leg."

The way he says it, it's like he really wants me to know this. I can't help but wonder if he'd be telling me this if he'd won the fight.

"I mean, I did, but it was Jack's idea. He didn't make me or anything. Sometimes it's just easier to do stuff, you know?"

I do know, and I get it. Jack's the leader of the team, and when the leader of something is a total asshole I've noticed that the people around them act like assholes too, either because they're scared or they want to make them happy, or because they don't want to be the one getting picked on. If everyone's laughing at someone else, then they're not laughing at you.

The problem is that at some point, you have to look at yourself in the mirror and realize that you're a coward as well as an asshole.

Not that I'm saying I'm a great guy or that I wouldn't have done some of the things if I were Todd. I just never had the option. That's something I'm grateful for now.

The light changes. I don't move for a second and a driver behind us lays on his horn. A second later he goes around me, flipping me off. I channel my inner Martese and don't react. The other guy must be in a hurry. Maybe he has a sick kid in the back or something.

I feel like Todd is waiting for me to say something.

"Whatever happened at school, it's done. We're good."

"We are?" says Todd, sounding a little incredulous.

"Yeah," I shrug.

I think about something Santana said to me before. "If you can't be the bigger person when you've beaten someone, you have a problem."

When we get to Todd's house there's nowhere to park. Every single space on his block is taken, and all the cars are new and expensive.

"My parents are having one of their parties," he says.

The way he says it I get the idea that they have a lot of parties. I can't remember the last time my parents threw a party. It must have been when I got out of the hospital, but it was super awkward because no one knew what to say to me and pretty much everyone left early.

"Just pull into the driveway," he says.

I pull in behind a shiny black BMW with personalized plates that read: *IJRY LWYR*. I guess that explains why they have such a huge house and throw lots of parties.

"Hey, can I leave my bag in your car and get it on Monday?"

"Sure."

As we both get out, the front door opens and a guy walks out. He has the same curly black hair as Todd and he's holding what looks and smells like a tumbler full of whisky in one hand and a cigar in the other.

"Hey, son, how was the party?" Todd's dad says, coming toward us.

He stops when he sees me. "Oh, hey—Dylan, right?"

I'm kind of surprised that he recognizes me. Then I remember I'm the kid his son was suspended for fighting with.

He does a doubletake as he sees Todd's face. "Oh my God, what happened?"

He spins around and calls back into the house. "Hey, Greta, get out here."

Todd puts up his hand. "Dad, don't."

Todd's father places his tumbler down on the walkway and rests his cigar on a ceramic planter.

"What happened?"

"It's nothing," says Todd.

My heart starts to pound out of my chest as I look from *INJRY LAWYR* to Todd's battered face and his father's horrified expression. If Todd tells him the truth, it's not just me that's screwed, it's Santana and Jared and Martese. If Todd's dad decides to sue, he could shut down the gym.

There's a scream as Todd's mom races outside.

I stare at Todd, wondering what he's going to say and how he's going to explain the cuts and bruises on his face. It doesn't look as bad as it did when it was covered in blood. Jared did a pretty good job of cleaning him up, but he still looks like someone who's taken a beating.

"Dylan was giving me a ride home. We stopped for tacos and these guys jumped us for like no reason."

More adults have started to gather on the front lawn.

"They mugged you?" says his dad.

"No. It was just, I dunno, there was no reason. I guess they were drunk or high or something."

Todd's mom looks at me. I'm scared that she doesn't believe Todd's story. Then I realize that she's staring at my eye.

"They hit you too?" she asks me.

"Yeah, it's nothing. We kind of fought them off and got out of there."

Her mouth is still open as she reaches up to cup Todd's face in her hands. She turns to look at my eye.

"Was it a gang or something? I mean, what kind of person hits a kid with one—"

She's about to say *with one leg,* but she must have remembered that her son hit me and stops talking.

"I'm calling the cops," says Todd's dad.

"No!" says Todd, panicking. "It's nothing, and they won't find them anyway. I don't think they were even from around here. They left in a car, they're probably miles away by now."

"We have to report this," says his dad.

"Well, okay, but can we maybe do it in the morning? I'm really tired and Dylan needs to get home."

"You won't remember in the morning. The longer you wait, the less seriously they'll take it."

"Tell us exactly what happened?" says his mom.

"I dunno," says Todd. "The party was kind of lame and Dylan was leaving so I asked him for a ride home. Then we stopped at this taco place."

"Where?" says Todd's dad.

"I don't even remember." Todd looks at me.

"I don't know," I say. "I can't remember the name of the place."

"Okay, what street was it on?" his mom asks me.

"Lankershim? No, Ventura? Listen, I'm sorry, I got hit pretty hard," I say, tapping a knuckle to my yellow-tinged eye and not lying about that part. "The guy really got me good."

"That's okay, we can figure it out. There can't be that many taco places between the party and here," his dad says.

"And they didn't want your wallet or your phone or anything?"

I shake my head. "Like Todd said, they were drunk and looking for trouble. It could have been anyone."

Another guy in slacks and a polo shirt, his belly spilling over his belt, has joined Todd's dad. His face is flushed from drinking.

"So these guys. What were they?"

I look at him. I think I know what he's working up to and where this is going, but wait for him to continue

"I mean," he stumbles, "were they Black, Hispanic, what?"

Seeing as we've already made up the whole story, I jump in. "No, they were definitely white."

The guy looks confused by what I just told him, not to mention a little deflated.

"It would have been worse if Dylan hadn't jumped in," says Todd.

"Listen, I really should be getting home," I say.

"Are you okay to drive?" Todd's mom asks me.

"Yeah, I'm fine," I say.

I think they've bought it, but I read once that a telltale sign of a liar is when someone starts adding lots of detail and ends up trying to sell their story too hard. Probably best to split while the going is good and hope that Todd doesn't decide to tell his parents what really happened. Although, I suspect there are a couple of reasons he doesn't want them to know the real story.

Todd's dad reaches out to shake my hand.

"Dylan, thanks for bringing him home and for jumping in. I'm glad you guys are buddies, especially after, well you know, what happened before."

"No problem."

As I get back into my car, I overhear Todd's dad talking to him.

"We need to get you some self-defense lessons or something. What's that place on Ventura? Resilient? A kid with one leg had to save you, for chrissakes. That's kind of embarrassing, son."

CHAPTER
Thirty-Seven

I PARK on the street and ease the front door open as quietly as I can. The house is quiet. I put my bag down in the hall and walk into the living room.

"Oh, hey."

Mom walks in from the kitchen. Dad is lying on the couch watching something on his iPad.

"Where have you been?" says Mom. "It's almost one in the morning."

"Your mom was worried you were at a party."

"No, just holding pads for Santana. Or trying to, anyway." I point to my black eye. They're going to notice it so I may as well explain it before they start asking questions.

My dad has only met Santana a couple of times, but he *loves* her. He thinks it's badass that a girl with one arm—well technically one and a half—wants to fight in the UFC.

By now my mom is way less shocked by the bruises and black eyes that I come home with.

"I'll go get a cold pack," she says, hustling back into the kitchen. "I think I have some arnica somewhere."

. . .

I take another shower, ice my eye, and dab some arnica cream around it to help with the bruising. Then I get into bed and lie there, staring up at the ceiling.

The soreness from the fight is starting to kick in. My body is tired, but my mind is buzzing.

There's a knock at my door.

"Yeah."

"Can I come in?"

"Sure."

My dad walks in and sits on the end of the bed.

"I don't want to say anything to your mom, but Todd's father called me about ten minutes before you got home. You want to tell me what happened tonight?"

I take a breath and tell him. I tell him how Todd took my prosthesis and hid it. How I challenged him to a fight. I tell him how the fight went, and how Jack split and I gave Todd a ride home.

He doesn't say anything until I've finished. Then he asks me, "You think Todd's father believed you?"

"I think so."

"That's good. Attorneys can be real jerks."

He gets up from my bed and walks to the door.

"You really beat the crap out of him, huh?" he says.

Now it's over, I'm not proud of it. I don't regret fighting him, and I'm glad I won, and happy I used my jits to get the tap, but I'm not proud of losing control like I did and messing up his face.

"I guess so."

He winks. "Good. He had it coming."

Thirty-Eight

BY THE TIME I wake up it's almost midday. I lie there and stare up at the ceiling. The missing part of my leg thrums. If I close my eyes and squeeze, I can feel my toes curl. My muscles ache and my eye throbs where Todd caught me. It's like my first week training BJJ, when I could barely get out of bed.

I hop into the bathroom to assess the damage. The skin around my eye is turning blue and I have some bruises, but all in all I'm not in bad shape. Sore, but that's not surprising.

I shower, brush my teeth, and put some clothes on. I have a bunch of homework that I need to get done before school tomorrow, but first I need to eat. Fighting gives you an appetite.

Mom's in the kitchen. She picks up my phone from the counter. I must have put it down when I came in last night and then forgotten all about it.

"You're very popular," she says, handing it to me.

I'm not sure what she means until I look at the screen and see I have a bunch of messages and notifications plus at least four missed calls from Santana.

I don't know what it could be, but something's up. I also have hundreds of new follows, likes and friend requests.

"Thanks," I tell her, walking back into the living room.

"You want some pancakes?"

"Sure, that'd be great," I say, staring at an Instagram post I've been tagged in.

It's a video, shot cage-side of me choking Todd out at the end of the fight. I know it's the fight because I can see my prosthetic leg lying on the cage floor at the very edge of the frame.

Todd taps, Jared jumps in, and the video ends.

I scroll down. There must be a few hundred comments and thousands of likes. I start reading.

OMG. That was crazy.

Kid with one leg KICKS ass. Lol.

Tap Machine Todd. LMFAO.

The leg! Hahahaha.

My screen lights up. It's Santana. I hit answer.

"You see it?" says Santana.

"Yeah, sorry, I just got up."

"You need to take it down. If Martese sees it, he'll flip out."

"I didn't post it."

"Then who did?"

From the angle and the fact I can see Santana on the other side of the cage, it could only be one person.

"Must have been Jack. The guy who was cornering Todd."

Santana goes quiet for a second. "Why would you post a video of your buddy getting choked out?"

"Because he's a jerk."

"You have a number for this guy?" Santana asks.

"I can get one."

"Good. Send it to me. I'll take care of it," she says, and ends the call.

I bet a message from Santana should do the trick.

"Was that Santana calling to apologize?" my mom calls through from the kitchen. "Your dad told me what happened."

My phone chimes again with a new notification. It's a friend request from Jenny Moran, the hottest girl in my grade.

THE GROUND ISN'T OKAY

CHAPTER
Thirty-Nine

IF I'D KNOWN all it took to be popular was to take off my leg and fight someone in a cage, I would have done it months ago. Even before I get to school, I have guys coming up to fist bump and high five me. Most of them have never even acknowledged I exist, never mind spoken to me before.

"Yo, that shit was sick, dude."

"Hey, Dylan, when's your next fight?"

"Oh man, I thought you were going to kill that guy."

"Can, like, anyone come down and train there?"

I even have a couple of juniors ask if they can get a selfie with me. I do the standard BJJ hand signal, fingers bunched into a fist with your thumb and pinkie finger sticking out. I've got no idea why jits people do it, maybe it's another Brazilian thing, but it's what pretty much every BJJ competitor does when they have their picture taken.

By the time I get into home room I'm feeling pretty good. A couple of guys fist bump me on my way to my seat and Jenny Moran is definitely checking me out.

She smiles at me as I walk past her desk. "You're coming to my party this weekend, right?" she says, flipping her hair.

"Sure," I say, although it's the first I've even heard about a party at her place.

"Great. Hey, you don't have a girlfriend right now or anything, do you?" she says.

"Right now? No."

"Good," she says, giving me this big smile before shifting around in her seat to face the front of the class again.

For the rest of the morning I keep waiting for everything to go wrong. To be called into the principal's office and told I'm being expelled. Or to get a message that Todd's father has found out what really happened and is suing my family and the gym for every cent they have.

But none of that happens. I just go through the rest of my classes like I'm a frickin' rock star, with guys wanting to talk about the fight and girls who always ignored me getting all flirty.

I'm not sure half the people who talk to me have even seen the fight. After Santana made Jack take down the video, it seems to have taken on an almost legendary status.

In truth, it was a pretty scrappy MMA bout between Todd, who pretty much had no idea what he was doing, and someone—me—who really isn't what anyone would call a cage fighter. My whole plan was to execute some kind of a takedown and then use my jits, but if I'd been up against someone with even halfway decent stand up, I would have been toast.

I don't know what fight people think they saw, but from the way some kids are talking about it, I know it wasn't the one I was in.

"Yo, when you like jumped off the top of the cage on top of him, that was crazy, dude," some kid who smells like weed says to me as I walk to lunch.

He must be thinking of professional wrestling where someone will jump from the top rope onto their opponent while he's lying down helpless. In MMA, if your opponent is lying flat on the cage floor unable to move while you climb the cage, the fight's over. The only time I've seen fighters climb on top of the cage is to celebrate at the end.

"I don't think that happened," I tell stoner kid. "But thanks."

"It was sick, dude!" he says, completely ignoring what I just said. Then he adds, "Those swim team guys are jerks," seeming to forget that I'm also a swim team guy.

Speaking of which, as I walk out to the picnic tables to eat lunch, Jack, who's sitting with the rest of the team, waves me over.

"Hey, Dylan," he says. "You can tell your friend that I took down the video, okay?"

"Sure."

"We all good?" he asks.

This is weird too. He's scared of me. Or maybe of Santana and Jared. But whoever it is, he's definitely scared.

"Yeah, I guess."

I don't know what else to say. He was an asshole for putting the video online, and for abandoning Todd after he lost. And if Todd was right and it was his idea to steal my leg, then I should still have a problem with him. But I don't have the energy for any of that. I just want what I've always wanted. To be left alone.

Only, maybe that's not true. Before now I thought I didn't like attention. But it turns out that I don't hate it either, as long as it's the good kind.

CHAPTER

Forty

THE TABLE where I sit is crowded so I start to look around for somewhere else to eat lunch. Then, as one of the guys sitting there waves at me, it hits me. It's crowded because it's where I usually eat lunch.

"Hey, man, scoot down, make room," someone says as I walk over to the table.

Kids rearrange themselves so I can sit in the middle. It's like being at a party where I'm the guest of honor. Kids offer me food while I get peppered with questions. Not just about the fight, but about training at the gym, and what BJJ is, and how it's different from MMA.

A senior who plays on the lacrosse team, and who a lot of the girls have a crush on, asks me about Santana and whether she's single.

"No, she has a girlfriend," I tell him, and he seems kind of bummed.

There are so many questions that by the time lunch is over I've barely been able to eat anything. Not that I mind too much. I could talk about BJJ for hours.

Just as the bell sounds for my next class, I spot Anna. I manage to catch up to her as she walks inside.

"Hey, sorry about the table. I'll save you a seat tomorrow."

"Don't worry about it."

Something seems kind of off. I know she thought that fighting Todd was a stupid idea.

"It's no problem. I like sitting with you."

She doesn't say anything, just keeps walking.

"Did you hear? I won the fight."

She stops and turns to face me.

"You did? I would never have guessed."

The sarcasm gets to me.

"What are you saying? I should have just gone through the rest of school getting picked on?"

"I saw what you did, Dylan. Someone sent me the video."

From the way she says it and the way her lip curls up, it's clear she wasn't impressed.

"Punching someone in the face when they're on the ground. It's disgusting. It's not something to be proud of."

"And what about when he did it to me?" I fire back.

"That was just as bad."

"Well then."

"I think some of your fans want selfies," she says, nodding to a group of freshman guys who are hanging back behind me, waiting for us to finish talking.

CHAPTER
Forty-One

"DYLAN, Santana, I need to speak with you."

Santana and I share a look as we walk over to where Martese is standing by the cage. His arms are folded and he looks super pissed. It's unnerving because Martese has to be the most chilled-out person I've ever met.

The whole week I had this feeling that life couldn't go on being this good. I'm not getting as many fist bumps and high fives as I did at school on Monday and my social media has calmed down from the initial frenzy, but my school life is still way better than it was before I beat up Todd.

Todd showed back up at school on Wednesday. His face was still kind of a mess. He got the opposite reaction that I got, like he had some kind of disease. No one wanted to go near him.

That might not have been strictly true. I tried talking to him, I even offered him some concealer, but he told me to leave him alone. I also saw Anna talk to him, while shooting me an ugly look as I walked past them.

But apart from me and Anna, Todd was an outcast. It was like that quote about victory having many fathers, but defeat being an orphan.

It wasn't just that people loved a winner, what they really loved was an underdog. In this case I'd been the underdog, because you know, the leg.

Anyway, all week I'd been waiting for my newfound popularity to come to a grinding halt. For my secret to be revealed.

"So," said Martese. "Anything you two want to tell me?"

As soon as he said it, I knew I was going to have to come clean. If he'd been a teacher or even my mom, I might have tried to play dumb. But Martese had gone out of his way to help me. He'd tracked me down, talked to my parents, and coached me pretty much every week. He'd made me part of the Resilient family and given me an amazing gift.

He helped me without treating me differently. He let me make mistakes and develop at my own pace. He made it so that having one leg wasn't a thing. At Resilient, I'm just Dylan.

I owe him. Big time.

I open my mouth to speak, but Santana beat me to the punch.

"The fight was my idea," she says.

"You really think I wouldn't find out?" says Martese.

"I'm sorry," I say.

Martese gives me a bowel-loosening look. "Oh, you will be."

"Same here, Coach. I'm sorry," says Santana. "I didn't want to tell you because if you didn't know it was happening then you couldn't be held responsible."

He gives her the same look he just gave me. "That's not how business liability works, Santana. It's my gym, I'm responsible for everything that happens here. Unless someone breaks in, which you didn't, since you have a key. A key that I gave you because I thought I could trust you."

"Is it Todd's dad?" I ask. "Is he suing?"

"What?" says Martese.

"The kid's old man is an attorney," says Santana. "Personal injury."

As soon as she says it, I realize this is news to Martese. "No, it wasn't him, thankfully. But I did get a message from another coach who saw the video before it was taken down. He wanted to know if I was bringing back the Vale Tudo challenge matches that we used to have back home in Brazil."

The whole idea of the UFC came from challenge matches that started in Brazil. Basically, anyone could walk into a gym and test their fighting style.

Back then there were gym wars and gym invasions. BJJ clubs were like street gangs and sometimes they went to war with each other.

"It was the kid I had a fight with before," I say to Martese.

"And this was you getting your revenge?"

"He wouldn't leave me alone."

"He was still bullying you?"

"Yeah."

"He stole Dylan's prosthetic and hid it, and dumped his clothes in the pool. The kid's an asshole. He deserved everything he got," says Santana.

Martese looks to me for confirmation. "He did that?"

"Yeah, it was pretty humiliating."

Martese seems to be weighing all of this information.

"He didn't have to agree to fight Dylan," says Santana. "He could have apologized and it would have been over with."

I'm starting to think that if Santana doesn't make it to the UFC, she'd make a pretty good defense lawyer.

"You gave him the chance to apologize?" Martese asks me.

"Yeah," I confirm.

There's a long pause before Martese says, "I had a similar situation when I was in school. A bigger kid who found out I trained jiujitsu wouldn't leave me alone. Every day it was something. Calling me names. Pushing me. Stealing my books out of my bag. Finally, one day I had enough. I told him to meet me after school and I'd fight him."

I can't imagine Martese ever being bullied by anyone.

"You won, right?" says Santana, who seems determined to push her luck.

"He was a couple of years older and a lot bigger than me, but yes, I won. And I took my time with him, just like Dylan did. I wanted to make sure that he wouldn't bother me again."

Martese doesn't say any of this like he's boasting. In fact, it sounds like he's trying to do the opposite.

"It was sad. I found out later that his stepfather used to get drunk and beat him. That's why he picked on other kids. He thought he could get rid of his pain by hurting people. I saw him years later—he'd become a drug addict. I was back home in Rio seeing my parents and he came up to me to ask for money. He was so out of it that he didn't even recognize me."

"What did you do?" I ask.

"What could I do? He was pitiful. I gave him all the money I had on me."

"You did?"

"Dylan, I don't have a problem with what you did. It wasn't like you jumped him. He showed up and got in the cage and I know Jared was here to make sure it didn't get out of control. But come on, you knew you were going to beat him, right?"

"I guess so."

"Of course you did. You've been training here for almost six months and this guy, he's the same age and about the same size as you."

I know he's trying to teach me something here but I'm not sure what he's getting at.

"You want to test yourself?" says Martese, handing me a flyer. "This is next month."

I look down at the piece of paper. It's for a BJJ competition that's happening in Long Beach.

He turns to Santana. I can see her wilt a little. She needs this place maybe more than I do and she can tell Martese is pissed that she arranged this behind his back.

"Look, I'm sorry," she says.

He puts out his hand, palm up. She digs in her pocket, pulls out the keys for the gym, and places them in his hand. She has the keys because she likes to train at weird times. Without the keys she has to rely on someone opening up for her.

Martese takes the keys and dangles them in the air for a few seconds. Then he hands them back to her.

"Do something like this again and I'll take them back for good. Understand?"

"I won't. I promise. Like I said, I'm really sorry, Coach."

Martese looks back at me. "Never make yourself feel better by making someone else feel worse. Jiujitsu is a gift. We have to know when to use it, but most of all, we need to know why we're using it."

CHAPTER
Forty-Two

BEFORE I LEAVE for the party at Jenny Moran's house, I text Todd to see if he needs a ride. I know kids are bringing booze, but even if I wanted to drink I can't, and not just because I'm driving. I have to be up early for a BJJ fundamentals class and then Santana's promised to help me start preparing for the BJJ competition in Long Beach.

Todd texts me back and I agree to pick him up him around nine. It might seem kind of weird to be helping someone I beat up a week ago, but I still feel bad about it. And I've been thinking about what Martese said. If his point was to make me feel guilty it totally worked.

Ever since the fight Todd has probably taken more abuse than I ever did. I feel bad about it, responsible even, but it goes beyond that too. A lot of it comes down to kids thinking that he shouldn't have lost a fight to someone with one leg, which is insulting to both of us.

Anyway, I figure that if some of the other kids see me hanging out with Todd they might just move on. It was two guys having a fight. One won, one lost. Not that big of a deal. At least Todd had the balls to step into the cage with me, which takes more guts than posting anonymous comments online.

. . .

Todd is waiting when I pull up outside his house. I'm relieved not to have to go through more questions from his dad about what happened.

He gets into the car with a bottle of Scotch that I guess he boosted from the family liquor cabinet.

"Hey, Dylan, thanks for the ride."

"No problem."

We fist bump.

"Hey, could you put that under the seat or something?" I say.

"Sure." He puts the Scotch down at his feet. "You must be psyched for this."

"I guess."

He twists around in his seat. "You guess? Jenny Moran is totally sucking your dick tonight."

"I don't know about that."

"I'm telling you, man."

I'm hoping we can talk about something else. I've never really been a fan of guys talking about girls like this. I mean I've gone along with it sometimes to fit in, but it creeps me out.

Back when I had a girlfriend, I never told anyone else about what we did together. I always thought it was disrespectful and kind of lame. Guys who talked about every detail of what they did with their girlfriend, or even a girl they just hooked up with, never seemed cool to me. They seemed like jerks. It was the same with people who talked smack about other people behind their back. It said more about them than the person they were talking smack about.

When we get to Jenny Moran's place (which is even bigger than Todd's), her parents are nowhere to be seen and everyone is sitting around the pool. The music's loud and kids are drinking from red Solo cups.

Jack is sitting at a table with a couple of other jocks from our class. He looks pretty blasted. He raises his plastic cup in salute as I walk over with Todd.

"Oh, isn't that sweet, look at the two of you," he says, and already I know this is not going to be good.

Sober Jack is obnoxious, but drunk Jack seems to be even worse.

"Hey, Dylan, is Todd like your girlfriend now? Is that how it works?"

The last thing I want to do is get into another fight, so I just ignore him and walk away, Martese style. Maybe I should get one of those wrist bands. *WWMD*. What Would Martese Do?

"Only kidding, man," he calls after me.

I walk from the pool into the house and end up in the kitchen. Like most parties where someone's parents aren't home, it's pretty jammed. Lots of guys, lots of girls, mostly sophomores but also some juniors and a couple of seniors.

"Yo, Dylan, you want a beer?" some guy from my year, one of the many who ignored me until he saw the latest video, asks.

"No, I'm good."

"Come on, man," he says, trying to press a cup into my hand.

"I can't. I'm driving and I'm training for a competition."

Usually this would be a whole peer-pressure thing, even if you say that you're driving, but as soon as I say competition, he stops trying to push the beer on me. It turns out that the guys like talking about MMA even more than they like talking about alcohol, drugs, or girls.

"Oh yeah?" he says. "That's cool. Like an MMA fight?"

"No, jiujitsu."

I feel a warm hand slip around my waist. I turn to see Jenny.

"You made it," she says. Her eyes are kind of glazed over, she seems pretty drunk. Drunk and flirty. "You want a drink?"

"No, I was just saying I'm in training for a jiujitsu competition down in Long Beach."

"A fight?" she says, her pupils wide. "That's so hot."

If anyone else uttered those exact words, especially the way she said it, I'd bust out laughing. But Jenny saying it while she hangs off me is different.

"Not really a fight. There's no striking."

She puts her arms around my neck, and whispers into my ear. "Come and find me later, okay?"

"Sure," I tell her.

Now I think Todd might be right. But she's already blasted, so by the time later rolls around she'll probably have thrown up or passed out, or both.

Not that I needed it, but I already had a huge lecture from Santana about consent. "It's like the tap, Dylan. You have to respect the tap. When someone taps, that's it. It's over. There's no debate. It's time to get off the mat, pack up, and go home."

I guess in this case, me doing something with Jenny when she was drunk would be like hitting an unconscious opponent. You just don't do it.

I really want to check out what's in the huge fridge and grab something to eat. I already had dinner but I'm still hungry.

"Hey, would you mind if I made myself a sandwich?"

"A sandwich?" she slurs.

"Yeah."

She makes a face. "You're so weird."

As she says it, she looks down at my left leg. It's like someone threw a switch and all of a sudden I know there's no way I'd hook up with her, even if she was stone cold sober and wanted to ride me like a one-legged pony.

The only reason she invited me, the only reason she was hanging off me a few seconds ago, was because I'm the school's flavor of the month. I'm still weird, only now I'm the popular kind of weird, like a passing fad.

I grab a cup, pour some sparking mineral water into it so that people stop trying to force alcohol on me, and head back outside to the pool. If anyone asks, I'll tell them it's vodka.

Outside, I scope the place out to see if I can spot Anna or someone else I can talk to like a regular human being. I don't see her. I doubt she was invited and even if she was, I don't think she'd come. This isn't her scene any more than it is mine.

I figure I'll hang out for a little while longer and then I'll sneak out. My dad, who told me he hates big parties, says it's called an Irish goodbye when you leave without telling anyone, although I have no idea what's Irish about it.

Todd is sitting with Jack and some other guys from the swim team. He's pouring them shots from the bottle of whisky.

It's kind of strange being stone-cold sober at a party where everyone is either drunk, getting drunk, or pretending they are so that they fit in.

"Yo, Dylan! Over here."

Jack waves me over.

"Show us that choke you used on Todd. What was it called?"

"A rear naked choke."

"Hey, Todd, stand up, see if you can get out of it without tapping this time."

Since the fight all Jack's attention has focused on Todd. Every time I walk into the locker room, he's ragging on him. It's relentless. I get now why Todd was the way he was. When I joined the team, he finally saw someone that would take the heat off him.

"I don't think so," I say, pulling up a chair.

"Come on, dude," says Jack.

I shake my head. No can do.

"Okay, okay, but he tapped like a wuss, right?"

I take a deep breath and look from Jack to Todd and back again.

"Fighters tap all the time," I say. "The only people who say things like 'he tapped like a wuss' are people who wouldn't have the guts to get in there themselves."

Some of the other guys let out a nervous laugh.

"I think Dylan just called you out, bro," one of them says.

"No," I say. "I'm not calling anyone out. I'm just saying that Todd had the guts to get in there in the first place, and that's worth respect."

"What's that? Some martial arts code of honor or something?" Jack says.

"It's called not being an asshole."

A couple of the guys crack up. I can see Jack's hands tighten and ball into fists. The way he's looking at me I know he wants to take a swing at me, but he's not going to. And the reason he's not is because he's not sure he could beat me in a fight.

He's taller than me. Heavier too. Stronger.

But BJJ is a leveler. The fact that I know it and he doesn't makes it an even fight. And guys like Jack don't like it when the odds are even.

One of the other guys throws back his whisky and his Dutch courage must kick in because he turns to Jack and says, "You are kind of an asshole sometimes."

"Yeah," says someone else, laughing.

I watch Jack's face. It's almost as if I can see the wheels turning in his mind. He's deciding his next move. His hands unclench and he tilts back in his chair, smiling, playing it off.

"Chill out. I was only joking," he says.

No one believes him. But no one wants a fight ruining the party either.

He slams his cup down on the table in front of Todd. "Gimme some more of that."

Todd dutifully tilts the bottle into Jack's cup and the moment passes. Someone starts talking about the next swim meet and how we're going to be up against our biggest rivals.

I can almost hear Martese's voice in my ear.

We learn to fight so we don't have to fight.

Then I hear Santana's.

Choke him out and throw him in the pool.

I decide to go with Martese.

Forty~Three

MARTESE TELLS me there's no way I'll be allowed to wear my prosthesis in the BJJ competition. There's too much of a risk that I'd catch someone in the face with the metal knee joint.

That leaves me with a big problem—how to start the match. If I start standing up on my good leg it will be really easy for my opponent to sweep my leg out from under me.

"We're going to have to get creative," Martese says as Jared and Santana stand on either side of him, studying me like I'm some kind of live martial arts experiment … which I kind of am.

"It's not all bad news though," says Santana. "He has a weight advantage."

"What do you mean?" Jared asks her.

"He's going to be competing at light featherweight."

I don't understand how this is good news as much as it's just news. "Yeah, but so will everyone else I'm going up against," I say, because that's how it works. You go up against people who weigh the same as you.

"Think about it," says Santana. "How much does your right leg weigh?"

I don't know, I've never really thought about it.

Martese nods. He steps back and now he's staring at my right leg along with Santana and Jared who look like they should be carrying clipboards and wearing white lab coats.

"That's a good point. Nineteen, twenty pounds," says Martese.

"It's not his whole leg," says Santana. "He has the Stump of Justice."

"Okay, fourteen, maybe fifteen then," says Jared.

I still don't get why this is an advantage.

"That's like the difference between light feather and feather," says Santana.

"How does that help?" I ask.

"You're up against light featherweights, but your upper body is that of a featherweight. That's a big advantage, especially if you take top."

I get it now. They're right—upper body-wise I should be bigger and stronger than everyone else. But I'd still have to take a top position, which is going to be hard when I'm starting the fight on one leg.

"Go in," Martese tells Santana who squares up against me on the mat.

Martese walks around us.

"I've got it!" he says.

We all look over at him.

"Combat base," he says, taking a knee next to me.

He shows me what he means, moving me around until I get the position.

"Here, you kneel down, you have your stump on the mat but you keep your right knee off the mat. You balance on your foot and you put your hand down like this to steady yourself."

He waves to Santana to come toward him like they're about to start a match.

"As your opponent comes in, shoot for the takedown."

I see what he's getting at. I'll already be close to the ground and my opponent won't be able to sweep my leg because I won't be standing.

My balance still won't be perfect, but the closer I start to the mat the more stable I'll be.

Santana comes in and Martese pushes off his right foot and grabs her ankle behind the heel, pulling down on the sleeve of her gi with his other hand. Then he brings her down onto the mat. He looks back over his shoulder at me.

"Now it's a scramble, but you knew it was coming, so you'll be ready."

A scramble is when neither person has established a dominant position and they're both trying to get control.

Jared nods.

"What do you think?" he asks Santana.

"Try it," she says to me.

I drop down so that the end of my stump and my left hand are on the mat along with my right foot.

"Tripod," says Jared.

"Precisely," says Martese like some crazy Brazilian jiujitsu scientist.

"I like it," Santana pronounces. "You'll have to keep your right knee up off the mat though, and lift your hand off the mat as you shoot otherwise you won't score for the takedown."

The rules say that you can't score for a takedown if you start from a grounded position, which means you can't have your knees or your hands on the mat when you shoot your shot.

"He won't have his hand on the mat anyway," says Jared. "He'll have to lift it to go for the ankle pick. We're thinking ankle pick, right?"

"Yes," says Martese.

"I dunno," says Santana. "Double leg could work too."

Martese nods. "Just be careful not to get caught with your head to the outside or you can get guillotined."

"Okay," says Santana, "let's start drilling it."

Martese and Jared retreat to the edge of the mats as I work out this new starting position with Santana. The first couple of times I lose my balance and fall to one side. She passes my guard and gets to mount.

If this happens in the actual match, I'm doomed. But if I've learned anything from training it's that you have to be prepared to get stuff wrong before you get it right.

The good thing is that here in the gym, no one cares. It's the same for everyone. Until you get good, you totally suck. Martese will demonstrate something and make it look super easy. Then you try it with your training partner and you can't manage the first part, never mind the whole move. Or you have your arm angled wrong. Or your hips are tilted in the wrong direction. And it doesn't work.

So you drill and drill, and Martese corrects you, and then finally, sometimes weeks after you first tried it, the move clicks and you have it.

But to get there you have to be prepared to fail. You have to deal with a mountain of frustration. Above all you have to be patient with yourself, which can be easier said than done.

After about twenty minutes I must have repeated the move fifty times. I'm still not getting it, but that's okay. I ankle pick Santana maybe twice out of those fifty attempts, but when it happens, I'm so shocked I did it that she quickly pulls me into her guard and it takes her just seconds to triangle choke or arm bar me, or we get into a scramble, which she inevitably wins.

Also, she keeps adjusting how she comes at me. This isn't like some other martial arts where a move will only work if your opponent is predictable.

A fight or a match is chaos.

After about twenty more minutes of this, we take a water break.

"How'd your party go last night?" she asks me.

I give her the highlights, or rather the lowlights. It's good to filter it all through Santana.

She pronounces Jenny 'a bimbo.' She laughs when I tell her about Jack backing down.

"Of course he did. Dude's a coward," she says.

When I tell her about how drunk Todd got, she doesn't say anything, but her expression darkens. I know Santana really doesn't like people who drink or take drugs. I think it has something to do with her family, but I don't want to ask.

Santana is fun and lively and like a cartoon character a lot of the time. But she has dark places that she goes to when she's in the cage. It's like there's a rage churning inside her that she keeps hidden.

"Here's the thing about high school," she says, leaning back against the gym wall. "All the cool people, that's as cool as they'll ever be. High school is like their peak. It's all downhill after that."

"You think?"

"I'm telling you." She taps my good leg. "Come on Stumpy, we're going to work on your baseball bat choke and then I need you to hold pads for me."

"Stumpy?" I say. "You're calling me Stumpy?"

Santana waves her half arm at me.

"Takes one to know one."

CHAPTER

Forty-Four

FOR THE NEXT three weeks my life consists of school, homework, swim training, a therapy session with Rich, and competition training at Resilient. I find out from Santana that Martese making me compete isn't a punishment so much as a requirement.

To be awarded your blue belt, you have to compete at least once. You don't have to win, but you have to get out there and test yourself. And I really want that blue belt more than I've ever wanted anything. Not for the belt itself, but because of what it stands for. Hard work, blood, sweat and tears.

Sometimes at night I lie awake and dream about standing on a podium, a gold medal around my neck, just having won my division. People don't usually win their first competition but it has to be possible, right?

If I can just score the takedown and take a top position, then I'll have the advantage. The idea that my one leg gives me an edge makes me feel almost giddy, like I have a secret that no one else knows.

After training as we're sitting on the mats, our gis so soaked that you could wring the sweat out of them, I ask Santana what she thinks. "Can I win?"

She looks at me like I just got hit in the head.

"What's the point of competing if you don't think you can win?"

I lie back and look at the ceiling. "That would be crazy though, right? I mean, if I could actually win."

"Why?" she asks me.

"Because, you know, the one leg thing,'" I say.

She chews this over for a moment.

"No one is going to be expecting to start against someone who's in combat base. They're probably all preparing for something else. You'll have the element of surprise."

"So, I could win? I could take gold?"

I can tell from her tone that she's eye rolling me. "What did I just say? Why compete if you don't believe you can win?"

I sit up. Now I'm kind of obsessed with the idea. I can see it in my mind's eye. The whole stadium going crazy as match by match I work my way through the division to a triumphant performance in the final.

"You don't think they'll go easy on me, do you? I don't want to win because someone feels sorry for me."

I don't think I've ever seen Santana laugh as hard as she does now. Her whole body shakes. She has to get up and walk to the wall and then come back, tears streaming down her face, snot coming out of her nose, and she goes into full blown hysterical laughter.

"Yeah, because that's going to happen in a jiujitsu match," she eventually says.

I don't see it as all that funny. I mean, someone might not want to beat up on a kid with one leg. Even if it made them hesitate, just a little bit, that might be all the advantage I'd need.

"It could," I point out.

She settles down and stops laughing.

"Oh, you poor, dumb, one-legged child. That's not how this works. Believe me. Someone sees you hop onto that mat they're not thinking, I'll give this guy a break. They're thinking, I don't want to lose to someone with one leg. Every single fight I've been in, my opponent goes even harder than they would normally. It's just human nature."

I guess she's right. "It was just a thought."

"Yeah, well, forget thoughts like that. No one is going to give you or me jack. You want to win? You're going to have to earn it. When I walk into that cage no one's seeing a future UFC champion. Either they see a freak, or they see some 'inspirational story' they can pat on the head," she says, air-quoting the *inspirational story* part.

"You want gold, you're going to have to take it. Just like everyone else. There's no shortcuts, no free passes, no special treatment. It's you and whoever's standing across from you, and that's how it should be. That's what makes this worth doing. Fighting is honest. It's the truth."

Forty-Five

I DISCOVER who my first opponent is the day before the competition. And when I say discover, I mean sit at school obsessively refreshing the competition website to see if the brackets have been released. Finally, in the middle of AP History, they are.

But as I'm scrolling down to see who it is, I hear the teacher clearing his throat and look up to see him staring at me. He walks to my desk and puts his hand out for my cell phone. My agony just got extended until the end of the day.

One of the kids sitting next to me, a surfer with long hair who seems like he's perpetually stoned, leans toward me.

"Yo, you should choke him out for taking your phone like that."

This has become a recurring theme with a couple of kids at school. Ever since the video of me beating Todd went briefly viral, some of them see me as some potential one-legged Chuck Norris vigilante type who should never take any crap.

I've tried explaining the phrase *learning to fight so you don't have to fight* to them, but they just look at me, disappointed.

At the end of the day I finally get my phone back and pull up the information.

The guy I'm up against first is called Ricardo Berardeli and he trains at one of the gyms in San Diego. I click on his name and see that he's competed a couple of times before. He has one win by submission and one loss on points.

I should leave it there. Both Martese and Santana have told me it's a bad idea to Google an opponent in a jits match. But now that I have the name it's like an itch I have to scratch, and I start Googling.

I don't find any videos of his previous matches, but I do find him on Instagram. He looks kind of skinny, and I instantly start to feel better as I remember what Martese said about me having an advantage competing at light featherweight.

I'm definitely bigger than this guy when it comes to upper body. Stronger too. All I have to do is get that takedown, get him to the mat and keep him there, and then not do anything stupid.

It's weird because BJJ is all about beating someone who's bigger and stronger than you, but both those things are still an advantage, assuming both of you have some training.

If your opponent isn't trained, you have a huge advantage. I already know that from my rematch with Todd. But if they are, you're looking for any edge you can find.

I drift through my classes then swim practice. Normally I'd be at Resilient on a Friday night, doing class and rolling afterward. But with the competition the next day I'm supposed to rest.

All I can think about is tomorrow and competing. I can feel my nerves starting to kick in. For the first time ever, I wish I had a session scheduled with Rich. A therapist is supposed to be able to help with nerves, right?

I should have asked him at our session on Monday. I did mention the competition, but all he asked me about was the same thing he always does, how I'm feeling.

I don't know what to tell him. I feel fine. Okay, maybe not fine. I still have the old one-leg situation going on, but school's okay. No one's going out of their way to make my life miserable, and my grades are good. Best of all Anna's talking to me again. I guess she heard about me sticking up for Todd or something, because now we eat lunch together most days.

Anyway, when I tell Rich that life's fine, he looks at me like he doesn't quite believe me and says, "That's great. I'm happy to hear it. But just be aware that adjusting to something like this is a process. Right now, you might be on an upswing but that doesn't mean there won't be more challenges."

Yeah, no kidding. I've got at least three or four matches to win before I even reach the final of the competition in Long Beach, and everyone I'll have to beat has one more leg than I do.

Wanna talk about a challenge, Rich baby? Try getting the timing right so you can ankle pick someone without getting guillotined. *That's* a challenge.

Forty-Six

DAD'S DRIVING me down to Long Beach. Mom said she'd be too nervous to watch, so she's staying at home and Dad's going to livestream it for her.

The drive takes a couple of hours and Dad doesn't say much on the way down. We listen to music, and I munch on a banana for energy and drink Gatorade to stay hydrated.

As the miles roll by, my nerves, which were already bad, get worse. Part of me hopes that we run into some traffic and end up getting there late, and I miss my weigh in. But it's early on a Saturday and we make good time.

I don't know how I can be so nervous when I just had a real fight. Then I remember that I had no idea Jack was filming it. I didn't want to lose but it wasn't like there were hundreds of people watching me. It wasn't like Jack and Todd hadn't seen me without my prosthetic on before.

We get to the venue, this huge sports complex, and my dad parks. He switches off the engine and looks over at me.

"Hey, I'm really proud of you, okay?"

I guess I should appreciate this special father-son moment and on one level I do. But as I look at people streaming inside, a lot of them in

BJJ gear or with the name of their gyms emblazoned across their T-shirts, all I can think is that I really wish that old Dylan hadn't agreed to this.

Inside, the venue is basically a huge gymnasium with bleachers along one wall. Barriers are set up around eight mat areas that are arranged into two sets of four. Next to each mat is a table where people record the points score for each fighter.

You can win a match by submission if your opponent taps or you choke them unconscious. Martese told me it's important not to talk or make any other noise (like yelling *ow*) because the referee can consider that a verbal tap.

For the most part though, matches are decided by points, or advantages. The number of points is meant to reflect how important getting to each position would be in a real fight. So things like getting to mount and taking someone's back and getting a takedown all score between two and four points. The referee can also award an advantage for attempting a submission or getting close to something but not quite pulling it off.

At the far end is the bull pen, where you have to wait before you're called down to the mat to take part in your match. Next to that is an area where you have weigh in and have your gi checked to make sure it meets requirements.

There are also big screens that show the order of the matches arranged by mat. When your match is highlighted, you have to go to the bullpen and wait to be called.

At the other end of the room is a small warm-up area.

People mill around drinking water or listening to music. Some people are already sitting in the bleachers with teammates or friends and family who have come along to watch.

I spot Santana and I point her out to my dad, who is super excited to meet her.

We walk over to say hi. I just hope he's not going to say anything dumb, like he thinks she's brave because of the whole arm thing.

He nudges me. "Should I shake her hand, or would that be considered rude?"

That's another thing people do now. They assume that because I have one leg, I'm some kind of disability-etiquette expert. Most of the time I'm just as clueless as everyone else. Like, we have a couple of kids with autism at school and I literally have no idea about any of that stuff. The only difference now is that I'm kind of embarrassed that before my accident I avoided people like that because someone who was different made me uncomfortable.

"Just be normal," I whisper, which in my dad's case is pretty much impossible.

"Hey," he says doing a hand wave thing at Santana as we get closer. "I'm Mike, Dylan's dad."

Santana puts out her hand to fist bump him. But he goes to shake, then realizes she's going for a fist bump and it's awkward.

He's also doing that thing of trying so hard to not look at her stump that he just looks weird.

"Hey, Mike," she says, and thankfully seems kind of amused.

"Are you fighting today?" he asks her.

"No, but I am competing."

MMA fighters get kind of touchy when people talk about a jiujitsu match being a fight.

"Right, of course," says my dad. "You know I did some boxing when I was younger. And Aikido."

Now Santana grins. Aikido is kind of a running joke in MMA gyms. Santana calls it Bullshido and there are a bunch of videos online of Aikido masters being mauled by BJJ players and wrestlers.

"Why don't you come in and try some jits?" she says. Then she leans in and pats his stomach. "It's a great way to get rid of the old love handles. We could turn you into a BJJ beefcake like Dylan here."

I have to bite down on my lower lip to keep from laughing.

"That sounds great. It kind of creeps up on you," he says looking down at his stomach. "Listen, Dylan, I'm going to let you guys go prepare or whatever it is you do. I'll be up in the bleachers if you need me."

As he wanders off, I turn back to Santana.

"BJJ beefcake?"

"Don't get too excited, I'm still really gay. How you feeling?"

"Like I might throw up."

She cracks up laughing. "Yup. First comp is really rough for nerves. Don't worry, they calm down once you have a few more under your belt."

"So how many comps before you started to feel calm?"

"Let me see." She tilts her head back, like she's counting. "Maybe two-stripe blue belt, so what was that? Twenty comps."

"Twenty?"

"What, should I just lie to you? Maybe it's not a fight, but the other guy is still going to try to choke the shit out of you or break your arm. But, hey, that's what you're trying to do to him, so it's all good."

This is not reassuring. Now I do really feel like throwing up.

"Just focus on the game plan. Combat base. Shoot for the take-down. Pass his legs, take top and if you can dish out a serious injury or get him to tap then all the better."

As she's saying this, I see a big guy lying on the mat writhing in pain, holding his knee. His opponent, another big guy, is standing next to him looking apologetic as the referee waves his hand in the air and shouts, "Medic!"

A couple of EMTs jog down the edge of the mats toward them.

"Relax, dude," says Santana. "Knee injuries are common at comps and you only have half the odds of that happening."

Forty-Seven

I DON'T KNOW if Santana was trying some reverse psychology or if she was just being an asshole. Either way she's done nothing to calm my nerves.

I retreat to one of the locker rooms and change. I strip off my regular clothes and put my gi with its one-and-a-half pant legs on. I had the pant leg on the left side cut off so that I can remove my prosthetic without having to take the pants off completely.

I usually wear a rash guard under the gi jacket but this time I leave it off. I'm sure I'm under the weight I need to be, but I figure that every ounce helps. As I'm putting on my belt, the door crashes open and this guy stomps in. He takes off his belt and gi jacket and throws them on the floor, then he starts cursing up a storm.

There are maybe ten people in there with us but no one asks him if he's okay. He's clearly not. And no one asks him what happened because we can all guess what happened. He lost, and losing sucks.

I throw on slides and pick up my phone, driver's license, mouth guard, and water bottle before heading back out. Checking the screens for Mat 4, I see that there are six matches ahead of me. The knot in my stomach tightens more.

It's weird, I don't think I've ever been this nervous about anything before. Not taking a test or going to the dentist. Not even either of the times I got into it with Todd.

Martese spots me and walks over with a couple of guys from the gym.

"Hey, Dylan, you feel good?"

I don't, but there's something about seeing him that does make me feel a little bit better.

"Listen, it's your first competition so no pressure. Just go out there and execute the plan. I'm going to be cornering you from the side."

The sense of relief I had a second ago fades. He'll be there, watching me, with Santana and everyone else. What if I totally screw up? I could get subbed in the first few seconds, which does happen. The match starts and *boom*, someone hits a flying arm bar and you're done.

That would be totally humiliating.

One of the other guys from Resilient, a purple belt, comes over to us from the bank of monitors.

"Santana's up next."

We follow him down the barrier to Mat 3, where Santana is already waiting at the table, bouncing up and down on the balls of her feet as her opponent stands on the other side. They're waiting for the match that's on the mat to finish.

I squeeze in at the barrier next to Jared, happy to have something to take my mind off my own match.

The match finishes, the referee raises the winner's hand, and then he calls Santana and her opponent onto the mat. They shake hands and move back. The referee chops the air as he says "Combache!" and it starts.

Santana drops down into a crouch and circles her opponent to the outside. After a few seconds of tentative circling, her opponent shoots for a takedown. At the same time, Santana drops down and pulls guard, wrapping her thighs around her opponent's waist.

There's a sudden flurry of activity as her opponent attempts to stand. Santana changes angles, hooks her opponent's ankle with her hand, and sweeps her backward.

Everyone from Resilient cheers.

"Pass guard!" Martese yells. "Yes, yes, now push her leg down, get to mount."

Even though they're both purple belts and the same weight, Santana is just way too good, not to mention strong. She passes from half guard into mount, cross faces her opponent by sliding her stump under the back of her head, then swiftly puts her good arm across her throat, grabs her own floppy gi sleeve and Ezekiel chokes her.

Her opponent taps. Santana stands up, then helps her opponent back to her feet. They hug and stand either on side of the referee while the ref raises Santana's arm.

Santana jogs over to everyone from Resilient at the barrier. First she hugs Martese, then Jared, me next, and then everyone else.

She has another match in a few minutes, so she heads back to the holding pen to wait. I look up at the screens and see that there are only four more matches on my mat before I'm up.

I swallow hard. This is it. Time to go weigh in. In twenty minutes, maybe a lot less depending on how fast the other matches go, it's going to be my turn.

I still feel like I could throw up.

CHAPTER
Forty-Eight

"ONE HUNDRED AND FORTY-SIX POUNDS. You're competing at light featherweight, right?"

Wait. What?

I look from the person in charge of checking everyone's weight—an older bald guy with a big white beard—to the display. He's right. That's what it says.

And the upper weight limit for light feather is a hundred and forty-one. I'm five pounds over, which means an automatic disqualification.

It hits me. Duh! I still have my prosthetic leg on.

I'm so nervous that I forgot to take it off before I got onto the scale.

"Hang on," I say, getting off the scale and quickly hitting the release button and sliding my stump out of the socket. I wobble a bit as I stand on one leg, lay down my prosthesis, and hop back onto the scale.

"Sorry," I say. "Forgot I still had it on."

A lot of people might freak out, or not let me weigh in again, but he doesn't seem phased.

"Guess that's one way to do a last-minute weight cut," he says. "You're all set. Good luck."

"Thanks," I say, handing over my ID to be checked before jamming my leg back on and walking through to the bullpen where a dozen or so competitors are waiting to be called down to the mat for their match. I look around to see if I can spot Ricardo, the guy I'm up against, but none of the guys in the pen look like the pictures I saw online.

Maybe he hasn't shown up yet. Maybe he got injured at the last minute. Or his car broke down.

The thought that he's not here and I'll win by walkover cheers me up. Then I turn and see a guy who looks just like the profile picture on social media walk into the pen behind me.

My nerves are back, even more dialed up than they were before. But there's nothing I can do now.

I sneak another glance at him. He's jogging in place, trying to stay warm.

I look at his belt. Four stripes. The most you can have before you get promoted to blue belt.

Okay, Dylan, stop psyching yourself out. I sit down, close my eyes, and try to focus on my breathing. I do the breathing exercises just like Santana showed me. Thirty deep breaths in, hold for as long as I can, take another deep breath and hold for a count of fifteen.

It works. Kind of.

I'd still rather be at home. I still hate old Dylan who signed me up. But I do feel calmer.

Combat base. Takedown. Pass guard. Take top.

I repeat it over and over in my head, like a mantra.

You can do this. Come on. I get my self-talk going.

"Ricardo Bardeli?"

I open my eyes and a girl with a clipboard is looking around the bullpen. She'll take us down to the mat.

I was right. The guy I thought was Ricardo walks over to her. She looks around again, "Dylan?"

My hand shoots up like I'm in class.

"Yeah, that's me," I say, trying to make my voice sound deep.

"Okay guys, Mat 4."

We follow her out of the pen and down the side of the barriers behind the desks to the mat at the far end. There's a match still going on.

I hear Martese's voice and turn to see him and Santana leaning over the barrier. I walk over and he grasps my hand.

"You ready?"

"Yeah," I lie.

"Great. Go do what we talked about. You got this!"

It helps. If Martese Terra says I've got this, who am I to argue? I might only be a dumb white belt but he's a legend.

I got this, I tell myself as the other match finishes up. I take my mouth guard out of its case and pop it in over my top teeth. I sit down to take off my prosthesis. I'm half waiting for someone to say something about it, but no one does. I know there aren't any rules against me competing. Some competitions even have whole para divisions but according to Martese, it's still not all that common.

The referee walks over to the score table. He's a chubby little guy with slicked-back, black hair.

He does a bit of a doubletake when he sees my missing leg but doesn't say anything apart from, "Ready?" to each of us in turn.

My heart pounds as I say yes and hop onto the mat. I shake hands with the referee and then Ricardo. We both back off, leaving the center of the mat to the referee. He asks us again if we're ready. I nod and then he says "Combache!" and steps out of the way.

Suddenly my vision narrows. I hear Martese shouting from behind the barrier, but it's muffled, like I'm underwater.

My mouth goes dry. Completely and utterly dry. My throat tightens and everything takes on a surreal quality, like I'm here … but not really.

I almost forget to crouch down into combat base. For a second my hand drops to the mat to steady myself. My opponent circles me but he doesn't close the distance.

He moves cautiously to my outside. I move as best as I can toward him, but he backs off.

We rinse and repeat. I move in, he circles out and away, keeping a good three feet from me.

I move in again. I keep waiting for him to rush me because if he does, he might catch me off balance. If he times it right, he could probably just push me over.

He doesn't. I move in. He circles to the outside and backs off.

An eternity passes. He's almost at the very edge of the mat. I back up as he looks over to his coach. He looks confused, like he doesn't know what he should do, and maybe even a little scared.

His fear is my confidence. He can't stay backing off for the full five minutes. He'll lose if he does that.

I keep going forward, basing my hand on the mat, and scooting forward, staying low. Finally he gets within range. As fast as I can, I close the distance, grab his sleeve, and shoot for his lead ankle.

Just as my hand closes around his ankle, the referee's arm comes in between us.

I look up at the ref, waiting for him to say something. I don't get it —I had a grip, I was mid-shot. I look at the referee for some kind of explanation of why he just stopped the match, but he's walking off the mat at top speed.

CHAPTER
Forty-Nine

I STAND UP, so does Ricardo. We don't say anything to each other. He looks as confused as I do.

I look over to Martese. He's asking me what happened, but I don't know. I was hoping he was going to tell me. Ricardo walks to the edge of the mat. I hop over to speak with Martese and Santana.

Other matches are still going on, but it seems like everyone spectating is looking over at our mat. A couple of tournament photographers appear, lenses pointed toward me.

I can see the referee down by the weigh-in area. He's talking to a guy in a suit who I think is the head referee for the tournament, like you have in tennis. He's gesturing as he crouches down. I have a sudden sinking feeling this is about my starting in combat base, but I don't see how it can be a problem.

When I shot for the takedown, my good knee was off the mat and the hand I'd been using to base had a grip on Ricardo's sleeve. The only parts of my body touching the mat were my foot and the end of my stump.

Another minute passes as he talks to the tournament referee. Both of them keep looking down toward the mat. Ricardo is talking to his coach who's demonstrating what looks like a guillotine. I make a note to keep my head inside so he can't get me with that one.

I'm deflated. I had the ankle pick right there.

It wasn't my fault that my opponent wouldn't engage.

The conversation between the referees wraps up. He speed-walks back to the mat, his head down. Martese calls out to him in Portuguese but the referee just motors past him and back onto the mat.

He motions for me and Ricardo to stand next to him.

He signals a penalty for Ricardo. It must be for backing off. I still don't get why he would have stopped the match though. I can't exactly reset mid-takedown.

He signals again, this time it's a penalty against me. Someone in the crowd boos. I can hear Martese shouting again in Portuguese. Santana yells too. "How can that be a penalty?"

The referee turns to me. "You were grounded. You can't shoot from that position. You can pull guard or you can start standing."

I don't believe it. With a couple of sentences my whole game plan has just been tossed out the window. If I sit down and pull guard, I'm toast—Ricardo will just pass on my left side. If I start standing, it's leg-sweep city. I haven't even prepped any takedowns from standing. I can try to level change from the outside and shoot, but that's about it.

But he's the referee. He makes the rules. Or interprets them, anyway.

He looks at me. "Okay?"

What am I supposed to say? This is my first tournament.

I had a split second of elation as I timed and shot. Now I'm back to square one, only worse. Way worse.

I feel sick. Not with nerves, but with the whole deal.

Screw it. I'll start standing.

We reset and I stay upright. I look at Ricardo. He doesn't look uncertain anymore. Far from it. Now he looks like he's loving life.

"Combache!"

The referee's hand chops through the air.

This time there's no hesitancy from my opponent. He rushes in and takes grips.

CHAPTER
Fifty

LESS THAN A MINUTE later the referee raises Ricardo's hand as I struggle to keep my balance, my calf muscle aching. The tournament photographers crowd the barrier, capturing my humiliation.

Leg sweep. Just like the Karate Kid, only this Karate Kid was already down to one functioning leg by the time the match started.

We turn around so the referee can show the winner to the other side of the arena. Finally it's all done. I hop off to the side and sit down to put my prosthetic back on.

I know Martese and Santana and the rest of the Resilient squad are standing at the barrier. I know I'll have to speak to them, even though I don't want to. I try to delay it as long as I can.

I knew I might lose. But this was way worse than losing. I feel like I've been cheated.

Behind me I can hear Martese talking to the referee in Portuguese. Martese isn't screaming or shouting, that's not his style, but I can tell he's angry. Way angrier than he was when he found out about Santana organizing the after-hours fight between Todd and me.

Santana jumps the barrier, catching a few looks before people see who it is and look away again. She comes over to me.

"What did he say to you?" she asks.

I tell her.

"Those aren't the rules. You didn't have a knee on the mat. That guy doesn't know what he's talking about."

I know she means well. I also know she's right, but I don't care. I just want to get out of here, away from people staring at me. Away from people feeling sorry for me.

I wanted my photograph to be taken today because I'd won, not because my match was stopped midway through because the ref thought I had a knee when I didn't.

I'm not even that mad at him. Not really. It is what it is. I don't care. If they didn't want me to compete in their tournament, which is what it feels like now, they should have stopped me when I weighed in instead of pulling some dumb interpretation of the rules out of their asses.

Or maybe if my opponent hadn't spent the first thirty seconds backing off and refusing to engage it wouldn't have been stopped at all. By the time we reset and I was standing, my head was pretty much gone. I knew I was going to lose, and I did.

I don't mind losing. I just didn't want to lose like that.

"Whatever," I say with a shrug, clicking my leg on and standing up.

I do the walk of shame back down along the mats. I get to the end and squeeze through the barrier, no longer a competitor. Dad is waiting for me.

There are lots of good things about my dad, and one of them is that he knows when I want to talk and when I don't. He pats me on the back and squeezes my shoulder.

"What do you want to do?" he asks me. "Hang out or go home? I'm good either way."

"Can we go home?"

Someone else might say I should stay and support the rest of the team. Or that I should suck it up. But he gets it. He can see this is about more than losing. I've lost plenty of swimming events, and other stuff too. But I've always taken it in my stride.

I don't even know why this feels different. It just does. Maybe because I thought this would be my thing. That I'd be able to compete, even if I didn't win.

"You wanna go straight to the car or you want to get changed?"

I still have my gi on.

"I'll get changed."

"Okay, see you out front in five."

I start walking toward to the locker room, then stop. I walk back over to Martese. After all the work he and everyone else did to help me prepare, I should at least let them know I'm leaving.

"I'm going to go," I tell him.

"Okay," he nods. "Listen, I think that decision was way off. I'm going to speak to the tournament director."

I shrug. "It's okay."

I mean it. Right now, I don't see myself competing again. It's like I left all the energy and enthusiasm I had back on that mat.

"See you at training? We can work on some other ways for you to start."

The ride home is quiet. Dad lets me stew.

I stare out the window. By the time we're back on the freeway, I start to feel embarrassed for leaving so soon. Maybe I overreacted. But I can't help feeling like someone's kicked me in the guts.

I know it's stupid to feel like this. People lose, life isn't fair—I get all that. I know I should toughen up. But understanding that doesn't seem to be helping. All the insecurities and anxieties and everything else are bubbling up inside me again.

Okay, I beat up Todd. But what was I doing thinking that I could beat someone with the same skills and two legs?

As we get closer to home, Dad looks over at me.

"It's up to you, but maybe take a break from the gym. You've been doing a lot."

Normally I'd get angry at the suggestion. I'd say no way, I'm going back at Resilient on Monday night, working with Santana to find another way to start a match. That BJJ is all about adapting. If one way doesn't work, then you find another.

But I don't say any of that. I don't have it in me to argue. Maybe he's right.

"Yeah, maybe I should."

Something hits me. Rich is going to *love* this. I can hear him now.

"How did that make you feel, Dylan?"

When we get home, Dad goes in first. By the time I walk in, I guess he's already told Mom it didn't go well because she doesn't ask me if I won. She just tells me that we're ordering Chinese food for dinner and asks if she should get my usual favorites.

I go to my room, open the closet and throw my Resilient training bag in the back, and close the door again. Then I go take a shower.

I stand there, the water beating down on me and tears streaming down my face, not even really sure why I'm crying except for the fact that it's all too much. I can pretend that it's not, but it is.

I look down at my stump and the space beyond it where my leg used to be. This is it. This is how I am. Nothing's going to change it.

I'm never going to be normal. I'll never be a regular guy. And who's going to love me when I look like this? I should face it. I'm a freak.

When the water starts to turn cold, I get out and towel off. My phone flashes with messages. I sit on the edge of my bed and stare at the screen, a towel wrapped around my waist.

A couple of people from school, including Todd, want to know how the competition went. There's a message from Santana asking if I'm okay and a picture of her standing on the podium with a gold medal.

I message her back with congratulations and tell her I'm okay.

She replies immediately, asking if I'll be at training on Monday.

I don't reply.

There's a message from Martese that says:

Hey Dylan, today wasn't your day, but there will be other days.

Below that he's written out this quote:

It is not the critic who counts; not the man who points out how the strong man stumbles, or where the doer of deeds could have done them better. The credit belongs to the man who is actually in the arena, whose face is marred by dust and sweat and blood; who strives valiantly; who errs, who comes short again and again, because there is no effort without error and shortcoming; but who does actually strive to do the deeds; who knows great enthusiasms, the great devotions; who spends himself in a worthy cause; who at the best knows in the end the triumph of high achievement, and who at the worst, if he fails, at least fails while daring greatly, so that his place shall never be with those cold and timid souls who neither know victory nor defeat.

Theodore Roosevelt

I don't know about daring greatly. I sure lost greatly.

I DON'T SEE Santana on Monday. Or any other day this week. My gi sits in my training bag in the back of my closet.

Martese messages me to ask why he hasn't seen at the gym. So does Santana. I tell them I'm taking a break. Just a week or two. Lick my wounds. Try to get my mojo back.

The truth is I don't know if I'll ever go back. As the training sessions I've missed start to stack up, walking back in to Resilient seems harder.

I didn't just lose. I lost and then I quit.

Teddy Roosevelt would have been straight back on the mats. But I'm not. I dared greatly. I lost greatly. Then I ran home and punked out.

I find a new rhythm to my days. I go to school and I swim. I come home and I watch Netflix or study for the SAT.

The week after I lost at the competition, I go to see Rich. Rather than being happy I've quit training, he seems kind of disappointed. He actually suggests I make a list of the good things about Brazilian jiujitsu.

"That should be easy, given how much you seem to love it," he says, smiling.

I guess I did go through a phase, when I first started training, that BJJ was the only thing I talked about. Santana used to joke that jiujitsu people were worse than vegans. You know, that joke about how do you know someone is vegan? Because they won't freaking stop telling you.

I promise to do the list then promptly forget about it. The next swim meet is coming up and now that Todd is back on the relay team, I think we might have a shot at getting a first-place win.

Things with the team have settled down. Jack is still an asshole, but now he's a quiet asshole.

Now that kids see that I don't have a problem with Todd, they've laid off him, which is good. I know they say that sometimes people who've been bullied can turn into bullies, but I never wanted to be like that.

Sometimes a kid at school will say something about my leg but I think by now everyone's kind of used to seeing me around so it's not a big deal. Don't get me wrong, I'm still self-conscious about it, especially around girls, but a lot of the time I don't think about it.

In a weird way, I think completely freaking out after the competition and sobbing in the shower helped. I know guys aren't supposed to cry and I know a lot of what I was thinking didn't make sense, but I felt better afterward. It's like when there's all this heat and humidity in the air and then there's a big thunderstorm and once it's passed everything is fresh and clear again and you can breathe.

The night before the next swim meet, I get a message from Santana.

"Dude, are you really going to quit because of one lousy referee decision at a dumb jits competition?"

I think of a dozen replies that I don't send.

Lying in bed, I can't get Santana's question out of my mind. Is that really why I haven't been back to training? Because something didn't go my way? Because the going got tough?

A few minutes later I reach for my phone, delete her message, and switch it to airplane mode. I need to get some sleep. Tomorrow's the swim meet and Coach wants us there early so he can tell us who's swimming what races.

He already took me to the side and told me to relax and just enjoy the event, which I hope means I'm not going to be swimming. I think he's finally realized that if I keep competing, the team has zero shot at winning.

Fifty~Two

COACH READS through the order of the meet and who's swimming what races. He checks the names off as he goes. I tune out about halfway through but then I hear, "fifty meter butterfly, Jack and Dylan."

He's got to be kidding. I'm not completely terrible at butterfly, but I'm not the best, not even second best. Jack is the strongest and I'm a good two seconds behind him over fifty and that's a canyon of time in a race that can come down to tenths of a second.

The other guys on the team look at each other. They must be thinking the same thing I am. Coach picks up on it too.

"Hey, now, let's not get ahead of ourselves here. I've spoken with the coaches from the other teams and we've agreed that because Dylan has a disadvantage, he's going to get a head start."

I hang my head and stare at the floor tiles. I'd rather lose by a full length of the pool than have a head start.

"Dylan, you're going to have a three second jump. I'll signal you first, then the whistle will sound three seconds later."

I can't believe this. It's awful. It's humiliating. Oh, let the poor little kid with one leg have a head start. I know that Coach thinks he's doing me a favor, but I have to say something.

"Coach, I really appreciate it, but—"

I feel a sudden jab in the ribs. It's Todd, and he's glaring at me. He leans in.

"It's lame, but we need the points, dude. Three seconds means you and Jack will be one and two. That pretty much guarantees the meet if we win the relays."

He's right. I'm slow, but I'm not three seconds slow. With that kind of start, and I go all out, I might even beat Jack.

Coach is staring at me. He's not exactly the most even tempered of guys so I can't imagine turning down his offer would go down all that well.

"Yes, Dylan?"

I look over at Jack. He's glaring at me. "It would be nice to win a few more meets this year," he says.

Public humiliation, or back to being an outcast—it's not much of a choice.

I bite down on my lip. Jack has a point. The team hasn't won all year because of me. Today I can change that. Not in a way I want to, but I can.

Todd leans in again. "Come on, Dylan. For the team."

"Okay," I say, finally.

"Great," says Coach. "That's settled."

I tune out again as he reads the relays. I guess I could ignore his signal, or hesitate until the whistle blows. But I've agreed, I've given my word.

As much as I hate everything about this, I'll swim as hard as I can. I'll get that first place. Not for me, for the team. But then I'm done. That's the promise I'm making to myself. I'll do it but I won't swim for the school again. I don't care what Mom and Dad say, I'd rather be an object of ridicule than pity. I'd rather lose than be handed a win.

I don't hear Coach's speech before we huddle up and put our hands in for the *win on three, win on me*. The words die on my lips.

As everyone starts to filter out of the locker room, Coach comes over to me.

"This took a lot of persuasion on my part, Dylan. A thank you wouldn't kill you, son."

"Thanks, Coach," I say, hating myself even more.

Fifty-Three

AS I'M on the starting block, I look over and see Anna. She smiles and waves. Damn, she's cute. I look away, trying to stay focused.

I wish I wasn't wearing speedos, and I hope this race starts in the next few seconds, because I really need to be in cold water sooner rather than later.

Thankfully, Coach gives me the signal. I dive off the block, my entry as smooth as I can make it. I kick hard, my arms straight out in front of me. I break the surface and settle into my stroke.

I hear the whistle and push on, losing myself in the rhythm of the stroke. I focus on my breathing. Any negative thoughts that come up, I shove to the back of my mind.

My body is in the water, but my mind is back on the mats. As my muscles start to ache, as the lactic acid starts to burn and my lungs feel like they'll burst, I keep going, finding comfort in my body's discomfort.

Keeping my head low I grit my teeth, willing myself through the water.

Just get to the end, I tell myself. Give everything. Empty the tank.

Work. Work harder. Find the reserve. Discover your rhythm.

You will not lose. You will not allow yourself to lose. No one will catch you.

I'm tiring, but I refuse to allow myself to slow.

I keep going.

Finally I touch the wall. My head snaps from one side of the lane to the other. I'm first home—I won. I can hear wild cheering. It sounds hollow to my ears. I put my head back under the surface where the sounds are muffled by the water and stay there until I finally have to come back up for air.

I won, but I feel empty.

Everyone else is so happy that the team has won so I do my best to plaster on a smile. Ever since the accident I've done that a lot—forced myself to smile so someone else doesn't feel bad. It's a lot harder than you would think. And this time it's really hard.

I think of Santana for a second. She would have refused the start. She would have waited. Or if by some chance she had agreed and won, she wouldn't have stood here grinning like an idiot.

With her, what you see is what you get. That's how she seems to me anyway.

Mom comes over and gives me a big hug.

"You were amazing," she says.

My time was a personal best. It would have been something to be proud of without the three second start. But then I would have come close to last, and the team would have lost the meet.

"I'm kind of tired. Do you mind if we go?"

"Oh no, sweetie, of course not."

We're just about to leave when I see Todd's parents and they're making a beeline for me.

"There he is," says Todd's dad to my parents. "Your son is one hell of a guy." He turns to me, "Great race, buddy."

"This is Todd's mom and dad," I say quickly.

"Oh, right," says my dad. "Great."

My mom stiffens. All she knows is that Todd was the classmate who was the one in the video who was punching me in the face my first week of school. I might have mentioned that we get on okay since then, and he did apologize, but parents, moms especially, don't let that stuff go.

Todd's mom and dad also look kind of awkward. I guess because most adults don't go around punching each other in the face and it makes for an uncomfortable social interaction when their kids do.

They do the usual 'nice to meet you,' saying their names stuff and then Todd's dad says to me, "One hell of a performance, Dylan."

"Thanks."

"I'm glad to see these two guys getting on," he goes on. "You know Dylan here really saved Todd the night they both got jumped."

My heart sinks as Mom looks at me. She's about to ask what the hell Todd's dad is talking about but my dad touches her arm.

"He sure did," my dad says to Todd's parents. "I'll bring you up to speed in the car," he says to my mom.

"Yes, you will," she says, shooting both me and Dad a frosty look.

"Oh, sorry," says Todd's dad. "I wasn't aware you didn't know. But it's not like they started it. Dylan here was just standing up for his friend."

"Honey, we should probably get going. We have that thing later, remember?" says Todd's mom, riding to the rescue.

"Right. Right," says Todd's dad. "Hey, good to meet you. Well done again, Dylan."

"Thanks," I say as I spot Anna over by the pool. "I'll be right back, okay?" I tell my parents, then walk over to Anna.

"I didn't think you came to the swim meets," I say to her.

"I don't," she says, a little awkwardly. "Great win."

I shrug. "I had a pretty decent start."

"Well, I thought you were amazing. Congratulations." She shifts on to her tiptoes and kisses me on the cheek.

Woah, where did that come from? I am so glad I've changed out of my speedos and that I have a long hoodie on because I'm totally getting a boner.

"Thanks," I tell her. "Hey, I gotta go. See you on Monday?"

"Sure," she says.

I yank the bottom of my hoodie down and hurry away before she notices. When I glance back over my shoulder, she's still standing there with a big smile on her face. She looks down at her own hoodie, then looks at me and tugs hers down over her jeans, giggling.

Oh my God, she noticed my boner. I want to go back and tell her that sometimes a guy's junk runs on autopilot, but that would just make things even more awkward.

I tug my hoodie down again and head for the exit as fast as I can before anyone else notices. What is it with me and stumps?

Fifty~Four

MOM WAITS until we're driving home before she mentions the conversation with Todd's parents.

"Was that the night you came home with a black eye and told us you got it helping Santana train?" she asks me.

"Yeah, but we didn't get jumped so there's nothing to worry about."

Apparently, this is not the right thing to say. Mom's mouth opens, then closes again. Her face goes red, and she looks like she's about to have a complete freakout.

I start to explain, but Dad cuts me off with a 'let me take this one' look.

He tells her the whole story of how Todd kept teasing me, and how I challenged him to a fight at Resilient and that I won but I got caught with a punch, hence the black eye.

As he winds down, I brace for Mom's fury. It's probably just as well I stopped training at Resilient while it was still my idea.

"Let me get this straight," she says. "You beat the hell out of that boy. In a cage. At the gym. In fact, you beat him up so badly you had to tell his parents that you were jumped by a bunch of older kids."

Her explanation of events makes it sound really bad. But it is factually correct.

"Yes," I say.

She goes quiet again. This is not good.

After what seems like minutes, but is probably only a few seconds, Mom says, "I guess this Brazilian juju stuff really does work."

Parents can surprise you. The rest of the ride home Mom peppers me with questions about my cage match with Todd. Eventually it's Dad that cuts her off and says something about how they can't condone the fight, but that they're glad I stood up for myself. Then he changes the conversation back to my race.

All the bad feelings about it sweep back over me. I don't want to be pitied. I don't want to be treated differently. I just want a fair shot.

My phone pings with notifications from kids at school congratulating me and the team. I'd forgotten what a big deal the swim team is at Meadow Grove.

Someone's posted a clip of the race. It's of the last ten yards, as I power home and make it to the wall first.

I start to read the comments, even though I know I should have learned my lesson by now.

The first few are good, they boost my ego.

Way to go, Dylan.

Yes, baby, Meadow Grove is back.

Before I know it, I'm scrolling my way down, soaking up all the praise.

Then, halfway down, someone's posted:

Embarrassing!

Then another dozen comments below that someone else has written:

What do you call a bunch of retards in a swimming pool? Vegetable soup.

Beneath that someone else has written:

He's not a retard. He's a cripple. Get it right, dude.

Lots of people react, saying how horrible it is to say stuff like that. I even see someone whose name I recognize from school post below that comment that they wouldn't dare say it to my face and that I'm a one-legged ass kicking machine.

It's like a couple of comments among a few hundred. But they hurt. I know they shouldn't. I know it's stupid to let some anonymous troll on the internet upset me, but it does.

Then my phone lights up with an actual call from probably the last person I want to speak to right now. Santana.

My finger hovers over my phone. I really don't want to talk to her. Not now. Maybe tomorrow. I know she's going to give me a hard time about not coming to train after the competition. I don't want to hear it, not after what just happened.

I stare at the screen. I can see her with her phone in her hand, cursing me. Santana once told me that the best defense is a good offense, so I go with that and answer.

"Hey, if you're calling to give me a hard time about not training then don't. Not today."

"Why not today?" she asks, in a tone that suggests that's precisely what she was about to do.

I tell her about the race, and how I was given a three-second head-start and how I won, but I feel like dirt.

Amazingly, she doesn't interrupt. She says *okay* and *uh-huh* and a few other things to let me know that she is actually listening. The silence comes when I finish. I have to look at my screen to make sure the connection didn't drop.

"Hey, are you there?" I say after another few seconds of nothing.

"I'm here."

"Did you hear what I said?"

I was half expecting her to have launched into some kind of major Santana speech about how patronizing it was to give me a lead. Or how she would have refused to swim. But I'm getting none of that.

"I heard you."

"So?"

"What do you want me to say?" she asks.

"I don't know, you're the one who called me."

I hear her sigh. It's the same kind of sigh I've heard from her during class when she'd show me a move a dozen times and I still wasn't getting it. Now that I think about it, I was the only person I ever heard her make that sound with during class.

"What do you want, Dylan? You complain when you're treated differently, but when you're treated the same as everyone else that's not good enough either and you go off and sulk."

I start to say that I didn't go off and sulk, that I'm taking a break, but I stop myself. If anyone knows BS, it's Santana.

"Do you know how many jits matches I've lost? Do you know how many Martese has lost over the years? Do you know how many every single person who competes regularly loses? A lot of times it's because a referee gets something wrong."

"Okay, but mine was stopped."

"Yeah, and Martese spoke to someone after, and they told him the referee got it wrong. That he shouldn't have stopped the match like he did, and you could have gone for the takedown. He made a mistake. It happens. It was a new situation for him too. Dude, it's one match. You don't up and quit just because you lose one match."

Sometimes in life you need to hear what you don't want to hear. This is one of those times. The truth can sting, but it's better than never hearing it and staying stuck in the same place.

Now it's my turn to be silent.

"You know what they say about BJJ?" says Santana.

"What?" There are lots of things people say about jits.

"That it's for anyone, but it's not for everyone."

That's like half the full quote. It goes something like, jits is for anyone, but it isn't for everyone. And after a few months it's only for half of those people, and after a few years it's just for a handful of rare savages.

"You do remember we have the charity rollathon for the kids camp next weekend, right?"

"Sure, I remember, but I kind of have something else going on."

"Hey, Dylan?"

"Yeah?"

"Not everything's about you. Sometimes it's about the people who're gonna come after you."

I don't know what that means, but I can tell she's not going to let this go. And it would be kind of fun to see everyone again.

"Okay, I'll be there."

"Yeah, you will. Oh, and make sure you get some of your buddies at that rich-kid school of yours to pony up some money. A lot of these kids weren't born with a silver spoon up their butt like you guys. I'll send you the link for the donations. I've put you down for ten rounds."

"Wait." Ten rounds? I haven't rolled in weeks. Ten rounds will kill me.

"Later, masturbator," she says and hangs up.

Fifty-Five

SANTANA DOESN'T DO invitations so much as thinly-veiled threats. A couple of minutes later she sends me the link to the fundraising website where people can donate. There's also a reminder that I've now *agreed* to do ten five-minute rounds. Under that she texts:

It'll be good practice for when you grade for your blue belt! :)

She may be the only person who would ever put a smiley face after telling you that you're going to have to roll for an hour.

I'm not gonna lie—when she said I was sulking, it hurt. A lot. But that was because if I'm being completely honest, I kind of was. Yeah, I was angry that my match got stopped, but Santana's right, it was just one match. I guess when it happened it brought a lot of stuff back to the surface.

I share the link to all my social media accounts with a picture of me standing in the middle of the cage at Resilient with Santana. If nothing else, it might stop everyone talking about the swim meet.

When I check the link later on, I'm amazed to see that I already have five hundred dollars in donations. Doing a doubletake, I swipe down the page and see that Todd's dad kicked in two hundred bucks. There are a couple of fifty-dollar donations and the rest are lots of five and ten dollar pledges from kids at school.

I guess I really am going to have to do ten rounds next weekend. I realize there's a method to Santana's madness.

For the first time since the competition, and definitely since the swim meet, I feel the cloud that's been hanging over me start to lift. Maybe it's because Santana reached out. Maybe it's because I know that I really love being on the mats more than I enjoy being in the pool. Or maybe it's because it's good to be doing something that's not just about me for a change.

CHAPTER
Fifty-Six

BY THE TIME I walk back into a packed Resilient for the rollathon, I've raised almost a thousand dollars, which makes me feel a little better about having gone AWOL. The rollathon is an open-house event, so anyone from any gym can come out and roll, as long as they throw some money into the bucket set up at the front desk.

The first person I see is Jared. He's in a slick, black gi and rocking his brown belt.

"Welcome back," he says, giving me a hug.

I haven't been away from the place that long, but I already forgot just how much people hug each other, and I'm not talking snuggle struggles. If you see someone you haven't seen in a while, you give them a hug. Even if a while might only have been a few weeks.

"Don't let Santana give you a hard time about that competition," he says. "When she lost her first no-gi final, we didn't see her for two months." He leans in. "But don't tell her I told you that."

"I won't," I say.

I can't imagine repeating that little nugget to Santana, never mind telling her who told me. It does kind of make me feel better that I'm not the only one to take a break though.

Martese walks into the middle of the mats, claps his hands, and everyone settles down.

"Guys, thanks so much for coming along today. As you know the summer camp that we organize is something that's close to our hearts. In a minute I'm going to set the timer for rounds. Five minutes a round with a one-minute break in between. So grab yourself a partner. We're pretty busy today so watch your space."

Watch your space means try not to kick someone in the head, or get kicked in the head, or let your partner get kicked in the head, which can happen when there are a ton of people rolling together. It's never intentional, but it happens.

A new white belt that only started training at Resilient right before my competition is standing next to me. He's about my height with a scraggly beard and I can see that even in the short time he's been training the paunch around his waist has started to melt away.

"Wanna roll?" I ask.

"Sure," he says. "I'm Jonah."

"Dylan."

There's not enough room for people to start standing so we sit down and wait for the timer.

"Everyone have a partner?" says Martese, scoping out the mat for any strays. "Okay, let's roll!"

The timer sounds for the start of the round. Ten rounds is a lot. I'm going to need to pace myself.

Bump, slap, and we're on. I immediately slip my stump through Jonah's legs and move to half guard. It's like my signature move. You can't stop a leg that's not there.

Jonah tries to buck me off. Like pretty much every new white belt, he's super tense and his breathing is way too fast. As he tries to push me off, I slide my hands under the collar of his gi, bring my elbows together, and finish a choke.

He taps. We reset and go again.

Soon I'm lost in the roll, unaware of anything apart from each passing moment. Before I even realize we're close to the end, the timer sounds and the round finishes. Jonah kneels on the mat, trying to catch his breath.

"You okay?" I ask him.

He shoots me a thumbs up and holds up his hand in a 'just catching my breath' gesture.

One down and nine to go. I feel good, like I'm home.

Jonah and I hug it out and I scan the mat for my next dance partner. It's like a weird mating ritual. You might find a higher belt looking at you and you avoid making eye contact with them because you don't want to get smashed. Or you'll choose a white belt and still they'll do the same thing to you. Then as people partner up and the choices diminish, you grab someone and off you go for another five minutes of murder practice.

The timer sounds for the end of the tenth round. My back is flat on the mat and I gasp for air, my heavy cloth gi soaked in sweat. Santana sits next to me, laughing, having just subbed me so many times that I lost count.

She pats my chest. "Good job, Stumpy."

"What was good about it?" I ask her, still gasping for air.

For the last five minutes I was a glorified grappling dummy as Santana worked through pretty much every submission she uses, including three—count them, three—different foot locks. But herein lies the magic. I'm smiling.

It was horrible. It was brutal. It was unrelenting. And, despite all of that, or maybe because of it, I loved it.

Santana stands up, reaches down, and grabs my arm with her good hand to haul me up onto my foot.

"Sorry about the foot locks."

"No you're not."

She laughs. "You're right. I'm not."

She hands me a water bottle and I suck down a big gulp.

"So what are the kids at this camp like?"

"They're awesome. You'll see."

Fifty-Seven

BIG NEWS—I have a date with Anna. Even better, she asked me.

"You mean like to study together?" I said when she brought it up, not quite sure what was happening.

"No, as in you and me go out and do something. Like a movie, or get something to eat, or just hang out or whatever. And because I asked, you have to pick what we do."

As soon as she says it, I totally know what we should do. But before I can get the words out, Anna says, "Something that doesn't involve rolling around on a floor. We can save that for later, assuming you don't screw up."

It turns out that Anna's sassy, and I love it.

"Can I think about it?"

She tilts her head to one side like she's confused. As if she's thinking, did this guy just turn me down?

"Not about the date, about what we do."

"Okay, but don't take too long. I might change my mind."

"Someone asked you out on a date?" says Santana, turning down the volume. "The Warrior's Code" by The Dropkick Murphys is playing on the gym's sound system as we go through some of my new moves for the next jits competition.

"Yeah."

"And she's hot?"

"Maybe more cute than hot."

Santana puts out her hand for my phone. "I'll be the judge of that. You must have a picture somewhere on there."

I pull up Instagram and hand the phone to Santana who does a quick swipe through Anna's feed.

"Huh," she says.

"What?"

"She *is* cute. So where you going to take her? And don't tell me you asked her if she wanted to come here."

"Never got the chance, she ruled it out as a possibility before I could ask. I was hoping you might have some ideas. Who better to ask, right?"

"Than a girl who dates girls?"

"Exactly."

"I need more information. What's she like? I mean what kind of girl is she?"

"I dunno. At first I thought she was nerdy, and she kind of is, but she's sassy too."

She chews this over for a while.

"Okay, first off, no food unless it's something where you can walk and talk. No one wants to look across at someone else scarfing down pasta on a first date."

"I was thinking maybe a movie."

Santana looks disgusted at this idea. "Worse than dinner. You don't get to talk and there's always this weird tension because you're wondering if you should make a move, which means neither of you can enjoy the flick." She chews at a fingernail, lost in thought. "I got it!"

"What?"

"Bookstore and coffee, then a walk on the beach. It's low key. It's no pressure. She'll think you're sensitive, which we both know is a lie because you're a horny teenage boy and by definition completely gross."

I ignore the jabs, partly because they are at least semi-accurate.

"A bookstore?" I repeat.

"Yeah, a bookstore. You know, shelves, books. Stuff to read."

"I know what a bookstore is."

"See what she likes reading and then if the first date goes well, buy her a book and give it to her on the next date. You'll definitely get some play if you do that."

"I will?"

"Newsflash. Girls like sex too. We just have to pretend we don't because if we're honest we'll get slut-shamed. Usually by boys who are way bigger sluts than any girl will ever be."

I don't have any better ideas, so I decide to go with Santana's plan. We're kind of short on beaches in the Valley so I'm going to take Anna to Santa Monica. Coffee, books, and a walk on the beach.

When I pull up outside her house her little brother runs out and starts peppering me with questions.

"Hey, are you Anna's boyfriend?"

"No, we're just friends."

"Do you really have one leg?"

"One and a third."

"What happened to the other two thirds?"

"A shark bit it off."

"Really?"

"Yup."

"Did you get it back?"

"No, the shark ate it."

A few months ago, all these questions would have bothered me but now I'm so used to making shark jokes with Santana that I find it funny too. We actually have a contest going to see who can get someone to believe the most outrageous story about what happened to us.

Currently Santana is at the top of the leaderboard with a good one about a plane crash in the Himalayas where they ran out of food and she woke up to find some of her fellow survivors chewing on her arm. It's completely unbelievable but Santana swears she had an old lady at a gas station believing it.

I'm rescued by Anna walking out of her house. As we get into my car, I look at her little brother. He's standing with his back to us doing that little kid thing of hugging his arms, so it looks like he's making out with someone.

"Sorry about him. He's the worst."

On the drive over to Santa Monica we mostly talk about school stuff—the SATs and college applications, that kind of junk. I haven't really given much thought to where I want to apply to, but Anna seems to have it all figured out.

When we get to the Third Street Promenade, I turn into a parking structure, and peer over the wheel as we creep along, trying to find an empty spot.

"What about that one?" she says, pointing to a wheelchair spot.

"Yeah, I don't like using those unless I really have to," I say, spotting an empty space halfway down the row.

"How come?"

"I can get around okay and sometimes there's someone who really needs it, like they have a ramp that they need the extra room to use."

She looks at me like she doesn't quite believe me but doesn't say anything.

As I start to turn into the empty spot a guy in a BMW 5 series whips round us, almost crashing into the side of the Dorkmobile, and steals my space.

"What the—"

I roll my window down.

"Hey, what do you think you're doing?"

He gets out of his car. He's a dorky looking dude, maybe a year older than me.

"Parking my car, what's it look like?" he smirks.

I start to open my door to get out. Anna leans over and grabs my arm.

"Just let it go, Dylan."

Punchable smirky face dude laughs. "Yeah, let it go, Dylan," he says in a high-pitched voice.

I'm lost in the moment. I can see myself getting out, double legging him, and grinding my titanium knee into his chest until he apologizes. Not hitting him, just giving him some knee-on-belly love.

Then I think of Martese and what he'd do. And how much Anna hates violence.

I take a deep breath, count to three, and decide to let it go.

I turn my head away from him and start to ease off the brake.

"That's right," he yells. "Why don't you and your slant-eyed girl-friend run along."

I stop and I look over at Anna. I can see what he said stung. As crazy as LA is, you don't hear stuff like that here often.

Or maybe if you're Asian you do, and I just don't know about it because I'm white. The same way someone with two legs would have no idea of the things I hear. Not that it's happened often, but even hearing that kind of stuff once is bad enough.

"That's way out of line. I'm going to speak to him. Unless you really, really don't want me to, in which case I won't."

She looks at me then over my shoulder to BMW douchebag who's standing with arms folded over a Hollister T-shirt and a self-satisfied smirk.

Anna looks back at me, then back at him.

"No, that's fine. People like that need to be spoken to."

I push the door open and start to get out.

"Dylan. Wait."

I stop.

"It's not really going to be a talk, is it. I mean, you'll say something, then he'll say something back and then you'll fight."

I get the feeling Anna doesn't want to hear all the technical details so all I say is, "Probably."

"Let's just go park."

I hesitate. I really want to kick this guy's ass. The only reason dudes like this behave like they do is because they don't get their ass kicked. I glance back over at Anna. I can tell she doesn't want me to do anything and throwing down with some random dude in a parking lot isn't a great start to a romantic afternoon together.

I get back in and close the car door.

"I really don't like violence."

"I get it," I tell her.

We park a little farther down the row and get out of the car. As we're walking to the exit, I hear the guy call out again. I don't catch it exactly, but I get the drift.

I turn back to look at him. He puts his fingers to his face and pulls at the corner of his eyes. Anna looks like she's about to burst into tears. I totally get her reaction. It's the same way I've felt at times since the accident.

"Stay here," I tell her.

She doesn't say anything or stop me as I walk back to the dude. He's still laughing as I shoot a double leg, use my good leg to trip him and smash him into the concrete. I grab his wrist to stop him from punching me and jam my metal knee into his solar plexus.

He thrashes around. I jam my knee into his chest even harder, pushing the air out of his lungs. All of his bravado seems to have evaporated for some reason.

I don't say anything. Still holding his wrist, I move my other knee so that it's jammed into the side of his neck.

"You done?" I ask him.

"Yeah, yeah."

"Okay, I'm going to let you up, but if you start any more shit, I'm going to choke you out. Understand me?"

"Okay. Yes."

I climb off him. He's looking at the knee that dug in under his rib cage. "What the hell is that thing?"

I walk back to Anna as he slowly gets back to his feet, rubbing at his neck.

"You okay?" I ask her.

I can tell she's still upset, but she doesn't want to ruin our date any more than I do.

"Yeah, I'm fine. You think he'll call the cops?" she says.

"And tell them what? That he said a bunch of racist stuff and then got put on the ground by some kid with one leg?"

"I guess you're right."

"Come on, let's not let that asshole ruin our day," I say, taking her hand.

CHAPTER
Fifty~Eight

"OH MY GOD, I LOVE BOOKSTORES."

Score one for Santana. We walk in and Anna goes to look at the stacks of new releases on the tables at the front. She picks a book up.

"Alice Hoffman. I love Alice Hoffman!"

"Have you read this one yet?" I ask.

"I usually wait for the paperback, it's cheaper."

She puts it down and picks something else up. She's like a kid in a candy store. I'm having fun watching her have fun. I don't want to crowd her, so I move to the next table. It's weird. I used to read a ton when I was younger, but I got out of the habit. I should get back into it. No, scratch that. I will get back into it.

I pick up a book with a purple and gold cover called *The Obstacle Is The Way* by some dude called Ryan Holiday. I turn it over and start reading the back. It's all about Stoic philosophy, whatever that is.

Anna looks over at me. "Thanks for standing up for me, and thanks for not hitting that guy."

"Jits is all about controlling the person, not hurting them." I see an opening. "You should try a class."

"No, it's okay. I like books, you like jiujitsu."

"You can like more than one thing at a time."

"True," she says, reaching her hand down and squeezing my butt. "Come on, let's go look at some more books."

We wander through the store. Anna points out books she's read. When she tells me about the story or why she liked it, her eyes light up and she comes alive. She's still the same Anna I know from school, but away from everyone else she seems lighter, happier, prettier.

Time seems to fly by. Eventually I tell her I have to go to the bathroom and sneak downstairs. I pick up a copy of the Alice Hoffman book she was looking at earlier and buy it.

I meet her as she's coming down the stairs.

"Oh, what'd you get?" she says.

I hand over the bag. For a second I'm worried that I'm coming off too eager.

She takes out the book and smiles.

"You shouldn't have," she says. "But I'm glad you did."

She stands on her tiptoes and kisses me on the cheek. "Thank you."

We get our coffees and walk down 3rd Street, past where I parked and toward the beach. There's a bridge that takes you across the Pacific Coast Highway to the water. I'm still not great on stairs, and it's slow going, but Anna doesn't seem to mind.

It's a perfect California day. Warm with an azure blue sky, miles of beach in either direction and the white tips of the waves rolling in.

We walk north along the path, drinking our coffee. It always seems weird when girls say, and it's always girls who say it, that they like long walks on the beach, but I get it.

It's like the breathing exercises Santana showed me. So simple that it's perfect.

"Hey, so what's it like being a badass?" Anna says.

The question catches me a little off guard. "You're asking me?"

She nods.

"I'm not really a badass."

"Yeah, right. You're like the only kid in our year that Jack doesn't talk smack to, and everyone knows why."

"I thought you didn't like violence?"

"I don't, but stop avoiding the question."

I take a moment. I have to think about this.

"The truth?"

"Of course the truth."

"It's kind of awesome."

She laughs.

"Can I ask you something?"

"Sure."

"Why did you ask me out?"

"What do you mean? I like you."

"Just like?" I say, raising an eyebrow.

She jabs a finger into my side. "Hey, quit that!"

"So when you used to come sit with me at lunch, I thought it was maybe because you felt sorry for me."

She doesn't say anything to that, and I get a sinking feeling that maybe I'm right. That she's asked me on a date because no one else has, and the reason no one else has is because, well, you know, the whole one leg deal.

"After I had that fight with Todd it was like you didn't want anything to do with me anymore. Then out of nowhere, you ask me on a date."

"You think it was out of nowhere?"

"Kinda."

"I've always liked you. That's why I sat with you at lunch."

"So why did you start ignoring me?"

"I didn't like what you did to Todd."

"It was a fight. He would have done it to me."

She stops and looks at me, like she's not buying it.

"Okay, maybe the last few strikes were too much," I say. "Does it help that I felt bad about it after?"

Anna takes a while before she says anything, like she's trying to get what she's thinking straight in her head first.

"I didn't like seeing you behave like that, but that wasn't all of it. All of a sudden you were popular. Jenny was all over you like a rash at the party. I guess I was jealous and I didn't want you thinking I wanted to go out with you because you were the cool kid. Does that make sense?"

"So you always liked me?"

"Yeah."

"And the leg thing? It doesn't bother you?"

"Dylan?"

"Yeah?"

"Please stop talking."

I stop. She puts her arms around my waist. I lean down a little and kiss her. It's freaking amazing. Like shooting the perfect takedown or grabbing a last second submission on the buzzer. Maybe even better.

Bookstore. Coffee. Beach.

I have to hand it to Santana, she really understands girls.

Fifty~Nine

"SO HOW'D THE DATE GO?" Santana asks.

There's only two weeks left until the next BJJ comp and we're on the mats working on my baseball bat choke. It's kind of sneaky and I've been catching a lot of people with it so Santana thinks if I hone it enough it might be my best weapon.

"It was good."

Santana takes a step back and smirks.

"What does that mean?"

"It means we had a good time."

"How good?"

"Good good."

"You get any action?"

I've never had a lesbian friend before, so I don't know if Santana asking me this stuff is because she likes girls as much as I do, or it's from hanging around a bunch of cage fighters for years. I actually don't think it's the last reason because none of the guys in the gym talk like Santana does.

She has no filter. None.

"I'm not telling you that."

"Such a gentleman," she laughs, doing a little curtsy. "Okay, just answer me one question."

I stand back and look at her. She's totally relentless, like a pit bull. That should be her fight name, because once she locks on to something, she won't let it go. "Go on."

"At any point during this date, did you take your leg off?" she asks me.

I'm starting to get annoyed. If Jack Kim had said this to me, I would have hit him by now. Of course, me getting annoyed only encourages Santana.

"Woah! Did she take it off for you? That's super hot. Did she like, kiss your stump?" she says, laughing.

"Hey, are we drilling this or not?"

"Okay, okay, Jean Jacques, take it easy."

In fact, I did get some action. Quite a lot of action, really. But I'm not sharing the details with anyone, and definitely not Santana.

More than the action, I like hanging out with Anna. The swim team is all guys, and most of the people at Resilient are also guys, so it's nice to have a break from that. And Anna has got me reading again.

The next Monday at school she gave me a copy of the Ryan Holiday book I was looking at in the store. It's all about how things that can seem bad at the time turn out to be valuable in our lives.

It's going so good that Anna is coming to my jits comp. So I have some extra motivation to kill it on the mats. Which I'll do, if Santana would focus on training. My game has made a jump. The time away from Resilient seems to have actually done me some good. I guess my body had a chance to rest and recover.

Martese has been assured there won't be a repeat of what happened at the last competition. If I need to, I can start a match in combat base, but since my last one kind of went viral and anyone I draw will have seen it, I have a different plan this time.

If I can pull it off, I'll be going viral again. But this time for all the right reasons.

If I lose, I'll be disappointed. I might be angry. I may be down about it. But I won't give up. I'll go again.

CHAPTER
Sixty

MARTESE, Santana, Jared, and Anna crowd the barrier as I wait to get called onto the mat by the referee. I have my game face on. Shoulders back, chest out, I hand over my ID to be checked for the final time by the two people keeping score.

I slip in my mouth guard, take a final sip of water, and take off my leg.

The ref waves me and my opponent onto the mat. The guy doesn't look as freaked out that I'm hopping. Or if he is, he's not showing it. Maybe he looked me up, which would be awesome, because he'll be waiting for me to drop into combat base and has probably spent the last week drilling guillotine chokes.

Once on the mat I crouch down, waiting for the referee to signal the start. Suddenly, I'm back in the tunnel. Everything in front of me is narrow and sharp. At the edges everything is black. I can hear voices, shouts, but they're muffled and indistinct.

Nerves give way to focus. I watch the referee's hand as it slices the air.

"Combache!"

I stay where I am, crouched down. As my opponent moves in, his hands up, I level change, coming up to fight for grips, my leg posted out behind me to avoid the trip.

We clinch. My right hand comes up and I snap down his neck, almost losing my balance, but I use my connection to him to stay stable. Palm down, my thumb eases in under the back of his gi collar.

Pawing open his gi with my left hand, I slide it in farther, palm-up as he goes for double underhooks, ready to take me down. Not that it matters.

Before he hits his takedown I make my move. I switch my hips and drop down, my hands gripping his collar as if they're holding a bat.

He panics as he realizes what's happening, but it's too late. My fall brings him down. He still has his legs under him but it doesn't matter. I slide in under him as we come down to the mat and I scissor my elbows together.

His hands come up to defend the choke. There's no space, the choke tightens. I stay close to him, keeping my head in tight. My elbows inch closer and the edge of my hands press into the carotid arteries on either side of his neck.

He thrashes, trying to push me off. I keep my grips, my fingers aching.

I feel his hand come down and tap against my side.

"Okay, okay," says the referee, reaching in between us.

I let go. The two of us sink down. He slaps the mat in frustration.

The sound of cheering comes like a wave. I cover my face with my hands. It's a moment of disbelief. I did it. I came in with a plan, I executed it, and I won.

We stand on either side of the ref and he raises my hand. I close my eyes for a second, savoring the moment as my teammates cheer. Then I hop off the mat, and hurry to put my leg back on as the next two competitors walk past and onto the mat for their match.

Over by the barrier, everyone from Resilient hugs me. I wrap Anna up in a hug. When I let go, Santana and Martese lean over to me.

Santana whispers in my ear, "You are totally getting some leg-off action later," then busts out laughing.

Martese says, "Don't get too giddy, you have another match in twenty minutes."

He's right. I need to refocus and work out my plan for the next one. It's a large division. To even get a shot at a medal I have a lot more matches that I have to win. The good news is I'm still completely fresh. I didn't even break a sweat.

Back in the pen, Anna comes over with some water and a banana for me.

"That was amazing," she says, handing me the bottle from the other side of the barrier.

I think Santana might be right. I could be getting some hot leg-off action later.

"Everyone's so friendly."

It's true. The crowd at a jits competition is completely different from an MMA crowd. For a start, everyone here is sober. And almost everyone trains. In other words, it's a room full of killers, which makes for a respectful and polite atmosphere.

"Santana's incredible. She really likes you too."

This is news to me. I mean, I guess she must—she spends enough time with me, and she's helped me more than anyone at Resilient, apart maybe from Martese.

"She does?"

"She said that if you win gold, I should definitely make sure you get," Anna throws up some air quotes, "some mind-blowing, leg-off sex."

I almost spray a mouthful of water over the barrier. My face gets hot.

Thankfully, Anna moves on.

"Maybe I will give this stuff a try."

I look up from my banana. "You will?"

"Sure, why not?"

This may be almost as exciting as the prospect of having sex. I've been trying to get Anna to try a class for weeks. She's nerdy in the best way possible, and that means she could get really good at it. Martese says jits is made for nerds because they're good at problem solving, which is what BJJ is all about. And they don't have a big ego about getting beat up, which also helps.

There's actually a whole BJJ nerd community. You don't realize how many of them there are until you come to an event like this. They tend to be small or skinny, and a lot of them wear glasses. Basically, they look like the kid who gets his head pushed into the toilet by the school bully. But the truth is they could absolutely destroy a regular person in a fight.

It's kind of cool, like a secret legion of Clark Kents.

My nerves return as I walk back down for the second match. Like me, the guy I'm up against has already won his first match. He's rocking a gi with a Gracie Barra patch on the back, so I know he'll be good. People who train at a Gracie Barra gym are known for being super technical.

I go through the same routine—leg off, final sip of water, mouth guard in.

The ref beckons us both onto the mat. I already have it set in my mind what I plan on doing. Take grips then go straight for an ankle pick. Pass his guard. Move to side control. Work my subs from there.

The ref asks if we're both ready. We are.

"Combache!"

I hop back as he circles to my outside.

He rushes in, fast. I startle. Just a fraction, but enough to lose my balance. I drop down into combat base, my right knee hitting the mat as I shoot straight for his lead leg, grabbing behind ankle to pull it out.

His arm comes down, sliding in under my neck. I drop my chin, but it's too late. He has the guillotine.

Martese and Santana shout at me from the side. I reach up to fight the choke as he falls back. His legs come up and over my back, his weight dragging me face-down onto the mat.

Face-plant or keep fighting the choke, two on one. I have to let go and base out with one hand.

He cranks the choke as he gets his leg onto my back. The pressure is crazy. It feels like my head is going to be separated from my body.

Black shapes swim in front of me as the choke tightens against my carotid arteries.

On my knee, I reach my other hand back up as he adjusts his position. The choke tightens another notch.

My head swims. I'm about to go out. I reach out and tap.

The ref steps in and I flop with my back onto the mat and stare up at the ceiling.

The ref's face hovers over me. "You okay?"

No. I'm not okay. I'm pissed because I lost, but I nod and haul myself up off the mat. The Gracie Barra kid kneels next to me.

"Oss!"

He gives me a hug, a sign of respect.

I stand on the other side of him as the ref raises his arm. He moves on to the next round. My race is run.

I'm still angry. I want to kick something, but I'd just fall over.

Back at the barriers, everyone from Resilient either shakes my hand or gives me a hug. No one says too much apart from Martese who tells me we need to work more on how I start and Santana who does her best to console me in her usual Santana-like manner. "Look on the bright side, I'm pretty sure you're still getting at least a blowjob."

Losing sucks. But not as bad as it did after my first tournament. And I still feel way better than I did after I 'won' at the swim meet.

I've won my first jits match, and now that I have a taste for how it feels, I want more. I lost the second match, and I'm annoyed I got beaten like I did, but, as everyone reminds me, it happens. I guess by winning a match, I have the monkey off my back. I know I can do it, which is pretty much the whole lesson of all of this: you can do a hell of a lot more than you think you can.

You win, you lose. You go back to the gym and fix the holes in your game. Rinse and repeat.

Anna and I hang out to support everyone else from Resilient who's competing. It's fun to watch the matches when you've already finished. I call my parents. Mom is delighted I'm alive and uninjured and Dad is psyched I won a match.

Anna and I get an açai bowl, which she proclaims a 'taste sensation.' We hang out at the comp all day. Resilient takes a bunch of medals, including a gold for Santana.

Martese gathers everyone together for a gym photo. Anna's about to take it but Martese grabs someone passing by to take it and she gets dragged into the middle of the group to be part of the photograph.

It's cool, like hanging out with one huge extended family. Maybe better, because everyone gets along, and the only fights that happen are on the mats.

On the mats, win or lose there's a handshake or a hug at the end of it, the way sports should be. The way life should be. No one's getting rich here, or famous. It's not about that.

It's about testing yourself. Seeing how deep you can dig. How much discomfort you can deal with and whether something works. Seeing how far you've come.

CHAPTER
Sixty-One

TODAY IS my final day as a junior. It's also my last therapy appointment with Rich. I never thought I'd say this, but I'll kind of miss him.

Last week he gave me my final therapy assignment. I have to do the same three lists that I did before. This time I'm going to start with the good things about having one leg.

I don't want to just repeat what I wrote before, so I decide to go with a different theme.

<u>*GOOD THINGS ABOUT ONE LEG*</u>

Easier to get to half guard.

Fifty percent less chance of being foot locked, heel hooked, or knee barred.

Huge upper body weight advantage.

I draw a line halfway down the page and move onto the bad things. Weirdly, this seems harder. I don't think a lot about the disadvantages these days. They're just there and you work around them. I'm pretty easy to push over on the mat with my leg off. I guess that's the biggest one, but even that can be used to my advantage, as that kid I baseball bat choked from standing found out.

Okay, let's get some of this down on paper.

Vulnerable to a leg sweep.

Easier for someone to pass my guard.

Less stability from standing.

That seems like a repeat of the leg sweep, but I decide to leave it in. After five minutes I can't think of anything else, so I put my pad back in my bag.

For the rest of the morning no one seems to be paying any attention to anything in class. Even the teachers seem distracted by the prospect of summer vacation.

I sit and have lunch with Anna. Neither of us are big into PDA like some couples, so we eat and talk and that's kind of it. I try not to eat too much because after I'm done seeing Rich I'm going over to her place and having Korean barbecue with her family.

"My dad is totally stoked to meet you," she says.

"Really?" I ask her.

"Yeah, this morning he kept asking me what you like to eat and stuff like that. I think he's just pleased that I have a boyfriend who doesn't have tattoos or drinks or takes drugs."

"I sound kind of boring when you put it like that."

She reaches over to steal a potato chip from my tray.

"Dads love boring boyfriends," Anna says.

"You think I'm boring?"

She laughs. "I don't think you'll ever count as boring."

"Think I should get a tattoo?"

"No!" she says. "Everyone has tattoos."

"I'm going to get one," I laugh. She's fun to tease. "Maybe one with, like, Chinese characters that the tattoo guy tells you means crouching tiger but actually spells out the word dork."

"In that case you should totally get one," she says.

"I'm going to run it past Rich later. See what he thinks."

"Good idea."

"I better get going. Coach wants to see everyone before we leave for the summer."

I lean over, kiss Anna, and grab my bag.

"What time should I be at your place?"

"Before eight if you want there to be any food left."

"Cool."

Coach's end-of-year speech went on so long that I'm running late for therapy. I park, get my bag from the back seat and rush inside as fast as one leg and a prosthesis will carry me, which isn't all that fast.

When I get inside, Rich's waiting. I sit down and apologize for being late, opening my bag to pull out the pad of paper with the new good/bad list I wrote this morning. But before I can find it, something stops me.

I wrote it as a goof, and suddenly it doesn't seem right. A few weeks back my dad told me that he knew that guys didn't like talking about their feelings, and he got that, but that I was lucky to have that chance. That there were kids out there who maybe weren't coping with life very well, and they never had the chance to speak with a therapist. So even if I didn't feel like taking it seriously, I should try.

Maybe it's because I'm getting older, but a year ago that advice would have seemed kind of corny and like something parents only say to you to get you to do what they want. But now I get it. I am lucky in lots of ways.

I peer down into the bag, let go of the pad of paper, and instead I pull out the book Anna bought for me. I'm reading it for the second time, and I've been highlighting quotes and things I like.

There was one passage that seemed to fit. It's not like a good and bad list. It's sort of the opposite, and it really made me think about everything that's happened to me since the accident.

As Rich looks at me, I flip through the pages trying to find it. I don't think I want to explain that it's better than a list of the good and the bad things about having one leg. Maybe I'll just read it out loud and see what he thinks.

It's something that Epictetus, a Greek philosopher who was born a slave, said, and ever since I first read it, I've been turning it over in my mind.

It's not what happens to you, but how you react to it that matters. When something happens, the only thing in your power is your attitude toward it; you can either accept it or resent it. Men are not disturbed by things, but by the view which they take of them.

I stumble through reading it. Rich stares down at the carpet for a while. He loves long, meaningful pauses. Just when it starts to get weird, he looks up. I've spent enough time in this room that I think I know what he's going to say before he says it.

"What do you think it means, Dylan, and why do you feel like you connect to it?"

I take a deep breath.

"I guess when I had my leg amputated, I resented it. I was angry. I was angry because it wasn't fair. I was angry when I got called names. I still get angry when people stare at me. But me being angry or sad or thinking it's good or bad doesn't change anything. It just is. When something bad happens, you have a choice. You can let it ruin your life, or you can make the best of it."

CHAPTER
Sixty-Two

THE ATMOSPHERE TONIGHT in Resilient is electric, especially for anyone like me who's rocking four stripes on their belt. Just because you have the four doesn't mean you'll be sent out into the middle to do the Iron Man. If Martese doesn't feel someone is ready, he won't call them.

I probably have a fifty-fifty chance of being graded tonight. I only got my fourth stripe after the last comp where I won my first match, so maybe I won't get my blue belt.

Before I drove over here, I promised myself that whatever happens, I won't give up. I won't allow my disappointment to overwhelm me. I've seen a lot of people not get promoted when they thought they deserved it and disappear. I don't want to be one of them. Not this time anyway.

The same goes if I do get it. People make jokes about the 'blue-belt blues'—when people get their blue belt and never come back. I've seen that too.

I guess for some people it's like checking a box. Once they have it, that's good enough.

The other reason, as Santana and Jared have both explained, is that a blue belt should really be called a blue target, because you're now in the crosshairs of every single three and four stripe white belt on the mat.

I figure I'll take my chances.

Martese asks everyone to quiet down. He runs through the same speech he gives at every grading. If you're not called out or you don't get a stripe, don't take it personally, keep training, your time will come.

Then he starts to call people out and pair them off for the first round before the Iron Man. If you're called out, you're being graded.

A four-stripe blue and then two other four-stripe white belts are called out and paired off with a purple and two blue belts. The idea is to roll with someone who's just a little above you to see if you can hang. They may sub you, they'll be doing their best to, but you have to at least cope.

I have pretty good defense, so I know I can survive. But he hasn't called me.

My throat starts to tighten with disappointment. Telling yourself that you'll take it on the chin and actually doing it are two different things.

"Dylan," says Martese.

As he says it, I see him exchange a look with Santana, like they already discussed picking me or something. If they did, now's not the time to ask her. Or thank her. She knows how much I want this, mostly because, as she said to me earlier this week, I won't 'shut the hell up about it.'

I take a final sip of water and pop in my mouth guard as Martese asks one of the younger blue belts to partner up with me. He's about the same size and he only got his blue belt last grading, so it should be a good match.

"Okay guys," says Martese. "If you didn't get called out it's because you might not be ready just yet. You need another competition, or a win, or more time on the mat. Don't be discouraged."

He turns his attention back to the four of us in the middle, ready to roll.

"You know the drill. Roll until I say so. Then it's Iron Man. Do your best, keep going, don't leave the mat. If you get injured or think you can't continue then let me know. If you really can't go on you'll be graded another day, but you can't receive a new belt tonight. Everyone ready?"

Along with the three others, I nod that I am, and then as Martese shouts Combache, it's on and I'm out in the shallows, the deep ocean in front of me, on the far horizon.

I get swept almost immediately, falling onto my back. As my teammate goes to pass, I manage to get my right leg up and bend it to form a knee shield. His weight bears down, crushing my hips into the mat.

Reaching up, I grip his collar and sit up. Shifting my leg, I pull him into a high guard and thread the thumb of my right hand in under the loop of his collar.

He moves to pass, and I twist under him, dropping the baseball bat choke. He pushes down and postures up. I keep my grips and scissor my elbows closer, tightening the choke.

His forearm comes down. It slams hard into my throat—offense as the best defense.

I tighten the choke, staying close and adjusting my position.

Then he taps. We reset and this time he smashes me hard into the mat and moves straight into side control. I frame out with my arms, denying him the cross face, and shrimp back, re-establishing space.

Now it's a dog fight. I try to get out from under him. He does his best to pin me so he can start working a sub. We go back and forth until he gets his arm under my neck to get the cross face. He goes to work with his shoulder, pressing it into the side of my neck.

He fakes going for a choke and as I move my hands up to defend my collar, he grabs my arm instead and swivels into an arm bar. His leg comes down hard over my head to secure the position.

I do my best to hitchhike escape, like I've been taught, but I'm too late.

His hips tilt up. My elbow strains.

I tap.

We bump fists and go again.

"Okay guys, switch," Martese announces.

My sparring partner gets up. The person at the top of the line, an eager white belt, jogs toward me as I sit up into combat base.

The conveyor belt has ground into life. Roll. Tap. Next.

After the first few opponents, I'm soaked in sweat and gasping for breath. The pace is relentless. Even when I tap someone, I don't get any time before the next person jumps in, fresh.

I find myself up against Martese. He sweeps me and takes my back. I hand-fight and keep my chin down as he tries to snake his arm under so he can choke me.

Cool, encouraging Martese is gone. This is black belt, I'll strangle you Martese.

Two on one I push his hand down. He transitions straight to mount then moves to knee on belly, grinding hard into my solar plexus. The last fragments of oxygen exit in a rush and I feel like I might throw up.

Then I remember that if I throw up, I won't be getting a blue belt. I tough it out, trying to control my breathing.

It's uncomfortable, I remind myself. When the submission comes in the form of a cross collar choke, it's a relief.

I tap.

Martese gets off me and slaps my shoulder.

"Good!"

Then the next person appears from the top of the line and I'm back in the water. It's deep water now. No signs of anything on the horizon, just a growing swell of waves.

I'm in a place beyond exhaustion. I can barely conjure up the energy to tap, never mind offer up much resistance. I stopped counting how many people I've rolled with a while back. It could be ten, it could be twenty. It could be more.

With every person that comes off the line, I feel myself struggling to keep my head above the water. Eventually I feel like I'm sinking, unable to summon the energy to kick my way back to the surface.

Another white belt comes off the line. Someone I must have tapped a dozen times. He's eager to get some payback. He comes hard, snatching for my arm.

Something about the way he does it makes me angry. I don't fight the feeling; I let it well up in me. It gives me a flash of energy that I use to reverse him. I move to mount.

I even find the air to talk.

"Can't stop a leg that isn't there," I whisper to him, as I slide grips under his collar and tap him with my trademark sub.

Someone else comes off the line. As we tap and bump and I get ready to go again, to keep going, Martese calls time.

I lie back on the mat, completely and utterly spent, my body vibrating with energy that seems to flow into me from the mats. I can feel the blood moving through my body.

I stay there as the room washes with applause. I look over to the other people who just finished their Iron Man. They're also lying there, completely spent and emptied out.

Santana hovers over me.

"You dead?"

I shake my head.

"No, I just wish I was."

"Sounds about right," she laughs.

Once everyone is back on their feet, Martese begins the fun part of the grading, getting another stripe or the next-color belt. Everyone lines up in order along the wall, no-stripe white belts at the bottom of the gym nearest to the door, black belts at the top.

I head up the white belt line, rocking my four stripes for the last time. I don't know if it's exhaustion, but I feel strangely emotional. I know I did well enough during the Iron Man to have earned my blue.

One by one, Martese calls out the white belts who are due an extra stripe. Some don't get one, but most do.

Santana cuts the stripes from a roll of tape and hands one to Martese as each person comes up. People applaud. They shake hands with Martese then walk down the line, high-fiving people as they go.

Belts are given out last, so I have to wait. I feel good. I didn't sub everyone—not even close. But I got through it. I endured, which is the purpose of the Iron Man.

All the stripes done, Martese calls forward the first person to receive their blue belt. Everyone, me included, goes crazy. To someone walking in from the street it might seem silly, but in here everyone knows what it takes to get that blue belt.

It might be the only place I've ever been where everyone is genuinely happy for every other person's achievement. There's no grading on a curve, no getting a B because others got an A.

The next person gets called forward. Martese takes off their white belt. Santana hands him a fresh, out-of-the-package blue belt and wraps it around their waist. They raise their hands in the air as we whoop and cheer. They jog down the line and take up their new place with the anointed, with the other blues.

I close my eyes. I should be next. This is it.

I step out of the line before I realize it's not my name that's been called.

"Stephen."

The blue belt who was grading for his purple belt walks across the mat.

I step back and join the applause. Martese must be saving me for last. Maybe torturing me one final time.

It'll be fine. I survived the Iron Man. I just have to wait a few more seconds.

Martese wraps the purple belt around Stephen's waist and people go crazy.

The guy next to me, nudges my elbow. A couple of people are sneaking glances at me from farther down the line. This is it.

Martese claps his hands together and keeps them there, palm to palm. I know. As soon as he looks at me, I know it isn't happening.

"Dylan, I'm sorry, I don't think you're quite there yet. You're close. Really close. Next time, okay?" he says.

I try to keep my face blank, but it's tough. Someone next to me pats my shoulder and gives it a squeeze.

"Good grading, guys," says Santana, avoiding eye contact.

She starts to clap and everyone joins in. So do I. Not getting my belt doesn't mean I'm not happy for everyone else.

People hug each other and pose for pictures. I get dragged into a couple and do my best to put on a brave face.

• • •

As I walk out of Resilient, my phone pings with a message from Anna:

How'd it go?

I put my phone back in my pocket, get into the Dorkmobile and pull out onto Ventura.

She calls me as I pull into my driveway.

"Hey," I say. That's all I have in me.

"Are you okay? Did you get injured? What happened?"

"I'm okay. I got through it, but Martese didn't think I was ready yet."

"You're kidding. They made you do that Iron Man thing and then they didn't give you the belt? How is that fair?"

I'm glad she's upset on my behalf. I appreciate it. But it's not about fair, it's about being ready.

"Hey, can I call you tomorrow?" I ask her.

"Sure," says Anna. "You're really okay?"

"Yeah, I'll be fine."

And I will. Not tonight, and maybe not even tomorrow. But I will. I'll get over it. I'll get back on the mats and I'll keep working. I'll get there.

Sixty-Three

THE DISAPPOINTMENT of not being promoted to blue belt hangs over me. My mom and dad and Anna say all the right things, but it doesn't help.

I don't fight the feeling. It sucks but I know it will pass. Or maybe it won't. Maybe it'll just go on sucking.

It's only a delay. I get that. Martese didn't say I would never get my blue belt. He said I wasn't ready yet. I guess it was just thinking that I would get it, building it up in my mind, that made it such a letdown. Along with seeing a bunch of other people get theirs.

Maybe more than anything, I'm just tired of being the odd one out.

In the end though, none of that matters. It's not going to be like after my first competition.

Either way, I need to get back to Resilient and onto the mats.

And I do.

Three days after the grading, when my body stops feeling like it's been in another car wreck, I throw my gi, my rash guard, and my mouth guard into my bag and drive over to the gym.

I've made a list of things I need to work on. I figure I can keep sulking or work, and only one of them is going to get me what I want.

. . .

When I push through the door and into Resilient, Jared is holding pads for Santana in the cage. They stop as I come in.

"You're still coming to the camp next week, right?" she asks, jumping over the cage fence rather than walking out through the door like a regular person.

"The camp is next week?" I say, teasing her.

Since grading, she must have messaged me twice a day to ask the same question. I don't know why it's so important that a lowly white belt like me is there, but it seems to be.

She comes up and waves a gloved hand in my face. "You'd better be joking. If you don't show, I'm going to—"

"I know, I know. You'll hunt me down like a dog. Don't worry, I'll be there."

"You'd better be," she snarls.

Any time I ask her why it matters that I'm there, she just says "you'll see" or something equally vague. I do know that kids are coming from all over the country, because Martese said he's picking some of them and their families up from the airport.

Santana stalks off to get changed for gi class. She just had another fight cancelled because her opponent pulled out at the last second, so that might be why she's in such a bad mood.

Whatever. I go get ready for class.

I know that as soon as I start to roll none of it will matter. When you're trying to escape mount, or stop someone from arm barring you, you're not thinking about the color of your belt or how many stripes you have. You're just doing your best to survive.

After class and five hard rounds, where I pretty much get pummeled in each one, I feel better. I ache and I'm sore, but my head starts to clear. I get submitted so many times I start to think Martese was right after all. Maybe I'm not ready to rock a blue belt.

As people begin to drift into the locker rooms to shower, he comes over and sits down next to me as I'm putting my leg back on.

"You okay?"

I shrug. "Yeah, I'm okay." And I am, kinda. I'm still not totally over not getting my belt, but it's not the end of the world.

"Good," he says, punching my arm. "Don't forget the summer camp, okay?"

Again with the camp.

CHAPTER

CHAPTER
Sixty-Four

ANNA SITS NEXT to me in the Dorkmobile. Her T-shirt says: *DATING HIM FOR THE PARKING*. When her mom saw it, she went crazy until Anna explained that, first, it was a joke, and second, I gave it to her.

Anna's come along to help with the registration and lunch break and junk like that. Also, even though I haven't been able to prove it, I'm pretty certain Santana messaged her to come along to make sure that I was going to be here on time. The first day of the camp is on the beach near Santa Monica, then the rest of the camp takes place back at the gym.

In the beach parking lot, all the disabled spots are taken.

"Joke's on you!" I tell Anna.

We get out. I think there are a bunch of activities planned but today the jiujitsu is going to be old school Brazilian, on the beach.

I grab some of my stuff from the back seat. I close the door, look up, and see this kid standing next to a car. He's maybe nine. Before I can stop myself, I do a doubletake. The same doubletake I get from people.

He's a double below-knee amputee, and on his left hand he has a thumb and a pinky finger, but no other fingers. He sees me looking and stares down at the ground as what must be his dad rummages around in the back seat.

It's weird. You'd think I'd know exactly how to act or what to say to someone missing some of their regularly assigned body parts, but I'm not sure I do. I'm as worried about staring or saying the wrong thing as everyone else.

Next to their car, a girl who's maybe in fifth grade is being helped into a wheelchair. In fact, pretty much everywhere I look I see kids who are missing limbs or seem to have a disability.

I look down and I'm glad I'm wearing shorts so that they can see my prosthesis, although I am kind of regretting my T-shirt choice of a shark swimming away from a cartoon guy with one leg with the words *TRUE STORY* underneath it. I feel like it might be less bad to stare at a fellow fake-leg wearer.

Anna nudges me in the ribs with her elbow. "Come on, let's go say hi and see if anyone needs help with anything."

Santana's already on the beach, surrounded by a gaggle of kids. They're all jumping up and down and asking her questions. It's like she's a rock star, which, to be fair, she kinda is. She just has an aura around her. I noticed it the very first time I saw her walking out of Resilient, before I even knew about her arm. Whatever *it* is, she has it and it seems like today she's totally in her element, the same way she is when I've seen her fighting in the octagon.

The kid with no feet is standing next to me.

"Hey," I say.

He's staring at me. "Did a shark really eat your leg?"

It seems kind of cruel to give my regular answer, seeing as he's one of my tribe and that we're at the beach and there may be swimming later.

"No, it was a car accident."

"Huh," he says. "I was born like this. No one knows why."

"I'm Dylan," I say.

"Jackson."

We fist bump.

"Hey, Jackson?"

"Yeah?"

"You want me to show you some Brazilian jiujitsu?"

"I don't know what that is," he says.

"It's like fighting, but on the ground. It's perfect for guys like us."

Now his eyes light up. "Fighting? Cool!"

But he hesitates and looks behind us to his parents.

"My mom doesn't like fighting. She worries I'll get hurt."

"I hear ya."

"But there's this one kid in my class who's always teasing me. You know, about my feet and my hand and stuff."

I look down at Jackson. I can feel myself getting angry at the idea of anyone teasing this kid. It's horrible.

"I'm supposed to ignore him, or tell him to stop, but he just keeps doing it," he says.

"Yeah, I had a guy like that at my school."

"How did you get him to quit?"

I don't want Jackson's parents to hear so I lean in and lower my voice. "I choked the shit out of him."

A huge grin spreads over his face.

While Martese talks to some of the parents, Santana and I demonstrate some BJJ techniques to kids who are interested. Then we break them up into smaller groups so that they can try stuff. I make sure Jackson's in my group.

My mind's already racing with how to adapt techniques. If he gets into jits he'll definitely have some advantages. For starters, no one's going to be able to heel hook him. Not that I'm going to say that. I can tell he's self-conscious about how he looks. A lot of the kids here are. But it has to help that they're somewhere they can see that they're not the only ones.

That's the thing with being like me or Santana or Jackson. In a regular school you're going to stand out. If you're the only kid with one leg or no feet or fingers missing, that's who you're going to be to everyone else. It's tough to break out of that box and be seen for who you are.

I show them how to close the distance and clinch up with someone to stop getting hit. Some of the kids are a little bit hesitant at first, I get the feeling they've been wrapped up in cotton wool their whole lives.

Once we get going, they all start to get into it. Jackson's kind of a natural. Even at his age, he's way better than I was the first time I went to Resilient. It's really cool to see how fast he's picking stuff up.

I show him what an overhook is. If he does gi jiujitsu, he might struggle to grip with that hand, but if he has a crazy good overhook like Jean Jacques Machado, it won't matter.

When we take a break, I get my phone and show him who Jean Jacques Machado is.

"Hey, his hand is like mine," he says, excited.

"Yeah, and he became one of the best in the world. That's the beauty of it, you don't worry about what you can't do, you develop the things that you can."

"What do you mean?"

I need a demo partner.

"Hey, Santana!"

Santana comes over and I tell her what I'm trying to explain to Jackson as the other kids start to crowd round us. Everywhere she goes, a bunch of kids follow, buzzing around her. She's like a crazy, one-armed, cage-fighting Pied Piper.

We sit down on the sand, Santana behind me, her heels connected to my hips to control my movement as she puts on a rear naked choke that's super hard to fight because she doesn't have a hand that I can grab.

"Your weakness can be your strength," she explains.

At lunch we get a demonstration of just how true that is. It has nothing to do with jits, but it's just as cool.

There's a little girl about the same age as Jackson who's missing both her arms. Right at the top too—not just above or below the elbow, but right up near the shoulder joint.

But she can do pretty much everything with her feet. It's freaking amazing. She can open a Ziplock bag, take out her sandwich, and eat it —all with just her feet. I don't know how she does it. I guess it's practice.

I catch Santana sneaking glances at her during lunch. Santana looks at me and I just know we're thinking the same thing.

"That kid could have an insane triangle choke," she says.

Everyone takes a little rest after lunch because you don't want to be rolling when you've just eaten. Then we do a little more on the mats before it's time to go swimming. The beach isn't my favorite place to swim because I don't have a swim leg and I have to hop out until the water is deep enough. But Martese is telling everyone how I'm on the swim team so I can't exactly not go in.

Some of the kids are good swimmers and some don't want to go all the way in, so they sit on the sand or paddle around in the shallow water. Jackson is actually pretty good. We hang out in the water and he asks me all kinds of questions about how long I've been training.

Finally, it's time for everyone to come out of the water and dry off. Martese calls us all together. There's another day of camp tomorrow at Resilient. I guess he wants to make sure everyone knows how to get there and stuff.

All the kids sit in a semicircle, their parents behind them. Santana and I, and a couple of the other guys from Resilient who've been helping out with the kids, stand next to Martese.

It's strange to be a coach, especially since I'm still only a white belt. But it's been fun and who knows, maybe one of the kids like Jackson will go home and start training and love it as much as I do. Or they'll see that whatever challenges they face there's always a way through.

And it's been a reminder that I don't have it all that bad. One leg and all my fingers makes things a lot easier than having no feet and only some fingers. It sounds cheesy, but it really does put my life in perspective.

"So, did everyone have fun today?" Martese asks.

All the kids cheer and laugh.

"That's good," Martese beams. "It's supposed to be fun. It's good to find joy in things, even if they're hard. So tomorrow we'll be showing you gi jiujitsu. Some people call it pajama jiujitsu. We'll have gis for everyone to take home so if you want to find somewhere to train where you live, you'll be all set. Or you can keep your gi as a memento."

I didn't know we were buying all the kids gis. I'm pretty impressed. It's cool that we raised enough money to do that.

"And," says Martese, "If you're like Dylan here, don't worry, you can customize your gi."

He reaches down into a big canvas bag and pulls out a pair of gi bottoms with half the left leg cut off. I take a second to register that they're *my* gi bottoms. He must have taken them from my locker. He throws them and my gi jacket and white belt to me.

"Put them on so we can do a little demonstration before we finish," he says, pulling his gi and black belt from the bag.

I'm not sure what's going on, but I put on my gi and tie my white belt around my waist.

"When Dylan first came into train with us, oh boy, a strong gust of wind could have blown him over. Now look at him. He's a killer."

Martese is teasing me, but it's okay. I know it's all from a place of love.

I finish tying my belt and click my leg off. Santana takes it from me.

I'm kind of psyched that Martese chose me. Normally rolling in front of people would make me nervous, but Martese is a black belt so I know it's going to be like a cat playing with a mouse. There's no way I'm going to beat him or even get close, so I might as well enjoy the ride.

I hop over to the mat and hunker down. So does Martese. We slap hands and fist bump, then start to circle each other.

I go straight down into combat base. He comes in and I shoot for his ankle. He lets me have it, but it's never that simple when you roll with a black belt.

Less than a second later, he flips me up into the air. I crunch up tight and roll, landing on my back, grateful for the soft sand under the mat.

Martese lets go of me and sits back into an open guard. He grabs my sleeves as I try to pass. His feet come up, pushing into my elbows as he puts me into a spider guard.

He sweeps me. As I try to scramble out, he takes my back. His leg slides over my waist and he hooks me into a body lock.

I do my best to defend the choke as he stays patient and waits for me to make a mistake or get impatient.

The strangest part of rolling with Martese is that he doesn't seem to do anything. He doesn't break a sweat. He may as well be sitting on the couch watching TV with a bag of chips, for all the energy he expends.

It's beautiful and effortless, like a dance.

I don't even feel his hand sneaking in under my chin. The choke comes on and I tap. Martese lets go before reaching over to shake my hand, the demonstration over.

He gets up and pulls me up next to him. Everyone claps and cheers.

I do a little theatrical bow and almost lose my balance. Martese grabs me and I steady myself.

"I hope you can all see that Dylan has learned a lot, but it wasn't always that way. He's learned and developed his skills through practice and perseverance. And, in return, jiujitsu has given him a lot. Not just how to fight, but also confidence in who he is. Strength. Health. And maybe best of all, like everyone who comes into a gym, he's learned that you can do a lot more than you might think."

He pauses, suddenly serious, like he's mad at me. "Although, and this is slightly embarrassing to have happen in front of all of our guests, he still doesn't know how to tie his belt correctly."

My face flushes—he's right. My belt is always coming loose.

"Here, I'll fix it for you," he says.

All I can do is shrug at the sea of faces as Martese reties my belt like I'm one of the third graders in kids' class.

"See," he says when he's done. "That's how you tie a belt correctly."

I glance down and back up, not quite registering what's happening.

It's only when Santana and Jared and the others from Resilient start laughing that I look back down and see it.

My white belt is gone, four stripes and all. In its place is a blue belt, stiff and new.

My mouth drops open. I can't quite believe it. Martese shakes my hand and gives me an enormous bear hug.

"Congratulations, Dylan," he says. "You know, I felt so bad at the grading, but maybe this is better, yes?"

"Sorry, dude," Santana pipes up. "It was my idea to save promoting you till now."

She comes over and gives me a hug. I look past her to the ocean. The last of the sunlight dances across the tips of waves that are as blue as the belt around my waist. I look back to Jackson, with everything he has to face ahead of him, and I know in this moment that Santana was right.

Sometimes it isn't about you, it's about who comes next.

Writing as Sean Black, David Young is the author of the million-selling Ryan Lock series of thrillers. He is a winner of the prestigious International Thriller Writers Award and his books have been translated into Dutch, French, German, Italian, Portuguese, Spanish, Russian and Turkish.

He took up martial arts in his forties and in 2019 became the first ever amputee in Ireland to be awarded a blue belt in Brazilian Jiu Jitsu. He competes internationally against able-bodied athletes and in 2022 took two bronze medals at the IBJJF European Championships in Rome.

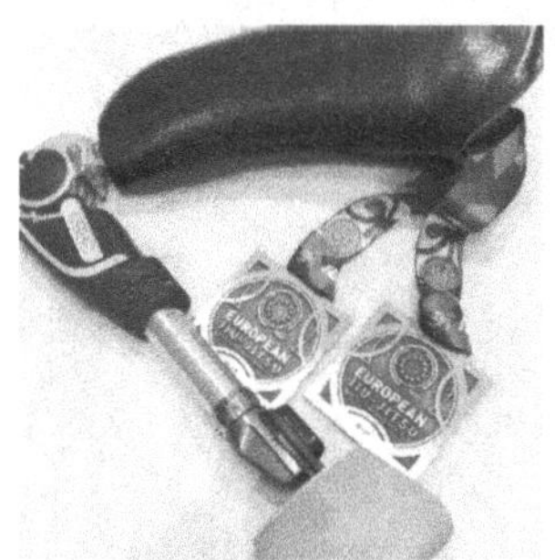

Did you enjoy this book?

If you enjoyed *The Ground Is My Ocean* you could do me a massive favor by posting a review online, sharing something about the book on social media, or recommending it to friends. Reviews and word of mouth are the number one way you can help an author.

I'm always happy to hear from readers. You can send me a message me via the contact page on my official author website www.seanblack-author.com/contact/